# ATRAYA

LONGSHOT BOOK 3

KEVIN J SIMINGTON

KEVIN J SIMINGTON

LONGSHOT
By
KEVIN J SIMINGTON



EDITOR: Sandra Simington

Created with Vellum

# PROLOGUE

The crippled starship hurtled toward the strange solar system, its rear end a mangled mess. For centuries, it had traversed the void between the stars while its occupants slept, safely cocooned in their stasis pods.

Back on Earth, 18 generations of people had lived and died, while those on board Longshot had barely aged at all. Wars had been fought and won, buildings had crumbled, nations had come and gone, and still the silent starship had flown on, its occupants oblivious to the passage of time. The starship was a mere speck of dust in the vastness of the universe, a piece of debris, battered and torn, adrift in an endless ocean of nothing.

Except now, after centuries of nothing, it was approaching a definite 'something'. The light from an orange dwarf star grew brighter, standing out from the sea of stars around it. Longshot's scanners detected the infinitesimal pull of its gravity and listened to the complex symphony of its electromagnetic emissions.

The ship's artificial intelligence began to waken the ship's systems from their slumber. Life support systems came fully online, warming the frigid air and circulating oxygen in readiness for the resurrection of the ship's sleeping occupants. Long-dormant relays clicked, and circuits hummed. Ice that had formed on hard surfaces melted, water dripped and metal creaked as the frozen ship thawed. The hydroponics and yeast farms came online, tended by robotic gardeners, themselves freshly woken from their own electronic slumber.

And all the while, the ship raced toward the looming solar system at one tenth the speed of light.

The occupants of Longshot had gone to sleep in the hope of rescue. Their disabled vessel, once an impressively powered starship, was now a rudderless life raft, destined to eternally drift among the stars unless someone intervened.

But intervention, when it finally arrived, did not initially herald the rescue that they had hoped for.

# 1

Daniel floated to the surface of consciousness. It was difficult to delineate when he ceased to be asleep and when he could be described as fully awake. It was a subtle and incremental transition. There was a short period of time when his eyes were open, but he was still more asleep than awake, his brainwaves predominantly in the theta and delta frequencies. Gradually, however, the infusion of chemicals worked their magic. Chemical scrubbers eradicated the last vestiges of sedatives from his system. Adrenal based stimulants sparked his autonomic system. Serotonin, oxytocin and dopamine flooded his synapses, supercharging his brain into alpha wave territory.

Over the previous 48 hours, all traces of the nanobots that had kept him alive for 370 years had been magnetically removed from his blood, and his blood chemistry had been stabilised. Internal organs that had lain dormant for centuries began functioning again. Lungs took their first breath. The heart pulsed with its first beat. Gradually, what had been a dormant collection of living tissues, suspended in cryogenic stasis, became a living breathing human once more.

Daniel blinked and looked around in confusion. It took a few moments for him to remember who and where he was. *This is Longshot, a crippled starship, and I've been in cold storage for centuries.* At least, he hoped he had been asleep for centuries. The last time he had awoken from cryogenic stasis he had expected to find that the ship had reached its destination, only to discover that they had been asleep for a mere three weeks. They had been woken prematurely by the ship's artificial intelligence in response to a crisis: a crisis that had almost killed them all and which had eventually crippled their ship. The back half of their ship had been blown off by an act of sabotage, completely obliterating their Vacuum to Antimatter Reaction drive. Without their VAR drive, the journey which should have taken them 38 years to complete was now destined to take 370 years. Their only option had been to re-enter cryogenic stasis and sleep away the centuries.

Daniel heard rustling and sighing in adjoining cubicles, and sensed others awakening and getting dressed. He eased himself out of his horizontal pod, its transparent lid open at an angle above him. The absence of a main drive meant no thrust and, consequently, no acceleration holding him to the floor. He floated to the plastic tub where his clothes had been placed and awkwardly began dressing, tumbling through the air as he donned various pieces of clothing. He heard the grunts and groans of others nearby, undergoing similar exertions. Finally, he slipped his feet into his magnetic boots and switched them on, activating the magnetic soles. Grabbing the side of his pod, he swivelled himself in mid-air and brought his feet to the floor. They connected with a dull thud and stuck. Now, at least, he could walk along the floor, even though his body felt as though it was perpetually falling.

He opened the curtain and stepped clumsily outside his cubicle, trying to get accustomed again to walking in zero gravity with magnetic boots. He saw several crew members emerging into the open area and he mumbled greetings to them as he clomped toward Kelly's cubicle.

"Are you awake yet?" he called as he stood outside her curtain.

"I'm not sure," she answered. "I'm still trying to decide."

Daniel heard the rustle of clothing from the other side of the curtain and heard her grunt several times.

"Doing some aerial acrobatics, are you?" he asked.

"Yeh. I'm currently executing a triple backflip in the pike position, while trying to pull my knickers up."

"I'd like to see that!"

"I bet you would. But not until you buy me a drink first."

"Just one? I would have thought it would take at least two."

"Good point. Remind me to increase my rate."

A few minutes later she drew back her curtain and emerged, wearing her space corps uniform, with warrant officer epaulettes on the shoulders. Daniel enveloped her in a hug and she clung to him tightly.

"I didn't die in cryogenic stasis," she murmured.

"Yeah, I noticed. Just like last time. What a fluke." He leant down and they kissed.

"Did you miss me?" she asked, a moment later. "It's been 370 years."

"Dreadfully," he lied. "Although, it doesn't feel like a day over 369."

"And why aren't my muscles weak or sore?" she asked, ignoring his flippancy.

"The wonders of modern technology," he replied. "Either that or we're all newly-created clones."

"Did we make it to Tama this time?" asked Jordan who drew level with them after emerging from her own nearby cubicle. Daniel glanced at the short, feisty shuttle pilot. She had long ago ditched her space corps uniform and was wearing all black clothing, to match her black spiky hair and multiple facial piercings.

Daniel shrugged. "No idea. I guess we're about to find out."

As if on cue, the ship's artificial intelligence announced, "Attention all crew. Please make your way to the dining area and scan your ID chip to receive a serving of rejuve juice. Mission team members and command centre crew are then to report to the command centre for a mission status debrief."

"I'm getting déjà vu," said Kelly. "I hope this is better news than the last time we woke up."

"Ditto," agreed Jordan.

As they clomped awkwardly toward the lifts in their magnetic boots, Daniel pointed to his lieutenant's epaulettes and said, somewhat facetiously, "I noticed that neither of you saluted me – again!"

"It's hard to salute someone who walks like a complete gumby," replied Jordan, whose discarded shirt with sergeant's insignia would probably never see the light of day again.

Kelly chuckled and said, "In my case, I think I was simply over-awed by the aura of your presence, my sweet."

Daniel merely shook his head and smiled.

A minute later they emerged from the lifts into the dining area along with several other crew members. More crew were milling around the automated food dispensers, built into several floor-to-ceiling columns throughout the expansive room.

A large woman dressed in voluminous flowing robes in brightly striped rainbow colors arrived behind them and gave each of the three a hug. "Hello my lovelies! How was your sleep?"

Daniel was enveloped in Pixie Rainbow's embrace and his muffled reply was lost in the folds of her flowing robes.

"Slept like a log," said Jordan, after she, in turn, emerged from Pixie's embrace. "And now I'm starving."

"You're always starving," said Daniel. "I don't know where you put it all."

"I've got a high-performance engine, Professor, so I need high octane fuel."

They chatted as they drank a cup of the pleasant tasting, but strangely blue-colored rejuve juice, and then Daniel and Kelly joined several others from the mission team as they headed back to the lifts to ascend to the command centre.

"How are you, Angus?" Daniel asked the wiry, red-haired chief of engineering, as they entered the lift.

"I'm as fit as a hungry whippet, sir," the Scotsman replied in his broad accent.

"Glad to hear it. Although, let's hope you won't be hungry for too much longer."

"Aye. I could eat the bahookie off a scraggly tup."

Daniel looked at Kelly, who interpreted. "He could eat the backside off a skinny male sheep."

Daniel raised his eyebrows. "I've had worse food since coming on board."

**2**

Captain Nash Anderson was seated in his captain's chair on the raised platform that served as Longshot's bridge, over-looking the rest of the command centre. Daniel, Kelly and Angus Fraser were the last of the mission team to arrive, and Daniel noted that most of the consoles throughout the command centre were now manned by crew members waiting for control of the ship to be handed over from the ship's artificial intelligence.

Anderson welcomed everyone and then address the AI. "Eric, I'm ready to receive your mission status report."

"Aye, sir," replied Eric, an acronym for Emergency Reserve Intelligent Computer. Longshot's primary artificial intelligence had become corrupt and had needed to be destroyed in a final, tense struggle for control of the ship, prior to the crew entering cryogenic stasis. "There is good news and bad news, Captain."

Several groans emanated from members of the mission team.

"Proceed," was all Anderson said, maintaining a calm demeanour.

"There are actually two pieces of good news. The first, is that we have reached the Tama system, and the second is that it is now inhabited. As we had hoped, humans have colonised the system, travelling here in much faster starships during the centuries while we coasted here in our disabled vessel."

"Very good. What's the bad news?"

"We appear to be having communication problems, Captain."

"Enlarge."

"We can hear them, but they don't seem to be receiving my communication attempts."

"What have they been saying?"

"There is a repeated message that is being looped. I will play it now."

There was a brief pause, then a voice in a strangely nuanced accent played over the ship's speakers.

*"Unidentified interstellar vessel, this is Tama System Control. Please identify yourself and state your purpose. Attempting to enter the Tama system without authorisation will be deemed to be an act of aggression and will result in terminal action."*

"How long have we been receiving that message?" asked Anderson.

"We began receiving it when we were one month from the outer edges of the Tama solar system. We are now one week away from entering their system and the message continues to repeat every five minutes."

"What attempts at communication have you made?"

"For the entire duration of our voyage, 370 years, 5 months and 11 days, I have been broadcasting the distress call and message that you recorded prior to going to sleep, Captain. Since receiving this message from Tama System Control, I have augmented your message with additional messages, identifying us and asking for assistance. After more than two weeks of failing to receive a response from them, I decided to wake the crew."

"What frequencies have you been broadcasting on?"

"All available frequencies, Captain."

Anderson turned to his XO, Commander Bryce Decker. "What do you make of it, Commander?"

"The most likely explanation is that our transmitter has been damaged, sir."

"I concur, Captain," said Lieutenant Olivia Alvarez. The tall, dark-haired mission specialist was now the acting chief of communications and computer systems, replacing the deceased Rajish Patel, who had been one of the saboteurs who was partly-responsible for their current predicament. "It was one of our worries after the explosion took out our VAR drive. We have two receivers – one at each end of the ship – or at least we did have two, before we lost the back half of Longshot. But the transmitter is located amidships, just above the damaged sections. The explosion must have damaged it."

Anderson considered this for a moment. "What are our chances of fixing it, Lieutenant?"

Alvarez screwed up her face in concern. "Not great, sir. Our external visual inspection immediately after the explosion couldn't identify any obvious damage, but we can certainly send out a crew to have a closer look."

He nodded then addressed Eric again. "Eric, exactly how long until we enter the solar system?"

"Six days, eleven hours, Captain."

"And what is our current trajectory?"

"Our course will take us within 537 million kilometres of Tama-B, and 286 million kilometres of Tama-C. Once we breach the outer limits of the solar system, at our velocity of 30,000 kilometres per second, it will take us 10 days and 18 hours to traverse the solar system and reach interstellar space on the other side."

"That's if they let us, sir," said Decker. "It doesn't sound as if they're very welcoming of strange vessels."

"No, it doesn't," agreed Anderson. "Where is their message originating from, Eric?"

"I have identified a satellite at the edge of the solar system as the source of the transmissions."

"Is it armed?"

"I cannot tell, at this distance, Captain."

"Give me our forward view on the screen."

A starfield appeared on the main screen, with one star in the centre, slightly bigger and brighter than the others, casting an eery orange light into the surrounding darkness.

"There it is," muttered Anderson. "Tama. A Type-K main sequence star."

They all gazed at the image of the star around which their potential new world orbited. But with no VAR drive, they had no way of decelerating and, therefore, no way of establishing orbit around the planet. Unless they could obtain assistance from the people now inhabiting this system, they were destined to fly straight past at ten percent of lightspeed and disappear forever into the void between the stars.

"Can you enlarge any further?" asked Anderson.

"The image is already at maximum magnification, Captain. At this distance there are no planets visible. Neither is the sentinel satellite visible to our visual scanners."

As they all continued to gaze at the image on the screen, Eric interrupted them. "Captain, I am receiving a new message. In fact, it is the old message with a new addendum. Would you like me to play it?"

"Go ahead."

*"Unidentified interstellar vessel, this is Tama System Control. Please identify yourself and state your purpose. Attempting to enter the Tama system without authorisation will be deemed to be an act of aggression and will result in terminal action. We have attempted to contact you for the last three weeks. At your current velocity, you are now one week from entering this star system. If you continue on your present course without identifying yourself, we will be forced to destroy your vessel when you reach the edge of our system."*

**3**

———

"The first step is to send someone outside on an EVA and visually inspect the transmitter," said Anderson, addressing the the mission team in the wardroom. "There could be damage that was not picked up in our previous visual inspection after the explosion."

"That's quite possible, sir," said Alvarez. "The previous inspection was done via a quick fly around with a shuttle. At that stage we were looking for hull breaches or major damage that would pose a risk for life support. I doubt they would have been able to pick up something small like a broken connector to a transmission dish."

"Well, this time they won't be using a shuttle to do the inspection," commented Angus Fraser, the chief engineer. The red-headed Scotsman was looking slightly strained, and he creased his brow as he spoke. "The two shuttles that we used to adjust our trajectory are still welded to the side of the ship, and the other two are permanently hooked up to the ship's power grid so that their fusion drives continue to power our deflector shields."

Anderson nodded. "Yes, we won't be using shuttles for this inspection. Someone will have to suit up and do an EVA. That's preferable, anyway, as it will have to be a detailed, close inspection to try to locate the damage. Unfortunately, the external camera that was near the transmission dish is not working, no doubt damaged by the explosion, so we can't identify the problem remotely."

"I'll get someone straight onto it, Captain," promised Commander Decker.

"In the meantime," continued Anderson, "let's work the problem from this end. Assuming the worst, and we remain unable to transmit, we are faced with a looming deadline with serious consequences. If the threat expressed in the messages is to be believed, we have a week to find a solution or risk being destroyed. What are our options?" He looked around the oval table at his mission team.

"The shuttles have comms," suggested Decker. "Could we use those to send a message?"

Science Officer Maria Vargas shook her head. "The shuttles only have short range transmission capabilities. A maximum range of about a million kilometres. At our current velocity of 300,000 kilometres per second, we would only come within effective transmission range three and a third seconds before arriving at the edge of the solar system. I suspect it will be too late by then." She raised her perfectly manicured eyebrows in a typically Brazilian expression, expressing her doubt about that particular course of action.

"Could the transmission capabilities of a shuttle be boosted?" asked Anderson.

"Possibly," admitted Vargas, pursing her lips together momentarily as she considered the suggestion. "We would need to mount a much larger transmission dish on the exterior of the shuttle and then significantly upgrade the transmission system inside the shuttle." She looked at the chief of engineering. "It would be a major job for Mr Fraser's team."

"Aye, Captain," agreed Fraser. "We'd need to rip the guts out of the cockpit console and give the whole system a major heart transplant."

"How long would it take, Mr Fraser?" asked Anderson.

"Hard to say, Captain. I'm not sure what spare components we have available and what we will have to make from scratch. Part of the problem is that the explosion that took out our main drive also blew away 17 of our 50 levels of storage. It depends where those kinds of spare components were stored."

"I see. Can you get onto that, straight away, Mr Fraser? Let me know where we stand."

"Aye, sir."

"In the meantime, let's get this visual inspection underway. The best outcome would be that there is a simple fix to our problem."

~

An hour later, the idea of a simple fix was no longer an option. Daniel was with Captain Anderson on the bridge when the comm call came through from the EVA team.

"Captain, do you copy?"

"Go ahead, Jordan."

"Sir, Ortega and I have reached the transmitter and we can see the problem."

"What is it?"

"There isn't one."

"There isn't a problem?"

"No, sir. There isn't a transmitter. Full stop. It's gone. The whole transmission dish has been sheared off at the hull."

"Why didn't we pick that up in our initial inspection?"

"Sir, that was my fault. I did the fly around in the shuttle. I was looking for major structural damage. I didn't even notice the missing transmission dish. From a distance of more than a few metres, all there is to see here is a perfectly smooth hull. I'm sorry, sir. I take full responsibility."

"No, you can't be blamed, Sergeant. I'm sure it was easy to miss. There's nothing more you can do out there now. Get yourselves safely back inside."

"Yes, sir."

Anderson closed the comm channel and let out a long sigh. "So, now we know why our transmissions haven't been received." His brow furrowed as he thought through the options, and those around him remained silent. He activated the comm again. "Mr Fraser, do you copy?"

"Aye, sir."

"How is your inventory check progressing? Do we have the necessary components to upgrade the shuttle's transmission capabilities?"

"Yes and no, Captain. We have a spare TTS transponder but no multiband modulator and no isotropic amplifier. I think I can scavenge Longshot's own amplifier from the communication console in the command centre, but we'll have to build the multiband moderator from scratch. That will take the best part of five or six days. Then we'll need to take the transmitter dish from Longshot and mount it on the shuttle."

"Mr Fraser, we've just discovered that Longshot's transmission dish is gone."

The captain waited for Fraser's response, but the comm remained strangely silent.

Anderson broke the silence. "Do we have a spare transmission disk, Mr Fraser?"

"No, Captain. Unfortunately, we don't."

"Could you build one?"

"No, sir. These dishes aren't anything like the oversized dinner plates of the past. They're packed full of micro-circuitry. We haven't got a hope in hell of producing one."

"Could you modify the existing one on the shuttle?"

"Sorry, sir, no. It's tiny. There's now way of modifying it to handle the power of the transmission we are trying to produce."

"I see. Do you have any other suggestions, Mr Fraser?"

"Right about now, my best suggestion would be to crack open any bottles of malt whisky you might have been saving for a rainy day. Begging your pardon, sir."

"Understood, Mr Fraser. As you were." Anderson disconnected the call.

There was silence around the bridge. The operators at nearby consoles had overheard the conversation and were now looking toward the captain, hoping that a solution to their dire predicament would present itself. Commander Decker and Mission Specialist Alvarez were also looking to the captain, hoping for a moment of brilliance.

Anderson sighed deeply, then summarised their predicament. "So, we can't slow down, we can't communicate with the outside world and our potential rescuers are threatening to blow us to pieces. Have I missed anything? Can any of you see something that I can't?"

There was silence again for a moment, until Daniel spoke up. "That's it!"

"What?" asked Alvarez, looking at him.

"Captain, you used the word, 'see'! You said, 'Can anyone see something that I can't?' That's the answer! They can't hear us, but they can certainly see us."

"I don't follow," Anderson replied, with a puzzled look on his face.

"We can't communicate with them audibly, but we can certainly communicate visually."

"Some kind of visual signal?" asked Anderson.

"Yes. Morse code."

"Never heard of it," commented Decker. "What is it?"

"An archaic form of communication, used in the 1800s, involving a series of dots and dashes to spell out letters to form words."

"I've heard of it," admitted Anderson, "but never seen it in operation."

"I assume the dots and dashes were audible in some way?" asked Alvarez.

"Yes. But in our case, we can use pulses of light to transmit the dots and dashes visually. A short flash of light is a dot, and a slightly longer flash of light is a dash."

"But do we have a bright enough light source?" asked Decker. "We are currently nearly 18 billion kilometres from the edge of the solar system. That's a hell of a long way to shine a light."

"There are a couple of parts to the answer," responded Daniel. "Firstly, although we can't yet see their sentinel satellite – or space station or whatever it is – they can apparently already see us and have been able to do so for the last three weeks. Obviously, their technology is centuries more advanced than ours. Secondly, given that they can already detect us, they should be able to also detect changes to our luminosity. By flicking lights on and off, preferably lots of them all at once, it should be pretty obvious."

"What lights?" asked Alvarez. "We don't have a whole lot of windows on board Longshot."

"But we do have four large shuttle bays: two on each side of the ship. We could open up the two shuttle bays on one side and get Eric to flick the lights on and off."

Decker shook his head. "But that would mean exposing the whole side of our ship to whatever micro matter – or even larger matter – that might be in our path. We would lose the protection of our front deflector dish and its LAF – the laser annihilation field. We'd be sitting ducks. If we ran into any debris while flying side-on at our current velocity, it would rip us to pieces."

"Yes, it would," agreed Daniel. He let his simple response hang in the air.

Anderson cleared his throat. "Your point is that we don't really have a choice."

"That's right, Captain. If we continue as we are, and do nothing, we will be destroyed. That appears to be a certainty. Turning our ship side on in order to send a visual signal is certainly risky, but it is the lesser of two risks. It is a choice between certain destruction, on the one hand, and only possible destruction, on the other, the latter bringing with it a high likelihood of success and survival."

They all considered his words carefully.

"Bear in mind," said Decker, frowning, "that the outer edges of most solar systems tend to accumulate tiny particles of debris, trapped by the star's gravity and locked into a slow orbit around the heliosphere. The closer we get to the edge of the heliosphere, which marks the edge of the solar system, the higher the likelihood of encountering stray particles."

"True," replied Daniel. "Which is why we need to start signally as soon as possible, before we get too close."

Anderson addressed a point in mid-air. "Eric, do you know morse code?"

"In anticipation of your request, I have just researched it in our history files and acquired it, Captain."

"Good. Let's quickly work on a simple message. Once we've settled on that, we will swing the ship around and start signalling."

"Of course, there's one other complication," added Daniel.

"What's that?" asked Anderson.

"It depends entirely upon the people of the Tama system recognising morse code and being able to decipher it. When Longshot departed Earth, it had been 500 years since anyone had used morse code. But we have also just slept for 370 years. Will anyone on Tama-B have any recollection of a communication system that is nearly 900 years in their past? Will they even have a record of morse code in their history files?"

Anderson nodded. "Let us hope and pray that they do."

4

———

A t an altitude of 28,000 kilometres above the planet's surface, an impressive mini city orbited. Looking like an over-inflated bicycle tyre with spokes leading to a multi-layered hub, the orbiting city maintained a permanent presence over the mainland below as it followed the rotation of the planet in geosynchronous orbit. At night, the city's lights were a reassuring presence to those below, a permanent star reminding the world's peaceful inhabitants of the watchful presence of those who were charged with their protection. Parents pointed it out to their children, assuring them that Angel City would keep them safe through the dark hours of the night. Lovers lay gazing up at it, attaching romantic symbolism to its ethereal, twinkling lights. Dreamers and science aficionados gazed at it through telescopes and followed it closely via its multi-channelled live stream.

Over an average day or week or month, the live streams held little interest for the average citizen of Atraya. The most popular broadcast channel was the weather report, helping them decide whether they needed to wear a warmer sweater or cancel their outdoor barbeque.

But this was not an average day. It had not been an average week or month. The news that an unidentified starship was approaching their solar system from the direction of Earth had sent shock waves around the globe. Panic had set in among the populace. Old fears, buried and forgotten long ago, rose to the surface once again. Speculation regarding the strangely silent spacecraft dominated the newsfeeds and was the focus of almost every conversation. After over a century of peace, would they now, once again, need to defend themselves from the hostile overtures of Earth? The scars of their last encounter with Terran warships were still etched into the landscapes of their planetary systems, like unhealed wounds. There were deep craters on Jumea, the third planet, and on its moon, Kronos, where human colonies had been blasted out of existence. One Terran warship had even made it as far as Atraya's own moon, Rios, where it had destroyed a military outpost before it had been crippled by defensive lasers, eventually crashing into the moon's surface. Its jagged remains now sat in eternal silence on the airless moon, a stark reminder of how close the Atrayans had come to losing their precious freedom and succumbing to the avarice of the over-reaching Terrans.

Now, as the silent starship drew ever-nearer to their solar system, images and telemetry data of its looming approach were relayed from the sentinel satellites at the outer edge of their solar system to Tama System Control, in the hub of Angel City. From there, the images and data were broadcast around the globe, keeping the populace informed of the unfolding drama. The starship was still too far away for much detail to be visible; all that could be seen was what appeared to be a large front deflector dish, similar to the design of the Terran vessels that had once tried to invade their solar system.

For the past three weeks, the comm screens in almost every home had been locked onto the relayed feeds from the sentinels as well as the continual speculation and debate on the news channels regarding the possible purpose of the mysterious vessel. Why was the vessel refusing to answer all attempts at communication? Surely, this inferred hostile intent. A starship with benign intentions would certainly have opened communication with them by now.

Debate raged as to what course of action should be followed. There were many commentators, and many within the general populace, who insisted that waiting until the ship breached the outer edges of the solar system before initiating defensive action was foolhardy. After all, the vessel had already been given three weeks to open friendly communication and had refused. Why should they risk allowing it to come any closer? It was already within striking distance of the sentinels' defence systems. Open fire now, before it had a chance to breach their defences and unleash its own weapons! Petitions had been raised and public campaigns mounted, calling for the authorities to act immediately. The ADF – Atrayan Defensive Forces – were on high alert, and its commanding officer was under increasing pressure to act decisively.

Others argued for patience. Perhaps the ship did not possess the long-range communication capabilities of the Atrayans. Or maybe the occupants of the vessel were all still in cryogenic stasis and the ship's artificial intelligence was not programmed to respond to external communications without authorisation from the crew.

And so, the debate raged.

But through it all, whatever side of the debate people were on, there was an undercurrent of fear. Their peaceful way of life was, once again, under threat. The Terrans, who had tried to violently seize control of their peaceful world through two failed coups and, finally, an outright assault, were once again on their doorstep. After 120 years of complete silence, they were back!

Now, as a new morning dawned across the continent of Northland, families were awakening to another day of speculation and drama. In the capital city of Jasper, directly beneath the orbiting Angel City, the rising sun was peeking over the rim of the Eastern ocean, painting the underside of the thin wispy clouds with deep orange and apricot, and infusing the ubiquitous morning mist with a dark orange, almost red, glow. It was a daily light show that the Atrayans had become accustomed to, but which had seemed eery and alien to the settlers who had arrived in the first starship, centuries earlier.

The red-shifted spectrum of light emanating from their star, Tama, meant that there were no true greens or blues. Everything was shifted toward orange. Grass was brown. The sky was apricot. This led to some strange conundrums. Could blue-eyed people still be referred to as blue-eyed? Their eyes were a rust-colored deep orange when they were outside, but blue again when they were under artificial white lights. Could you still say that someone was 'green with envy'? Surely, they were now 'brown with envy'? The inhabitants of Atraya had long since become accustomed to the changing nature of colors from indoors to outdoors and had even developed art forms and colors that celebrated the inconstant nature of spectral frequencies.

Keelor Trantum padded into the kitchen of the family domicile, glancing out the window at the dark orange early morning mist that hung over their farm. He heard the lowing of their cows as his father herded them into the milking shed, accompanied by the enthusiastic barking of their dog. Rusty liked to think he was a working farm dog, but somehow, the instincts of his breed had sidestepped him, leaving him clueless. He tended to run around the cattle randomly, barking and even running between their legs. The cattle, for their part, had learned to ignore him altogether, as if he were no more than a mildly annoying insect. Keelor heard his father calling Rusty to heel which, he knew from experience, would only be effective for a few brief moments until the dog's exuberance overcame his obedience and he rushed enthusiastically into the fray once more.

"I don't understand why Dad doesn't tie Rusty up while he's getting the cows in," he commented to his mother.

"You know your father. He's got a soft spot for that dog. Besides, it's company for him as he does the milking."

Keelor's father was one of several farmers in the area who preferred the pure-bred Earth cows, directly descended from the frozen embryos brought to Atraya by the first settlers. He argued that the creamier taste made up for the slightly lower milk yield, compared to the genetically modified breeds.

"Two eggs and bacon on rye toast," Keelor said to the food dispenser, yawning and stretching as he did so.

"You stayed up late last night," his mother commented.

"I was trying to work out if there is any kind of meaning behind the flashing lights on the Terran ship. The pattern repeats every 157 seconds. The same pattern, over and over again. It's been repeating like that for the last six days."

"If TSC can't work it out, I doubt that you'll be able to."

"Gee, thanks for the vote of confidence," he said as a chime announced the arrival of his breakfast. He opened the door of the dispenser, took out the plate of food and sat at the kitchen bench. "The staff at Tama System Control aren't infallible, you know," he said, a moment later, speaking through a mouthful of bacon and eggs.

"I'm just being realistic, my darling. They've been trained to deal with this sort of thing. If they say there is no meaning behind the pattern, there mustn't be one. And don't talk with your mouthful."

"But what if they're wrong?" he continued, stuffing another forkful of bacon and eggs into his mouth. "They say that it must be some kind of electrical fault in lighting relays that has set up a cyclical fault pattern. But what if the ship isn't from Earth? What if they're aliens who don't communicate verbally, but use visual patterns to communicate? If we destroy them, we could be about to start a war with another sentient species."

"I doubt that," said his mother as she placed her used coffee mug in the sonic auto washer. She pulled it out a few seconds later and replaced it in the cupboard. "The ship's trajectory shows that it has definitely originated from the Terran system. So, it must be Terran. Besides, you've got more important things to think about, haven't you? Tomorrow is your big day."

He walked to the drink dispenser and ordered a coffee from the dispenser. "What could be bigger than the first encounter with people from outside our solar system for 120 years?"

"It's your enhancement day! I'd say that's a pretty big deal."

He shrugged. "I guess."

"I know you didn't want a party, but your grandparents and your uncle and aunty are coming for dinner tonight, and your cousin Sia. It will be a low-key family send off for you before you leave in the morning."

Keelor started to complain, but his mother cut him off. "This is not open for debate. It's your 21$^{st}$ birthday, for goodness' sake, and your family want to celebrate it with you! Now, hurry up and finish your coffee and go and help your father with the clean-up."

A few minutes later, Keelor emerged into the crisp morning air and trudged up the hill toward the milking shed. The orange mist was beginning to disperse, and the sky had lightened into a pale apricot. Rusty saw him and raced excitedly to him, jumping up at him and wagging his tail furiously.

"Good boy," Keelor said, absently patting the dog. He continued up the hill with the dog running in circles around him, but Keelor's attention was elsewhere. He couldn't stop thinking about the mysterious starship and its curious flashing lights. He couldn't shake the feeling that by destroying it, as TSC was planning to do, they were about to make a terrible mistake.

**5**

———

Longshot shuddered and an alarm began to sound throughout the ship. It was a little after 2:00 in the early hours of the morning, and the crew were all asleep. Daniel came awake with a start and sprang into action. He launched himself from the top bunk and slipped his magnetic boots on with practised ease, quickly activating them.

"That doesn't sound good," said Kelly, blinking her eyes as she extricated herself from the lower bunk and began dressing. "Did you feel the tremor?"

"Yes," responded Daniel. "I'm guessing we just suffered an impact. It's what we've been worried about, as we draw closer to the edge of the solar system." He donned his shirt and clomped toward the door. "I'm heading for the command centre. I'll see you there." He walked awkwardly down the hallway to the lifts as a ship wide message advised all crew to get to their appropriate stations. He took a lift up to the command centre, sharing it with Jordan who was rubbing sleep from her eyes, smudging her dark eyeliner as she did so.

"Nice morning for an emergency," she said.

"Lovely," he agreed. "Where are you headed?"

"Command centre. The boss messaged me. I'm guessing it's something to do with the shuttles."

"Maybe he just loves the pleasure of your sunny disposition," Daniel replied.

"They say that sarcasm is the lowest form of wit."

"I like to pitch my conversation at the level of my recipients," he replied.

"You're hilarious."

The lift doors opened onto a scene of controlled panic. Various console operators were trying to determine the extent and location of damage, and people were talking across each other. Captain Anderson walked in from the second lift and ordered quiet.

"What's our status, Ensign?" he asked a female console operator closest to his chair on the bridge.

"Sensors indicate that we took a direct hit amidship, sir," she answered, still furiously tapping and swiping on her screen. "It looks like ... yes, a projectile has gone clean through Level 68, Recreation Level 1. In one side and out the other. We've lost atmosphere to that entire level. The bulkheads sealed it automatically."

Commander Decker had arrived as she was talking and he asked, "Were any essential systems damaged? There are power and life support conduits running the length of the ship."

"There's no damage to any systems evident, Commander."

The Captain addressed the ship's artificial intelligence. "Eric, why was there no warning?"

"My sensors can identify a single piece of debris of one centimetre in diameter at a maximum range of 100,000 kilometres, two centimetres at two hundred thousand kilometres, and so forth. Our current velocity of 300,000 kilometres per second is such that I would get a one second warning of a three-centimetre object at a distance of 300,000 kilometres. The object that pierced us showed up in my scans 0.76 seconds before it impacted, therefore inferring that it was 2.28 centimetres in diameter."

"How close are we to entering the solar system?" Anderson asked.

"We are 648 million kilometres from what would be deemed to be the edge of the solar system. At our current velocity, we will enter the solar system in six hours."

"And still no response to our morse code message?"

"None, Captain."

"What is the position of their satellite?"

"My sensors now indicate the presence of two large satellites, both 650 million kilometres distant: one to port and one to starboard. The second one has moved into position over the last 12 hours."

"I'd like to think it's a friendly welcoming committee, but I doubt it," offered Alvarez.

"Sir, we can't risk flying side on any longer," said Decker. "There is almost certainly going to be more debris around the outer edge of the heliosphere: stray particles of matter captured by the star's gravitational field and held in a permanent orbit. If we continue like this, we are almost certainly going to suffer a much more devastating broadside."

Anderson nodded, thoughtfully. "Unfortunately, you're right, Commander. I think we've done all we can in attempting to communicate. I can't expose the side of the ship any longer. Plus, lining us up behind our deflector shield might give us a little extra protection if we are fired upon. The downside is that our flashing lights will no longer be visible behind our deflector dish."

"It can't be avoided, sir," said Decker.

Anderson nodded reflectively and sighed deeply, as he weighed up his final decision. "Eric, bring the fusion drives of both the shuttles welded to our hull online. Prepare to swing us around."

"Aye, sir."

"Jordan, seat yourself at Console 4. I want a trained pilot casting an expert eye over the manoeuvre. I don't want to leave anything to chance."

"Yes, sir."

"Captain, if you don't mind me asking, how long will it take to bring the shuttles online?" asked Daniel.

"Eric?" asked the captain, deferring to the AI.

"Approximately seven minutes."

"Sir, a suggestion," said Daniel.

"Go ahead."

"Change the message we are broadcasting via morse code for these remaining seven minutes."

"To what?"

"S.O.S."

"You think it will make any difference?"

"It can't hurt, sir. The changed pattern might jog someone's memory – or at least give them a second pattern to consider."

Anderson nodded. "Very well. Make it happen, Eric."

"Done, sir," replied the artificial intelligence.

"Save our souls," muttered Anderson. "How appropriate. Now all we can do is wait and pray."

6

———

Tama System Control was situated at the very heart of Angel City, in the hub of the huge wheel-shaped space station in orbit around Atraya. The city had a diameter of approximately one kilometre from outer rim to outer rim, and the central hub was a cylinder of 100 metres diameter, attached to the main wheel-shaped structure via spokes of varying sizes. The headquarters and training academy for the ADF, the Atrayan Defence Force, occupied the top 12 levels of the central hub, with the very top level devoted to Tama System Control. Its 360-degree panoramic windows gave a magnificent view of space to one side and the planet to the other. Not that the duty crew had much time for gazing out the windows.

TSC was the hub for communications throughout the Tama system. There were bases on Jumea, the third planet, Kronos, its moon, Rios, Atraya's moon, and two space stations in orbit around Helios, the tidally locked first planet. As well as all that, TSC also tracked and controlled the 12 sentinel satellites that were permanently patrolling the outer edges of their solar system. After the near disastrous surprise attack by the Terrans 120 years ago, the Atrayans were determined to never again be caught unaware.

"Commander, the pattern of flashing lights has changed."

Commander Shila Hansen walked briskly to the console operator who was currently monitoring the signals from the two sentinels that were watching the approaching intruder.

"Show me."

She looked at the screen, over the operator's shoulder. Three short flashes, three long flashes, followed by three more short flashes, then a long break before the pattern repeated.

"What do you make if it?" she asked the controller.

"No idea, ma'am. Except that it can't be dismissed as random any longer, surely. Could it be some kind of message?"

"Perhaps. But it's more likely to be an automated external lighting system that kicks in when the ship approaches a new solar system – like a flitter flying at night on Atraya, for identification purposes."

"But if they're hostile, why would they want to identify themselves, ma'am?"

"Maybe they've forgotten to turn the system off. Or maybe it's more sinister than that. Perhaps this is a sign of them arming their weapons for attack."

The commander paused, considering her options.

"How far from our sentinels is it now?"

"A little under six hours, at their current velocity."

"Bring the weapons systems fully online and await my orders."

"Yes, ma'am."

Hansen moved aside and activated her personal comm. "Colonel Forster, do you copy?"

"Yes, Commander. And I know why you're calling. I can see the new light pattern on my feed, here in the situation room. What are your thoughts?"

"There is a slightly increased possibility that they are trying to communicate with us, but I still think the most likely scenario is that they are hostile in intent. The lights are probably an automated system of some kind."

"Not a very sensible strategy if they are trying to sneak up on us, though, is it?" commented the Colonel.

"I think, by now, they know they aren't sneaking up on us, sir.

In fact, they may well be trying to confuse us into thinking they are attempting to communicate, so that we will hold off firing until they can bring their own weapons to bear."

"Yes. I suspect you're right. I'm getting enormous pressure from the senate to blow the ship to pieces immediately."

"What are your orders, sir?"

There was silence for a few moments, and Hansen could hear the colonel breathing heavily, as if he was carrying a heavy weight on his shoulders, which, of course, he was.

"Can we get a visual on the ship yet?"

"It's still only a dot at the fullest extreme of our cameras, sir. We'll start to see some detail when it is about two hours out."

"Mm." The colonel paused, again. "Damn it! I don't like having to do this, any more than you do, Commander, but we've got the safety of our whole population to consider."

"Just a moment, Colonel!" interrupted Hansen. "Are you seeing this? The flashing has stopped."

"Yes, I can see it. But it doesn't change anything. In fact, it just confirms that the flashing must have been some kind of auto-mated system. I'm authorising you to open fire with deadly force when their vessel is two hours out from our sentinels."

"Confirming authorisation of deadly force in ..." she looked at the countdown timer running on her console, "...3 hours 54 minutes."

"Confirmed. You are authorised, Commander."

"Yes, sir."

"Do us proud, Commander."

"I will, sir."

**7**

———

The party was in full swing, to the limited extent that any party solely comprised of two parents, two grandparents, an aunty, an uncle and a 17-year-old niece could legitimately be described as 'swinging'. The night before an individual's enhancement was usually an occasion for big celebrations, marking the end of adolescence and a person's entry into fully integrated adulthood. Along with binding, when you bound yourself to a life partner, it was arguably the most important occasion in a someone's life. Some families hired bands and invited hundreds of guests to celebrate the impending enhancement of their son or daughter. Many of the young people, themselves, spent months planning their enhancement party and negotiating with their parents regarding how many they could invite and how extravagant they could make the celebrations.

But not Keelor. He had always been a solitary, reclusive type, and hadn't wanted a party at all. If he'd had a complete say in the matter, he would have preferred to spend the evening as he usually did, roaming the data streams and exploring the colony's archives.

His family, however, had other plans, and they were not to be denied. Keelor's grandmother had baked a cake in the shape of

'21', and his aunty had cooked her famous pumpkin pie. After dinner was finished, Keelor was made to sit through a visual collage of videos and images set to music, showing his development from a wobbly toddler to the young man that he was now. Following that, his father gave a short speech, expressing his pride in the fine young man that Keelor had become. Keelor was then made to stand in the centre of the room and the family pronounced the formal enhancement blessing upon him. Each person in turn stepped forward and placed their hand against the back of his head and said, "May your enhancement bless our community." A toast was then made, with everyone downing a hefty gulp of stava, an aromatic alcohol that was produced from the fermentation of a local flower. Keelor noticed that Sia, his 17-year-old cousin, topped her glass up with a hefty second serving and drank it down enthusiastically.

Eventually, the adults progressed to reminiscing about old times, drinking stava and laughing, and Keelor was able to slip into his room undetected. At least, he *thought* his departure had gone undetected.

"Hi Keelor," said Sia, as she opened his door and stood in the doorway. "What are you doing?"

"Nothing much," he said, opening one of his favourite data streams and scanning the latest news.

Sia stepped into his room and closed the door behind her, leaning back against it.

"Do you ever get lonely?" she asked.

"Not really, I enjoy my own company."

"I get lonely. We live way out of town, and we hardly ever see anyone." She moved and sat on the bed beside him as he used a remote to scroll down the large screen built into his bedroom wall. Sia sighed and looked around the room. "You don't have many interesting decorations in here."

"No."

She sighed again and gave up trying to find anything interesting in his room. She looked at him instead. "Have you ever had a girlfriend?"

"Not really." Keelor continued to read the screen, barely noticing his cousin.

"Not really? What does that mean?"

"It means no."

"Have you ever kissed a girl?"

Keelor paused and looked at her, wondering why she was suddenly so interested in his romantic life. He briefly contemplated making up some stories to impress her, but then felt that he couldn't be bothered. Besides, she probably already knew the truth.

"No."

He resumed reading the screen.

"Would you like to?"

He shrugged. "Sure. What guy wouldn't?"

"I've never kissed a boy, but most of my friends have. It's easy for them, they go to school in town. I have to do school remotely."

She shifted closer to him, so that her thigh was touching his.

"I'd sure like to try kissing." She paused and looked at him. "Would you like to kiss me?"

He frowned, without looking away from the screen. "But you're my cousin."

"So? Cousins kiss all the time. Don't you find me attractive?"

He looked at her now, as if seeing her for the first time. She certainly had blossomed over the last 18 months. She was no longer the spindly young girl that he remembered. She was a fully developed woman now, and the dress she was wearing tonight, with its plunging neckline, confirmed it. His eyes strayed to her breasts and he also noted how her short dress had ridden up so high that he could almost see her underwear. He felt a surge of excitement and looked away awkwardly.

Sensing his mood change, she placed her hand on his thigh and leaned in toward him, purposely allowing him a better glimpse of her cleavage. This was not a spur of the moment thing for her. She had plotted her attack all afternoon, choosing the low-cut dress and glossing her lips in anticipation. She was determined to experience her first kiss tonight, even if it was with her cousin.

"I won't tell, if you don't," she said, reaching her other hand to his own and twisting him toward her. "There's no harm in it," she murmured, leaning closer still and brushing her lips lightly against his.

Keelor was completely out of his depth. This was his cousin! But she had also grown into a beautiful young woman, with curves in all the right places. And her lips looked so inviting, so sweet. He glanced furtively toward the closed door.

Sensing that he was crumbling, she whispered, "They'll never know. Kiss me. Please!" She parted her lips and ran her tongue briefly across her top lip, like she had seen women do in movies.

Keelor's last defences crumbled, and he leaned in and kissed her. Their lips came together, and he felt their softness against his own and smelt her flowery fragrance. They stayed like that for several moments and then he drew back, his heart thumping in his chest. He saw that Sia's cheeks had a blush to them now and she was breathing a little faster.

"That was nice," she said. "Do you want to try something else?"

He nodded, unable to speak and not wanting to break the spell.

She leant in toward him again and they kissed once more, but this time she parted her lips and her tongue slid between his own. Keelor felt a surge of excitement as he savoured the exquisite sensation of her slippery tongue inside his mouth, and he found himself aroused more than he could have imagined. He responded in kind and their clumsy kissing became more passionate. New sensations swirled through them both, leaving them breathless and giddy. Eventually, they came up for air and drew apart. Both were flushed now.

"That was ... umm ..." said Keelor.

"Nice?" suggested Sia.

"Yeh."

Sia bit her bottom lip uncertainly, then asked, "Would you like to touch my breast?"

Keelor shot to his feet and turned to stare at the screen on his wall. He had glimpsed something out of the corner of his eye and now he faced the image directly. He had dedicated the top left corner of the screen to the feed from the sentinel satellite, showing the sporadically flashing lights of the strange starship.

"What is it?" asked Sia, looking between Keelor and the screen, uncertainly.

"The new starship. It's blinking in a steady pattern now."

"So?" she asked, starting to feel a little frustrated.

"It's got to be a message; it's just got to be!" Keelor mumbled to himself, as he continued to stare at the screen. "Three short, three long, and three short again."

He sat at his desk and mirrored the wall screen to the desk's transparent top. He began swiping and typing, scrolling and tapping, muttering to himself as he did so.

"Why are you so interested in a boring old starship, anyway?" Sia asked as she came to stand beside him, hoping that her proximity would remind him that they had unfinished business to attend to. "If there are people in it, they would be centuries old," she continued, as if that was the definitive argument for the vessel's irrelevance.

Keelor paused in mid-action, his brow furrowing as he considered her last words.

"Yes. Yes, you're right! They would be centuries old! And so would any of their communication codes! How old ... how old ... how old?" he repeated to himself as he called up a calculator. "We know their current velocity, and we know the distance to Earth, so if they maintained that velocity for the whole journey, they would have left Earth ... 370 years ago!"

He cancelled the calculator and sat thinking for a moment. "That's nearly 160 years before the first colonists arrived here. Whatever code they're using predates our colony." He bit his lip. "I need to access the old Earth archives."

He swung around and discovered that Sia had gone, and his bedroom door had been left open. He experienced a moment of regret, but then shrugged it off. This was more important. He turned back to his desk and began typing.

## 8

---

Keelor opened a separate window and considered his next move. The Earth archives were off limits. Earth history wasn't taught in schools and people weren't encouraged to investigate their pre-Atrayan origins. This policy didn't arise from some kind of totalitarian desire to editorialise the past or erase history. It was simply because the violence of Earth's past was regarded by Atraya's peace-loving colony as being utterly repugnant and detestable. The new society that they wished to build and maintain was one of love, respect and mutual understanding, and the study of Earth's rapacious past was considered to be potentially counterproductive and undesirable. As a consequence, Earth's history archives were locked away and password protected.

Keelor sat and contemplated what he was about to do. It was serious. He could get into trouble for this. He sat poised with his hands hovering over the screen. Then he noticed another new development in the stream from the sentinel. The mysterious ship had stopped flashing its lights. He scanned various newsfeeds and listened to several commentaries, speculating on what was happening. Everyone seemed to be of the opinion that the flashes were meaningless or, at most, part of the strange ship's autonomic functioning.

But Keelor was convinced otherwise.

After a final moment of hesitation, he took the plunge. He activated an encryption program that he had developed as part of his major project at university and which he had modified further over the last 12 months. It would render him invisible to the T-Net security algorithms. It took a few moments before a green light appeared in the top right corner of his new window, indicating that his identity and location were now untraceable.

Keelor went to the T-net archives and found the repository labelled, 'Earth Archives'. He selected the repository and was immediately confronted with a stern warning: 'Earth Archives is a sealed repository. Access is restricted to authorised personnel. Unauthorised access is a serious offense.' Immediately underneath that message were two blank ID boxes: one for 'name' and one for 'authorisation password'. It was an antiquated identification system, as most secure sites used iris identification these days, but the Earth archives held little interest for the average Atrayan and no one in authority regarded them as needing state-of-the-art security. For the most part, these ancient records of Earth sat in a dusty, neglected corner of the digital world, probably not accessed from one year to the next.

Keelor typed in his uncle's name and password. He paused before finally entering it. His uncle, Sia's father, was a Level A T-Net Systems Analyst; part of the team of experts responsible for maintaining the security and integrity of T-Net, the Tama data network that permeated the entire solar system. Keelor had stumbled across his uncle's password during a family visit to their home, six months ago. He had walked past the door to his uncle's study and saw him logging in to his work site. His password was ridiculously simple, a combination of his dog's name and his wife's birthday. Keelor's sharp, analytical mind had filed that information away, and not long afterward, he had made a tentative sortie into the Earth Archives, just to see if he could do it. After a few minutes of curious browsing he had quickly exited, feeling slightly guilty but also giddy with adrenaline after his first experience of illicit online activity.

Now, however, he had a purpose. He felt justified because he was convinced the authorities were missing something. There must be some kind of visual code in Earth's past that would make sense of these strange flashes from the Terran vessel.

He took the plunge and entered his uncle's login information. Instantly, the archive's folder structure was revealed to him, and he quickly scanned the huge list of folders. There were hundreds! Where should he start? He decided to begin with a global search. He entered 'visual communication codes'. A long list of results appeared:

- graphic images
- infographics
- applied visual arts
- visual design
- motion graphics
- typography
- advertising
- animation
- emoticons
- ASCII art

The list continued in that vein, and none of it seemed to lead in the right direction. He had a sudden thought. What if the code the Terrans were signalling with wasn't originally a visual code system? What if it was an auditory one that they were adopting in a visual format? He tried a different search phrase: 'ancient long-distance communication'. The first result caused him to sit up and lean forward. He selected the link and read the description.

'Morse code was developed in the late 1880s by Samuel Morse and others as the first viable long distance communication code. Letters of the alphabet were transmitted electronically as a series of dots and dashes, short and long signals, which formed words and sentences.'

"Short and long! Dots and dashes!" he muttered to himself. "That's it! It must be!"

He scrolled down and found the morse code alphabet key and quickly located the three dots and three dashes.

"S.O.S. What does that mean?"

He did a global search for 'morse code SOS' and found the answer: 'Save our souls, an international distress signal.'

He exclaimed aloud, "They're in trouble! They're not threatening us; they're asking for help!"

Keelor replayed the video of the previous, much longer sequence of long and short flashes of light from the starship. He began translating, and as each letter accumulated and grew into words and whole sentences, his excitement grew. Finally, he had the complete message typed onto a separate window:

*"This is starship Longshot from Earth. Unarmed colony ship. Transmitter and main drive destroyed. No way to slow down. Help."*

Keelor stared at the message, his heart racing and his mind whirling. The authorities needed to be told! They were about to murder a colony ship full of innocent people!

He pondered his predicament. How could he communicate the deciphered message to those in authority, without revealing his identity and his illicit activity? He had no idea who to contact, and even if he did know, they would probably not listen to an insignificant nobody like him. He decided on a blanket approach. He would flood the T-Net with his deciphered message.

He quickly opened a blank message and copied the morse code key and the text of the deciphered messages onto it. Then he typed an introductory message of his own:

*"Urgent! The Terran vessel that is about to enter our solar system is not a threat. They are innocent people in desperate need of our help. The flashes of light are an ancient form of communication known as morse code. The key to the code is shown below, along with the deciphered text of both of their messages: their original longer message and their recent, shorter one. Please convey this to the appropriate authorities, urgently!"*

He then spent nearly thirty minutes sending it to every newsfeed, every public broadcaster, every discussion board and every social media platform that he could find. Finally, he sat back in his chair, his eyes bleary from staring at the screen. He had done all he could do. Now he had to hope that the authorities would take notice before it was too late.

"What if it's a hoax?"

Keelor spun around and was surprised to find Sia sitting quietly on the bed behind him. She had slipped into his room again, unnoticed by him as he had laboured at his urgent task.

"What if they are just trying to lull us into thinking that they are harmless?" she persisted. "They could be trying to fool us until they reach Atraya and then launch an attack."

Keelor stood up and in two strides was standing over her as she sat on the bed. He leant down and grabbed her by the shoulders.

"Sia, you can't tell anyone about this!"

"But you've just told a whole lot of people."

"What I mean is, you can't tell anyone that it was me who sent this message."

"Why not?"

"Because ..." he paused. "I snuck into the Earth archives to find the key to the code."

She stood up and faced him.

"That was a bit naughty of you." She blinked her eyes at him, flirtatiously.

"Sia, promise me you won't tell anyone!" He was still gripping her shoulders.

She smiled, coyly. "I'll promise. If you'll kiss me again."

It was an offer too good to refuse.

9

Commander Shila Hansen was staring at the countdown timer. In just six minutes, the intruders' starship would be two hours away from breaching their solar system, at which point Tama System Control had an authorised order to employ deadly force. Shila was a newly promoted commander, still finding her feet in the role and had not anticipated such a dramatic turn of events so soon. The ADF – Atrayan Defence Force – had not fired a weapon in anger in over 120 years. Ten predecessors, previous commanders of TSC, had come and gone without ever having to activate a weapon. But now, after only a month on the job, she was about to destroy an entire starship.

The burden of responsibility weighed heavily upon her, and she couldn't help thinking about the people on board the starship. Were they all tyrannical fanatics? Surely not all of them. There must be many ordinary people within the ship's crew who were simply carrying out their duties, tending to engines, servicing life support systems or preparing meals, caught up in a cosmic conflict that they had no say in. Ordinary people about to be killed as a result of an order that she now had to give: an order that she had no say in either. This was the sad reality of war: senseless killing and violence between people who, in the normal course of life, had no reason for mutual animosity, but who were forced into deadly conflict by the pugilistic whims of their political leaders.

Shila shook her head and exhaled deeply. She had a job to do and she had to carry it out, for the protection of her own world and her own people. Right now, there were families going about their daily lives on Atraya – taking children to school, tending their gardens, buying groceries and planning the evening meal – ordinary people who were living peaceful lives and were trusting her and her team to keep them safe.

"Weapons check," she said.

"Weapons are online, ma'am," said a console operator.

"Targeting?"

"Both sentinels are locked on."

"Distance at zero count?" she asked.

"We've moved both sentinels forward, ma'am. At the zero count, the distance to target will be 1.6 million kilometres, well within the kill zone of 2 million. At the intruders' current velocity, they will be less than one minute from us at that point."

"Very good." She paused and breathed deeply again. "Set the laser canons to maximum power. You have authorisation to use deadly force."

"Please confirm authorisation to use deadly force, ma'am."

"Confirmed."

"Confirmation acknowledged," replied the weapons operator.

Shila glanced at the countdown timer again. The green digital numbers read 04:52. Less than five minutes until she had to give the order to fire. She felt a sheen of sweat break out on her brow.

"Ma'am! You need to see this!" cried the comm officer, sitting in front of a different console.

In two strides, Shila was looking over his shoulder. Multiple windows were open on his screen, each one showing a message claiming to have deciphered the mysterious starship's flashing lights. She read the message quickly, and her heart rate went through the roof. Could this be true? Were they about to destroy a starship full of innocent people?

"The same message is all over T-Net, ma'am! It's being broadcast through newsfeeds and social media platforms."

Shila activated a comm channel. "Colonel Forster, do you copy?"

"Yes, commander."

"Sir, have you seen the deciphered messages?"

"It's a hoax, Commander. Disregard."

"Sir, it looks genuine. Have we checked with Intel?"

"That's my call to make, not yours. This whole morse code thing is probably just a prank. Besides, those eggheads at Intel haven't got the balls to make the tough decisions. I've got the safety of an entire world to consider, and I can't risk letting a hostile vessel slip through our defences. Your orders stand, Commander. Carry out your duty!"

The comm line went dead, and Shila glanced at the countdown timer, which now read 03:18.

"Get me Intelligence Department! Now!" she ordered.

A moment later, a voice came over the comm. "Intelligence."

"This is Commander Shila Hansen at TSC. I need to speak with Major Maxwell, urgently!"

"Patching you through."

There was a moment's pause, then, "Maxwell."

"Major, this is Commander Hansen at TSC. Are you seeing these deciphered messages?"

"Yes, Commander. My team is working on them right now."

"I need an immediate answer. Is the deciphered message accurate?"

"Yes, ma'am. There is such a thing as morse code, and the flashes from the vessel do, indeed, translate to the message that is currently being circulated around T-Net."

"So, the message is accurately translated?" she repeated.

"Yes, ma'am. I was just about to contact Colonel Forster and tell him."

"Do it! We're running out of time!"

She disconnected and looked at the timer. 02:24.

"What do you want me to do, ma'am?" asked the weapons operator, looking at Shila uncertainly.

"Remain locked onto target and await my order to fire."

"Yes, ma'am."

Shila thought furiously, then turned to her comm operator.

"Comms. Send a signal to the vessel. 'Starship Longshot. Your message has been received and understood. Please confirm that you need assistance and that you offer no hostile intent. Signal four long and four short flashes."

She listened while the comm officer typed the message into the automated voice transceiver.

"Done, ma'am. The message is being broadcast now."

Shila glanced at the countdown timer. 01:38.

A comm channel chimed and Colonel Forster's voice boomed throughout the TSC control room.

"Commander Hansen!"

"Yes, Colonel."

"I don't appreciate you bypassing me. I just had a call from Intel."

"Sir, I have a duty to ensure that I only engage a hostile enemy."

"You have a duty to obey my damn orders!"

"But sir, the message is genuine."

"No, Commander! The translation may be accurate, but the message is almost certainly a ruse. They are trying to slip through our defences. This is my call, and we can't risk the safety of our world based on a series of flashing lights. You have your orders. Now carry them out!"

The countdown timer now read 00:31.

"Ma'am! I have a visual on the vessel now. It's pivoting!"

The image of Longshot appeared on the screen. The image was shaky, as the TSC cameras struggled to keep the vessel in focus as it raced toward them at ten percent of lightspeed. Its massive deflector dish had hidden the ship from view, but as it slowly began to pivot, three things happened simultaneously. The first was that the horribly damaged rear end of the ship came into view. Secondly, a series of lights along the side of the vessel started to flash on and off, four long, followed by four short. The third was that the countdown timer reached zero.

"Ma'am? Permission to fire?"

"Hold your fire!" yelled Shila.

"Countermand that order!" yelled Colonel Forster over the comm. Shila had forgotten that his comm line was still active. "Open fire, now!"

"Colonel, I have visual confirmation of significant damage to the starship. It confirms their message. They are genuinely in distress and pose no threat to us."

"It is a ruse, Commander! I am ordering you to open fire!"

"Ma'am," called the comm operator. "They are continuing to flash: four long and four short."

"I can see that, Ensign."

Shila looked at the timer, which was now counting upward from zero, showing how long it had been since the starship had reached the prescribed zero point. The timer read 00:35. In another 25 seconds the Terran vessel would flash past the two sentinels at 300,000 kilometres per second. After that the starship would be in range of their weapons for only another minute, after which it would be beyond their reach and headed into their solar system.

She continued to stare at the digital counter.

"Fire those damn weapons now, Commander! That is a direct order!"

The weapons operator turned in her chair and stared at Shila.

"Ma'am?"

"Hold your fire, Ensign."

The counter reached 01:00 and kept counting, and the image on the screen was lost momentarily as the starship streaked past the two sentinels, which were placed only a few thousand kilometres to each side. The image on the screen refocused, and now they were seeing the rear of the starship as it raced into their solar system. It had realigned itself so that its deflector dish was in front, and it was continuing to flash in patterns of four. The damaged rear section of the ship was now completely visible, and it was a truly horrendous sight.

Colonel Forster's abrasive voice boomed through the control room's speakers, slightly distorting them. "Commander Hansen, you are relieved of duty! Stand down immediately. I am assuming remote command of TSC. Weapons controller, you are ordered to open fire on the enemy vessel immediately!"

"Belay that order!" shouted Shila as she came to stand beside the now trembling ensign. "I have visual proof that this is a stricken civilian vessel with no visible signs of weapons. Under the constitution of the ADF, it would be a war crime to fire upon an unarmed civilian vessel."

"Damn it, Ensign! Fire that weapon!" Forster's voice had risen to fever pitch and the poor ensign in question had turned pale and was trembling with fear. Forster continued to yell and threaten but his voice was suddenly cut off as Shila belatedly cancelled his call. The room was suddenly eerily silent.

"We're doing the right thing, Ensign," assured Shila.

The weapons officer merely nodded and continued to look terrified. It would not have entered her mind that morning that she would end up directly disobeying a colonel.

Every eye in the control room stared at the timer as it climbed steadily toward the two-minute mark, the point at which their weapons would be ineffective because, by then, the starship would be too far away. Finally, the clock reached 02:00 and continued to climb. Shila switched it off and turned to the Ensign at the weapons console.

"Power down all weapons, Ensign."

"Yes, ma'am." Her hands shook, but she managed to power down efficiently.

Shila turned to her comm officer.

"Comms. I want multiple audio copies of those comm calls, copies of the video feeds showing the damaged vessel, plus full transcripts of everything that was said in this control room over these last six minutes."

"Yes, ma'am."

"I'm going to need them for my court martial trial."

## 10

Alarms were sounding again throughout Longshot. The final pivot manoeuvre that had enabled them to flash their lights as they raced past the sentinel satellites had cost them dearly. A small particle of matter, estimated by Eric, their artificial intelligence, to be approximately 3.2 centimetres in diameter had ripped through their unprotected side. At 15,000 times the speed of a bullet, it had gone straight through the ship and out the other side. Despite its small size, the inertial mass and velocity of the object had punched a hole the diameter of a large dinner plate in both sides of the hull and the resulting explosive decompression of that level had widened the holes even more.

"Shut off the alarm!" called Anderson, over the din. A moment later the command centre was relatively quiet again and they could now start to assess the damage.

"Where were we impacted?" the captain asked.

"Level 57, sir. Life support systems."

"That can't be good," whispered Jordan to Kelly, both of whom were standing next to Daniel on the bridge.

"Commander Decker, get a team down there to assess damage," Anderson commanded.

"Right away, Captain."

"Sir, we're getting another message from Tama System Control," advised the comm operator.

"Put it on speaker."

"Aye, sir."

A moment later, a woman's voice could be heard.

"Starship Longshot, this is Commander Shila Hansen of Tama System Control. We are sorry it has taken us so long to respond to your morse code message, but we have only just deciphered it. We have visually confirmed your obvious damage and we acknowledge your predicament. Be assured we will be seeking to implement a rescue mission as soon as possible. We will keep you updated regarding the specific details of that mission. In the meantime, we recognise your inability to respond verbally to our messages, but now that we have identified your visual code, you may continue to communicate with us in that manner. There is no further need to adjust the angle of your spacecraft in order for us to see your lights, as our sentinel satellites are now directly behind you and can see your lights clearly. They can relay your messages to us here at system control. That is all for now. Good luck."

"Well, that's one bit of good news," said Alvarez, who was standing near the captain.

"Yes," agreed Daniel. "At least we're not about to get blown to pieces anymore."

About ten minutes later, they realised that there wasn't going to be any more good news for a while.

"Captain Anderson? It's Angus Fraser. Do you copy?"

"Go ahead, Mr Fraser," replied Anderson, who was allowing the comm call to be on speaker.

"Sir, I've got a team in spacesuits on Level 57. We'll be able to patch the walls, and get atmosphere back in there, no problem. But we've got a wee bit of a bigger issue to deal with."

Anderson winced. "Go on."

"The bonny wee rock has gone clean through our bank of $CO_2$ scrubbers. It blew the whole bank of scrubbers to kingdom come, sir."

"Are they fixable?"

"They're scrap metal, sir. Beyond salvage or repair. It was a direct hit. The velocity of the wee bugger must have been like a bomb going off. The whole level is filled with tiny floating pieces of debris."

"Copy that. Is anything else damaged?"

"Not that we can see, Captain. But we'll know more once we seal the hull breaches and get some atmosphere back in here."

"Get to it, Mr Fraser. Out."

"And the hits just keep on coming," said Jordan, shaking her head. She looked at Daniel. "Remind me next time to stay home and binge watch reality TV shows from the 21$^{st}$ century."

"I wouldn't wish that on my worst enemy," he replied. "You'd be brain dead within half an hour."

Another alarm started sounding urgently, and people at consoles began furiously tapping and swiping, trying to identify the problem.

"Shut it off," commanded Anderson, and the alarm died a moment later. "What's happening now?"

"I can't find the problem, Captain," said a puzzled ensign.

"Eric, can you identify the issue for us?" asked Anderson.

"Yes, Captain. Prior to puncturing Longshot, the object also punctured the shuttle that is welded to the hull directly outside Level 57. As the object passed through the shuttle it damaged the fusion drive."

"Specify the damage."

"The magnetic confinement coils were destroyed resulting in uncontrolled dispersal of the low-density hot plasma. This plasma has infiltrated the fission reactor at the core of the fusion drive and there is now a runaway chain reaction that I am unable to stop."

"Can't you power down the reactor?"

"I'm sorry, Captain. No. The plasma has eaten through the fuel rod casings and there is now an escalating reaction that will inevitably result in an explosion."

"How much time do we have?"

"Based on the current rise in temperature, I estimate two hours."

"What size explosion are we talking about?"

"Only one kiloton, Captain, but that will be sufficient to destroy Longshot," responded Eric, calmly.

Anderson activated his comm. "Angus! Forget the holes in Level 57. We have an uncontrolled meltdown happening in the fusion drive of the shuttle welded to the hull outside that level. I need you to cut that shuttle free, urgently!"

Daniel noted the captain's use of Angus's first name, a sign of the urgency of their predicament.

Angus's muted voice came over the comms. "Shite a brick out of me boghole!" There was a pause, followed by muted muttering. A moment later, Angus said, "Sorry, Captain. I think I may have inadvertently neglected to mute the comm."

"You've expressed our sentiment perfectly, Mr Fraser. How soon can you cut it loose?"

"How long have we got, sir?"

"Two hours, maximum."

"We'll get it done in 90 minutes, Captain, or you can boil me head fer a turnip."

"Get to it, Mr Fraser."

"Aye, sir."

Anderson turned his attention back to the artificial intelligence. "Eric, will you still have remote control of the shuttle?"

"Yes, Captain. But the fusion drive will no longer function. I will have to use the manoeuvering thrusters to move the shuttle a safe distance from the ship."

"That's going to be slow," interrupted Jordan, who was Longshot's most experienced pilot. "The two rear manoeuvering thrusters at full power only generate a combined acceleration rate of 0.1 metres per second squared."

Anderson addressed the AI again. "Eric, what safe distance will the shuttle need to reach?"

"200 kilometres would be optimal. 160 kilometres would be the bare minimum."

Daniel spoke up. "0.1 metres per second squared for 30 minutes will get it to 162 kilometres."

Anderson got straight back on the comm to Fraser. "Mr Fraser, do you copy?"

"Aye, sir."

"We've done some more calculations. Every second sooner than 90 minutes would be a blessing."

"Aye, sir. We'll go like the clappers."

Kelly whispered to Daniel. "How fast do clappers actually go?"

"That really depends on who's doing the clapping."

**11**

———

Angus Fraser and his team 'worked like the clappers' and they succeeded in cutting the damaged shuttle free from the outer hull in exactly 87 minutes. The only problem was that the nuclear meltdown had not progressed linearly. Despite Eric's optimistic predictions, by the time Angus and his team were cutting through the last strut that held the nose to the outer hull, they had only 12 minutes left until the fusion drive would reach critical mass and detonate.

"How far away can we get the shuttle in 12 minutes?" asked Anderson.

Daniel calculated rapidly. "25.92 kilometres."

"Is that all?" asked Anderson.

"That's how constant acceleration works, Captain. The velocity steadily increases, but you don't cover much distance in the early part of the time period."

"I see. Eric, what will a 1 kiloton explosion at a distance of 25 kilometres do to us?"

"It will be lethal, Captain. I'm sorry."

"You're bloody kidding me!" muttered Jordan.

There was silence around the bridge. Everyone had been

pinning their hopes on getting the shuttle clear, and now it seemed that all hope was gone.

Jordan started walking toward the lifts, unbuttoning her shirt as she did so.

"Where are you going?" asked Kelly.

Jordan stopped and turned to face her friend. "I'm going to dance naked on one of the dining room tables. Remember? I always said if I knew it was the last day of my life, I would dance naked on a table." She turned and started walking toward the lifts.

"Wait! That's it!" said Daniel.

"What's it?" asked Jordan, turning back again.

"The table! Our shield! We've been calculating the safe distance of an explosion to port or starboard of Longshot. But our front shields can absorb a lot of energy for a short period of time."

"By God, you're right!" exclaimed Anderson. "Eric, what is the minimum safe distance for a 1 kiloton blast directly in front of our deflector shield?"

"I apologise, Captain. I should have thought of that. 20 kilometres should be a safe distance."

"Do it!" yelled Anderson. "Get that shuttle out in front, now!"

"I'm manoeuvering it around the deflector dish as we speak, Captain." A few moments later, Eric announced, "Initial manoeuvering and alignment is complete. Initiating linear acceleration now."

An image of the shuttle, viewed from the rear, was now displayed on the main screen, firing its two rear manoeuvering thrusters continually. The shuttle began to move forward, agonisingly slowly at first, but gradually gaining precious velocity. A countdown timer was now running in the corner of the screen, and as the shuttle began to move slowly ahead of the starship, the timer went under 11:00 minutes.

"It's going to be very tight," muttered Daniel, working the numbers in his head.

"So, should I go to the dining room, or not, Professor?" asked Jordan. "I need plenty of warning, because I've got a whole routine worked out, but I'm gonna need some limbering up first."

"Why don't you give us a quick demo, now?" he suggested without taking his eyes off the screen.

She shook her head. "Nope. It's a one-off performance."

"In that case, you'd better save it for when we're really in trouble."

"If this isn't 'really in trouble' I'm not all that keen on experiencing the genuine article."

The minutes counted down and Eric gave regular updates on the state of the fusion reactor's escalating chain reaction. Captain Anderson also compiled a morse code message to warn the people of the Tama system of the impending explosion.

As the countdown time went below two minutes, all conversation in the command centre ceased and every eye was fixed on the screen. The image of the shuttle was still very clear, made apparently closer by Longshot's high-resolution magnification. The Captain opened a comm channel and briefly warned everyone to secure themselves.

At the one-minute mark, Daniel announced, "18 kilometres." His eyes stayed riveted on the screen as he watched the timer, and he kept a steady calculation of acceleration and elapsed distance running in his head.

At 30 seconds to the predicted detonation, he announced, "19.8 kilometres."

The seconds counted down.

With 12 seconds remaining on the timer, the screen went white and Anderson yelled, "Brace for impact!" A moment later the whole ship shook, and they were all thrown forward as the shock wave from the explosion slammed into them, resulting in instant deceleration. An alarm sounded briefly but shut itself off moments later. The shockwave quickly passed, but it took several minutes for order to be restored. Several crew who had not secured themselves properly had impacted the front screens in the nil-gravity environment and had to be helped back to the floor from where they were now floating in mid-air.

"Damage report?" asked Anderson.

Crew members scanned various consoles, but no one could find any indicators of damage.

"All clear, Captain," they reported, one by one.

Anderson breathed a sigh of relief and looked at Daniel. "How many is that, Daniel?"

"How many what, sir?"

"How many times has your quick thinking saved all our necks?"

"I'm sure your necks would still be in fine shape without me, sir."

Anderson gave him a sceptical look. "And that's the first disingenuous thing I think I've ever heard you say."

Jordan slapped him on the back. "It's a shame, Professor. It was gonna be a damn fine dance. You don't know what you're missing."

Daniel smiled at his friend. "No offence, but I'll be very happy to miss it for a long time to come."

## 12

———

Keelor awoke to the newsfeeds announcing that the Terran vessel had been revealed to be an ancient colony ship from Earth, predating even the Terrans' earliest attempts to attack and subjugate Atraya. Furthermore, the newsfeeds were abuzz with speculation regarding the origin of the morse code decipher that had kept the military from destroying an innocent colony. Some said it must have come from a government employee; someone who had access to the Earth archives. Others speculated that it must have been a super-hacker.

The visual images of the stricken vessel were all over T-Net, and the video footage of the exploding shuttle and the starship's close scrape with disaster added to the drama. Of course, there was a small minority who suggested that it was all still a ruse by the crafty Terrans. Perhaps they were carrying a super-bomb, a planet killer, which they would detonate when they got within range of Atraya. Or maybe they were carrying a Trojan code which they would insinuate into T-Net and which would bring the solar system's technology to a standstill, rendering the Atrayans helpless. Keelor shook his head in disbelief. Some people just loved conspiracy theories.

As he continued to scan the newsfeeds, his overwhelming

emotion was one of elation. He had played a part in saving the visitors from destruction! Literally hundreds of people's lives had been spared because of his intervention! It was, without a doubt, the most important moment of his otherwise boring life, and he felt an upwelling of pride and immense satisfaction.

There were calls for the secret decoder to come forward, and several government officials commented that they were keen to speak with the author of the morse code document, but Keelor wasn't fooled. He knew he would be in trouble if he was ever identified, and he was determined to remain anonymous.

"Good morning, sleepy head," his mother commented as he entered the kitchen and ordered a coffee. "How did you enjoy last night?"

"It was fine."

"Yes, it was lovely for us to all be together." She paused. "Sia has certainly grown into an attractive young woman, hasn't she?"

"I guess," he commented as he took his cup of coffee and sat at the kitchen bench.

"I noticed you two spent some time together last night."

He shrugged. "A bit."

"Did you know she was adopted? She's not your blood cousin."

He looked up at his mother in shock. "Really?"

"Yes. They told her only last month. Your aunty and uncle weren't able to have children of their own."

"Wow! That must have been a big shock for her."

His mother placed her used breakfast bowl in the sonic cleanser for a few seconds. "She seems to have coped with the news remarkably well." She took the clean plate out and replaced it in the cupboard, then sat on the opposite side of the kitchen bench to Keelor and took a sip of her own coffee. "You could marry her, you know?"

Keelor blushed in embarrassment. "Mum! She's my cousin! Besides, she's much younger than me."

"There would be nothing stopping you getting married, and the age difference isn't that great. Look at your father and me; he's six years older than me but it hasn't made a scrap of difference."

"But she's only 17!"

"I was 17 when I married your father," she persisted. "And you have to admit, Sia is now a fully grown woman."

Keelor certainly couldn't deny that. He shook his head and sighed. "Why do parents always try to get involved in matchmaking!"

His mother looked at him, discerningly. "Is she a good kisser?"

"Mum!"

"Don't deny it. Your bedroom door was ajar when I went to the bathroom."

Keelor blushed even more and didn't know what to say. His mother reached out and placed her hand on his forearm.

"I'm not trying to embarrass you, and I'm certainly not trying to influence you in any way. You've got to make your own way in life and make your own decisions. But I just want you to know that your father and I would not have any objections if you and Sia ended up together. In fact, in some ways, it would be a lovely way of tying our family together."

She stood up. "But enough of that! Today is your big day! Are you packed?"

He shrugged. "Almost."

She nodded and pushed back a stray wisp of hair that had fallen down across her eyes. Keelor noticed the streaks of grey they were becoming more prominent and the deep wrinkle lines around her eyes and mouth, and it dawned on him that she was growing old. Everything seemed to be changing so quickly and he had a sudden sense of the onrushing tide of time, sweeping him forward unrelentingly and washing away the sandcastles of his life that he had thought would always be there.

As if sensing his mood, his mother squeezed his arm and said, "Nothing stays the same forever, son. You're going to do us proud, I'm sure of it."

"Thanks, mum." For some strange reason his eyes welled up with tears and he looked down into his coffee cup to hide them.

"Eggs and bacon on rye toast?" she asked as she stood up and walked to the food dispenser.

"Yes please."

His mother placed the order and a few moments later she placed the meal in front of him. He began eating hungrily, listening to Rusty's enthusiastic barking as his father herded the cattle into the milking shed.

"When you're ready, your father and I will fly you into town. Are you sure you don't want us to fly you directly to the island? It would be no trouble."

"No. I like the ferry. Besides, it looks like it will be beautiful day, and the crossing should be pretty calm."

"Okay. If that's what you want. The ferry leaves at 09:00, so we will need to leave by about 08:15."

He nodded and stuffed another forkful of egg and bacon into his mouth. The front door chimed softly, and his mother frowned. "Who could that be at this time of the morning?" She fastened her dressing gown more securely around her and padded to the door, futilely brushing her sleep-ruffled hair with her fingers.

"Security view," she said.

The door changed to one-way transparency, revealing two people in military uniform: a man and a woman. A sleek black flitter was parked on the front lawn, and she noted that she hadn't heard it land. She knew that the military had flitters that could engage silent mode, but this was her first close encounter with one. She saw her husband emerge from the milking shed and begin walking toward the house, frowning.

"Can I help you?" she asked, activating the door comm.

The male officer, a lieutenant, held up his military ID and said, "Mrs Trantum? We're sorry to intrude so early in the morning. We need to speak with your son."

Keelor's eyes widened in shock and his heart began to pound. His day, which was already shaping up to be momentous enough, had just become a whole lot more complicated.

## 13

"You're taking him to Angel City?"

"Yes. To military headquarters," responded the lieutenant.

"Why? Is he in trouble?" Keelor's mother had deep lines of concern etched in her brow.

"We just need to ask him a few questions, ma'am."

"Can't you ask him here?"

"Major Maxwell would like to talk with him, personally."

"But today is his enhancement day," she persisted. "He's meant to go to Corfu this morning."

"We're aware of that. If necessary, we can reschedule it."

Keelor's father was a man of few words, more comfortable in the company of his dog than with people. He cleared his throat and spoke hesitantly. "Is Keelor under arrest?"

"No, sir, he isn't."

"So, he doesn't have to go with you, then."

"That's not exactly true. The military has the authority to detain any person deemed to be relevant to its investigations. Your son doesn't have a choice."

"But what's it about?" persisted Keelor's mother.

"I'm not at liberty to say, ma'am," said the lieutenant.

The female officer, an ensign, smiled at Keelor's mother. "You have nothing to worry about, ma'am. Your son will be treated well. We'll look after him."

The lieutenant addressed Keelor. "I suggest you pack your bag as if you were going to Corfu, as planned. You might be gone for a similar length of time."

Ten minutes later, Keelor watched his family farm shrink below him as the flitter rose smoothly into the air and accelerated toward the city. His last glimpse of his parents was of them standing on the grass in front of the house, shielding their eyes in the morning light as they gazed up at him, while Rusty ran around in circles, yapping excitedly. He watched them until he could no longer crane his neck around far enough, then turned his attention to the two military personnel accompanying him.

The young woman's badge simply said 'Cartwright'. The lieutenant's name was Bridges, and he appeared confident and well spoken.

"So, can you tell me now? Am I in trouble?"

Lieutenant Bridges answered, "That depends on your definition of 'trouble'. Are you going to be arrested or sent to prison? No. But your recent actions will definitely bring certain consequences."

"What kind of consequences?"

Bridges adopted an enigmatic expression. "That's for Major Maxwell to say. I suggest you sit back and enjoy the trip."

The lieutenant had a point. It was not every day that a 21-year-old was taken to Angel City. Sure, there were wealthy people who holidayed there, staying in the Casino, playing in the zero-grav games rooms and visiting the observatory, but not many sons of farmers ever made it up there.

Keelor marvelled at how quiet the flitter was. There was only the mildest of hums, so quiet that the predominant sound was the whooshing of air as they sliced their way toward Jasper City Terminal. Keelor's family lived in a rural community, on the outskirts of Emerald, a small, provincial sea-side town, 35 kilometres south of Northland's capital city. Keelor had studied at Jasper University, and although most of his work could be done remotely, he had needed to attend in person several times each semester. The trip to Jasper City usually involved a five-minute tube ride in a superfast bullet-pod. He had never seen the city from the air, however, and now as they approached from the south, he marvelled at the forest of impressively tall, slender skyscrapers, rising to over a kilometre in the mild Atrayan gravity. The skyscrapers glittered and sparkled in the apricot morning light and flitters of all shapes and sizes darted between them, carrying early morning workers to their offices and industries.

The spaceport was on the north-western edge of the city, away from the coast, and their flitter now banked in that direction. As they approached, Keelor saw a heavy-lift rocket readying for launch, perhaps taking a payload to Angel City, or to Rios, their moon, or even further to the bases on their sister planet, Jumea, and its moon, Kronos. To the south of the heavy-lift launch pads were the private space jet terminals where the space yachts of the rich and the commercial jets that catered to the middle-class tourists could be found. This morning, as always, the private terminals were abuzz with activity, as jets and passengers prepared for lift off.

Their flitter swung around the western outskirts of the expansive spaceport and further still to the north-west. Now the MPS terminal came into view, sitting at the end of a maglev rail that ran due East, toward the coast. At the end of its eight-kilometre length, the maglev rail climbed a man-made hill and ended abruptly at the summit, with the end of the rail pointing skyward. The magnetic propulsion system was the fastest way to get into orbit. A shuttle that was accelerated along the maglev rail and launched off the top of the hill would achieve a velocity of 5.8 kilometres per second within one minute and would be in low Earth orbit at the end of an additional 30 seconds. Of course, all this was only possible because of the wonders of the shuttle's inertial dampening system, which enabled passengers to sit comfortably in a space vehicle which was being accelerated at 10G without feeling any acceleration at all.

Their flitter circled a small landing pad at the rear of the MPS terminal and landed gently, executing a perfect vertical touchdown. The flitter door slid open and the three passengers quickly made their way across the tarmac and into the terminal building. The MPS launch system was run by the military as a fast and efficient means of transferring up to their headquarters in Angel City, so it was not surprising to Keelor that he was the only person in the terminal not in military uniform.

A private met them at the door and informed them that the shuttle was being held for them, on Major Maxwell's orders. He escorted them through the terminal to a sliding doorway marked, MPS Boarding Platform. They walked through and Keelor got a brief glimpse of the shuttle before he was hustled on board. The undercarriage of the shuttle was straddling a maglev rail that was almost two metres wide and the shuttle itself was a long, sleek craft with minimalist swept-back wings, both of which had vertical stabilisers. Two impressive jet engines were situated where the wings met the fuselage, and Keelor had the impression of their immense power.

They walked up a retractable ramp into the shuttle interior and quickly took empty seats at the front. There were about twenty military personnel already on board, with at least another twenty seats empty. The shuttle's door sealed shut and, a few seconds later, Keelor felt an instant change in the air pressure on his ear drums.

"Do you know how this works?" asked Cartwright, who was seated to his left. It was the first time she had spoken to him, directly. He glanced at her and thought that she didn't look very much older than him.

"A little," he said. "The maglev accelerates us along the rail initially and the jet engines only kick in at the last moment, as we reach the launch ramp."

She smiled. "Yes." She held out her hand. "I'm Maran, by the way."

He shook her hand. "Nice to meet you." He looked at her more closely. She had short blonde hair and, now that they were out of Tama's orange light, he noticed her bright green eyes.

She explained the system in a little more detail. "The magnetic propulsion system accelerates us at 10G, and the jets, when we get airborne, will continue accelerating us at the same rate. It'd be an intense ride if it wasn't for the inertial dampening system."

"That's the part I'm not entirely conversant with," he admitted. As he spoke, he felt a strange tingling throughout his entire body, as if an electric current was passing through him.

"That's it coming online now," she said reassuringly. "It operates at the sub-atomic level, creating a field that ensures that changes in momentum act upon every atom of your body evenly, so that you don't notice that you're actually accelerating."

Keelor was looking out the window to Maran's left and thought he noticed the platform and terminal sink by a few centimetres. She saw him looking and commented, "That's the maglev coming online. We're now floating above the rail. I'd say strap in and hang on, but there's really no need, as you're about to see. Just keep watching out the window."

Keelor didn't quite know what he was meant to be watching for, but a few seconds later it became abundantly clear. The platform and terminal building disappeared behind them in a flash. The world outside the window began racing past them at ever-increasing, ever-more astonishing speed. Meanwhile, inside the shuttle he felt absolutely nothing. He could have been holding a full cup of coffee without spilling a drop.

"Pretty cool, eh?" said the now chatty Maran.

"It's incredible!" he admitted. "It's like the world is moving, instead of us. Or like we're watching a video of motion through the window."

"It's the only way to fly, in my opinion." She smiled at him, and her clear green eyes sparkled.

He looked back out the window and was amazed to see that the world was now tilted below them, and they were streaking upward through the air.

"We've already left the maglev rail!" he exclaimed.

She smiled again, vicariously enjoying the novelty of his first flight. "Yes. At an acceleration of 10G, it took us just 13 seconds to get to the end of the 8-kilometre rail. By then we were travelling at 1.3 kilometres per second."

"Wow. That's ... fast!"

"And we're going a lot faster every second," she continued.

Daniel kept looking out the window and saw the sky begin to darken. Gradually the orange / apricot hue of Atraya's atmosphere turned a dull brown, then faded to black.

"The Karman line," offered Maran. "We've just officially crossed into space. It's taken us 45 seconds to get here and we're now travelling at 4.4 kilometres per second."

"How do you remember all this stuff?"

She shrugged. "I'm a math nerd. There are plenty more like me, in Intel."

"And that's where we're going now?"

She glanced nervously at Lieutenant Bridges who was sitting to Keelor's right and whispered, "Yes. Major Maxwell heads up Intel. He's keen to meet you."

Keelor dropped his voice to match hers. "Should I be worried?"

She shook her head. "Just be honest and be yourself."

"That's easy," he replied. "I'm the only person I know how to be."

Maran laughed, and Keelor felt a lift in his spirits. Maybe today wasn't going to turn out so badly after all.

## 14

I t took 23 minutes to reach Angel City, which was in geostationary orbit at an altitude of 28,000 kilometres. A variety of vessels were docked along the spokes of the wheel-shaped city. Some were small private craft, the space yachts of the wealthy. Others were larger tourist cruisers, ready to return people to Atraya or take them on extended sightseeing trips to other marvels in the solar system. Keelor took particular note of two sleek sun divers, needle-like vessels with shiny, mirrored surfaces that promised tourists the thrill of briefly diving through Tama's super-charged chromosphere.

Their shuttle, however, avoided the cluttered busyness of the spokes and flew directly to the base of the city's hub. A large military cruiser was docked directly underneath, and Keelor could see small drone units flying around its outer hull, along with numerous space-suited workers performing various kinds of maintenance. A large bay door opened toward the base of the hub and their shuttle was drawn inside by an automated parking system. For the last few minutes of their flight, once they were no longer under acceleration, Keelor had experienced true weightlessness for the first time. But as soon as their shuttle entered the shuttle bay, even before it touched down, Keelor had plonked firmly down into his seat again. He looked at Maran with raised eyebrows.

"Artificial gravity," she said, stating the obvious. "Gravity generators produce an artificial gravity field throughout the whole city, so it doesn't have to spin."

Keelor had known this already, but he had assumed the shuttle would need to be in contact with the floor of the shuttle bay to come under the influence of the gravity field. He decided he would have to find out more about how the gravity generators worked.

The bay door closed and atmosphere was restored. The pilots stretched and chatted together as the passengers disembarked, and a group of new passengers waited patiently to board for the return trip. It looked like it would be an almost full load going back.

The arriving passengers exited the shuttle bay into a spacious foyer with several corridors leading in different directions and a bank of lifts against the far wall. The military personnel dispersed in different directions, although most headed for the lifts. A few moments later Keelor found himself squeezed into a lift with about a dozen personnel, some of whom were chatting amiably as they headed to their stations for their shifts. There were buttons for 30 floors, but the lift occupants all selected floors between floors 19 and 30.

Lieutenant Bridges guided Keelor out of the lift on the 20th floor and led him along a wide corridor, finally entering an outer office with a male ensign at a console guarding an inner door. The sign on the door read, 'Chief of Intelligence, Major Cole Maxwell'.

"Is the Major in?" Bridges asked without any preamble.

"Yes, sir. He's expecting you. You can go straight in."

Bridges knocked on the door and, without waiting for a reply, opened it and led Keelor and Maran into the inner sanctum. It wasn't a huge office. A large desk had multiple screens, and there were screens all around the walls, but there was only room for two visitors' chairs. Major Maxwell sat at this desk, frowning at a screen. He looked up as they entered and immediately Keelor felt himself being evaluated by a piercing, intelligent gaze. Maxwell looked in his mid 40s, with short hair going prematurely grey. It was his piercing blue eyes that stood out, however.

"No handcuffs, Lieutenant?" he asked.

"No, sir. But I had my sidearm and I was prepared to shoot if he tried to escape."

Keelor looked between the major and the lieutenant, and couldn't see even the hint of a smile, but he caught a subtle wink from Maran, and he relaxed slightly.

Maxwell nodded. "Very good. I won't hold you up any further, Lieutenant. I'm sure you've got things to be doing."

"Yes, sir." Bridges left the room and the major pointed to the two chairs. "Take a seat, both of you."

Once they were seated, Maxwell gazed at Keelor intently, as if mentally sizing him up. Keelor, tried to return the major's gaze confidently, but his heart was hammering and he felt completely out of his depth. Less than an hour ago he had been on his family's sleepy farm, listening to the cows lowing as they were milked, and now he was sitting in front of the Chief of Intelligence for the Atrayan Defence Forces.

"You are the author of the message that drew everyone's attention to the Terran's Morse code signal."

It wasn't a question. Keelor remembered Maran's advice to be honest.

"Yes, sir."

Maxwell nodded and regarded him carefully.

"You used your uncle's log in details to access the Terran history archives."

Again, another statement, without the hint of a question.

"Yes, sir."

"And you knew that doing so was in direct contravention of civil regulations."

"Yes, sir."

"Why did you do it?"

Keelor considered his answer carefully. Had he been trying to show off? Was he bored? Was it simply the thrill of solving a puzzle? Perhaps a little of the latter. But that certainly wasn't his primary motivation.

"Because I was convinced that we were about to make a big mistake."

"What convinced you?"

"The repeating pattern of lights, particularly the second pattern. It was too coincidental to have two sets of repeating patterns. They had to be messages."

"So how did you manage to find the code, when my team couldn't?"

Ah! Here was the crux of the matter! Military intelligence had been trying to decipher the messages but had failed.

"They were searching the archives, too?" Keelor asked.

"They were. So how did you find it and they missed it?"

"They were probably searching for visual codes."

Maxwell tapped and swiped on his screen for a few moments, and then nodded. He looked back at Keelor.

"But it wasn't a visual code, was it?" asked Maxwell.

"No, sir. Morse code wasn't visual; it was an audio code. The starship just adapted it in a visual format."

Maxwell nodded again. "Mm," he said, noncommittally.

"To be fair, sir, I started out searching for visual codes as well. It was an easy mistake to make."

"Why didn't you try to contact us directly?"

Keelor bit his lip. "I ... I didn't want to be found out."

"But we did find you out, didn't we?" Maxwell leaned forward and focused a particularly searching gaze upon Keelor. "How do you think we did that?"

That was, indeed, the very question that Keelor had been considering during the whole trip to Angel City. How had they located him? He was very confident in his encryption coding. Not even his university lecturer had been able to crack it. There could only be one answer.

"My cousin," he said simply.

"Go on," encouraged Maxwell.

"You must have checked who had logged in to the archives

over that period and you probably interviewed them. There wouldn't be many. Maybe only one, because I don't think anyone bothers to go there. When you contacted my uncle, he would have indicated that he hadn't accessed them, and you would have suspected that someone else had used his password. The first logical step would be to check with immediate family and I'm guessing that Sia caved in pretty quickly."

"What makes you think we didn't just trace your computer trail back to your home?"

It was, indeed, a possibility, and Keelor had racked his brain during the shuttle journey trying to think of any weak points in his coding. He couldn't think of any, but perhaps he was just being arrogant. After all, this was military intelligence: the best of the best. If anyone could crack his encryption code, they could. Despite these doubts, he shook his head.

"I don't think so. I'm fairly sure my encryption was watertight."

"Really?" asked Maxwell, raising his eyebrows. "You're that confident, are you?"

"Not completely confident, sir. I'm sure you have very competent people on your team. But I'm guessing it would take much longer than just a few hours to break through my encryption. The shorter and easier route would have been my blabbering cousin."

Maxwell grunted and sat back in his chair. He was silent for a few moments, as if pondering what to do.

"How did you get your uncle's password?"

Keelor shrugged. "I was walking past his office one day, and I saw him type it in."

"And you remembered?"

"I have a good memory, sir."

The major sighed. "What am I going to do with you? You've broken the law. You realise that, don't you?"

Keelor swallowed. "Yes, sir. I'm sorry, sir."

"Are you? Are you truly sorry?" Maxwell raised his eyebrows again.

Be honest, Keelor thought to himself. He took a deep breath. "No, sir. I'm not sorry."

"Why not?"

"Because it was worth it to save innocent people's lives."

"Mm. That's my dilemma as well. Because you're a criminal and a hero at the same time." He paused. "You realise that people are calling you the 'masked decoder'?"

"No, sir. I haven't seen that."

There was a longer silence this time, as Maxwell pondered his predicament.

"Tell me three things about yourself, and one of them has to be a lie."

Keelor was caught off-guard at this puzzling change of direction. He frowned, and then shrugged.

"My dog's name is Rusty. My mother sings in a local choir. I kissed my cousin last night."

Maxwell leant forward and stared at him intensely, and Keelor returned his gaze. Finally, the major sat back in his chair.

"I can't tell. Which one was the lie? I'm guessing it's probably the last one."

"My mother is tone deaf; she can't sing a note."

Maxwell's eyebrows shot up to new heights and he tried unsuccessfully to cover up a smile.

"So, you really did kiss your cousin last night?"

Keelor blushed slightly. "I probably should have thought of something else to say."

"Hmph!" the major grunted. He leant forward. "I've reached a decision. We can't have civilians running around breaking into forbidden data files. It doesn't look good for us. So ... I'm going to recruit you into military intelligence."

Keelor was stunned. He had been expecting some form of punishment or, at the very least, a severe warning. But not this.

"You're inviting me to join the military?" he asked.

"No. I'm not. It's not an invitation. You don't have a choice, son. I could go through the courts, bring you up on charges of civil disobedience, and then they would probably sentence you to 12 months community service. At that point I would step in and acquisition you for 12 months service in military intelligence.

That's how it would go down. No question. I'm simply short cutting the system."

"So, I don't have a choice?"

"Cheer up. It's not that bad. A lot of people your age would do just about anything to get a chance like this. What were you planning to do with your life, anyway?"

"I have no idea, sir. I guess I was probably just going to eventually take over my family farm."

"And that would have satisfied you?"

"No. Not really."

"Didn't think so. You've got a brain, son, and I plan to help you use it productively." Maxwell stood to his feet. "Ensign Cartwright, take our masked decoder down to the intake office and stay with him while they process him. Then show him around and get him settled into temporary quarters. There's a week-long induction course starting tomorrow for new recruits. Make sure he gets there."

"Yes, sir," she said.

As they walked down the corridor toward the lifts, a few moments later, Maran turned to Keelor and asked, "So, is she a good kisser? Your cousin?"

Keelor blushed slightly. "Honestly? I have no idea. I've got nothing to compare it to."

"You mean ...?"

"I mean, I'd never kissed a girl before last night." He shrugged with awkward embarrassment.

"Well, well, well. Aren't you a find? The girls on the base are going to love you. You're going to have to beat them off with a stick."

## 15

Commander Shila Hansen marched into the military courtroom and snapped to attention. In front of her was a long, high bench, behind which sat a solitary figure, General Lorn Claymore, Commander in Chief of the Atrayan Defence Forces. They were on Level II of the central hub in Angel City, in orbit directly above Jasper City.

"At ease, Commander. Take a seat."

Shila stepped to her right and sat in the solitary chair, facing the general. To her left, sat Colonel Forster, who had initiated the court martial proceedings, and behind them both, in the public seating area, the rows of wooden bench seats were packed with military personnel who had come to see the show. The near destruction of the Terran vessel, saved only by Shila's defiance of her immediate superior, were the talk of the whole base.

Claymore let out a long, slow sigh, and cast his discerning gaze around the packed courtroom.

"Well, this is a fine pickle, isn't it?"

Shila raised her eyebrows in surprise. It wasn't exactly the start to proceedings that she had expected.

Claymore tapped the screen on his desk and read the official opening statement.

"This is a duly convened military court, convened to hear court martial charges brought by Colonel Ty Forster against Commander Shila Hansen; General Lorn Claymore presiding. Commander Hansen, I take it you have decided to forgo legal counsel and defend yourself?"

"Yes, sir."

"And have you had a chance to read the charge sheet in full?"

"Yes, sir."

"So let me cut to the chase. You are charged with deliberately disobeying a repeated direct order from Colonel Forster on the occasion of the Terran vessel's entrance to our solar system. How do you plead?"

"Guilty, sir."

A ripple of murmurs went through the spectators, but Claymore seemed unsurprised and unperturbed. He merely nodded and looked toward the Colonel.

"Colonel Forster, do you wish to speak to the charges?"

Forster stood. "Yes, General, I most certainly do!"

"Keep it brief, Colonel."

Forster began a detailed exposition of Shila's crimes, explaining her refusal to obey his repeated command and her undermining of his authority by contacting Intelligence Department behind his back. He was winding himself up into a passionate tirade and starting to use words like 'insolence' and 'outrageous' when Claymore interjected.

"Colonel Forster!"

Forster paused in mid-flow. "Yes, sir?"

"Do you have anything of substance to add to the documents that have already been tendered to this court?"

Forster seemed slightly taken aback. "Well, General, I would like to say that if this sort of wilful disobedience is allowed to go unpunished, it will undermine the very fabric of our military institution. The order of rank and the respect of those in authority is the very essence of ..."

"Yes, yes, yes, let's take that as a given. But do you have

anything of *substance* to add to the detailed report I have already received?"

Forster was clearly flustered at having his tirade cut short and being so gruffly dealt with by the general. His face was flushed, and he glared at the general for a moment before conceding, "No, General, I do not."

"Thank you, Colonel Forster, you may be seated."

He turned his attention back to Shila. "Commander Hansen, do you have anything to say in your defence?"

Shila stood and cleared her throat. "Sir, I take it that you have listened to the audio, and watched the video log, and read the transcripts of the events surrounding these charges?"

"I have. And I remind you that I am the one doing the questioning here, not you, Commander. So let me repeat my question. Do you have anything to say in your defence?"

"Yes, sir. I submit to you Article 7, Section 3, paragraph 6 of the Military Code of Conduct, which states, *'All military personnel must obey an order given by a superior officer except when such order either contradicts a higher superior's order or is in direct contravention of the Atrayan Convention of Civil and Military Rights'*. I further submit the relevant excerpt from that convention which states, *'Military action which deliberately seeks to harm civilians or which, by inaction, allows avoidable harm to befall civilians, shall be deemed a war crime'*. It was on the basis of this military code and this convention that I disobeyed Colonel Forster's order."

Shia sat down as a ripple of murmurs swept across the spectator gallery once more. Claymore glared at the spectators and said, "The next person who mutters an uninvited word in my courtroom will be cleaning the latrines in the trainees' barracks with a toothbrush for a month!"

In the icy silence that followed, he addressed Colonel Forster again.

"Colonel Forster, do you have anything to say in reply to Commander Hansen's defence?"

Forster stood. "Yes, I do, General! At no point did Commander Hansen have any solid evidence that the Terran vessel was a civilian vessel. The fact that it was proved to be such, subsequently, does not exonerate her from a court-martial offense."

Forster sat back down, wearing a smug expression, as if he had just presented the most scintillatingly brilliant, irrefutable legal argument.

General Claymore peered at him for a moment. "So, the fact that she was right, and you were completely wrong, should not be taken into consideration?"

"Well, I wouldn't put it quite ..."

"In fact, you believe that this court should punish Commander Hansen for saving you from murdering a ship full of innocent civilians. Is that your view, Colonel?"

"Well, it's the principle, General. She ..."

"The principle? The principle, Colonel Forster? Surely the highest principle is that the military exists to protect and preserve the lives of innocent civilians and to do all we can to save life, rather than take it!"

"But she had no solid evidence, sir."

"No solid evidence? There was a clear message. There was a badly disabled ship with no weapons, which was not even remotely similar to a military vessel. There was your evidence, Colonel! Verbal and visual! Clear and incontestable! And you, Colonel, chose to ignore it all!"

Forbes sat glowering. He had come to the court believing that he would be exonerated and his cause upheld, but instead, he was taking a battering.

General Claymore turned back to Shila.

"Commander Hansen, please stand."

Shila stood to attention, ready to face whatever consequence was coming.

"Commander Shila Hansen, you have pleaded guilty to the charge of disobeying a direct order of a superior officer. This court rejects your plea. Under the terms of the Military Code of Conduct and the Atrayan Convention of Civil and Military Rights, which you have appropriately drawn to the court's attention, there is no guilt attached to your decision to disregard your superior officer's orders. On the contrary, you are to be commended for your initiative and clear thinking, which undoubtedly saved the lives of hundreds of civilians. Accordingly, the charges brought against you in this court martial hearing are dismissed. Furthermore, in recognition of your decisive leadership in the face of great pressure, you are hereby promoted to the rank of Captain."

A buzz of excitement swept around the court, and this time, Claymore let it go, with a twinkle in his eye.

Shila couldn't quite believe what had just happened, and she stood there in shock.

"You may sit down, Captain."

"Yes, sir. Thank you, sir."

"Colonel Forster, please stand." The general waited until Forster stood reluctantly to his feet. "Colonel Ty Forster, you are charged with gross incompetence that endangered the lives of innocent civilians and you will face a court martial hearing at a date yet to be determined. You are relieved of your command while you await your hearing. I suggest you seek legal representation."

Forster looked thunderous.

General Claymore thumped his gavel on his desk and announced, "This hearing is now closed."

**16**

———

General Lorn Claymore brought the emergency meeting to order. Present were Major Cole Maxwell, Chief of Military Intelligence, Commodore Gil Bronson, captain of the ADF cruiser, Ulysses, and the newly promoted Captain Shila Hansen, commanding officer of Tama System Control.

Claymore didn't beat around the bush. "How do we rescue these people?"

Shila spoke up. "It's going to be difficult, sir, given their current situation."

"Which is?"

"Travelling at 30,000 kilometres per second, they will traverse our entire solar system and be out the other side in five more days. It will take us longer than that to catch up to them."

"How long?"

"Commodore Bronson can best answer that, sir."

"Commodore?" Claymore asked Bronson.

Bronson was a sharp-nosed, compact man, with a completely bald head and a no-nonsense military bearing.

"Well, General, the Ulysses is our best bet, and it's already here on base. With its inertial dampening system, we can accelerate comfortably at 5 gravities. At that rate it would take us 7 days to match their velocity. But of course, by then, they will be about ..."

He tapped on a data pad in front to him.

"... 4 days ahead of us. That's 10.4 billion kilometres. To bridge that gap, which would involve continuing to accelerate and then decelerate again as we caught them, it would take ... let me see ..."

He did some more calculations,

"... an additional 7 days 8 hours."

Claymore nodded. "Two weeks to catch them and dock with them. That sounds doable. What then?"

"Their ship is a right-off," continued Bronson. "And we would have no way of slowing it down, anyway. We'll simply need to get the passengers and crew onto Ulysses, and then come home."

"And how long will that take?"

"Let me see," said Bronson, speaking as he tapped away on his data pad. "It will take another 7 days to decelerate to zero velocity, relative to Atraya, at which point we will be ... 362 billion kilometres away. The return journey from that point, accelerating at 5G to the midway point and then decelerating, will take ... an additional 714 hours which is ... 30 days."

"Mm," contemplated the General. "14 days to catch them, 7 days to come to a stop and another 30 to get back. 51 days. It's a big assignment."

"We don't have a choice, General," urged Shila. "There are nearly 240 souls on board Longshot."

"I realise that," agreed Claymore. "There's no possibility of us not rescuing them. But it is a big commitment for the crew of Ulysses. Are you up to it, Commodore?"

"Absolutely, sir! It will be the most important thing I've done in my whole career. And I know my crew will all feel the same way. We'll need a skeleton crew, to make room for the newcomers, which means we will be working longs shifts, but we'll manage."

"Good. How soon can you get underway?"

"Over the last 24 hours, I've recalled all my key crew. They're on standby, awaiting your order. We can leave within the hour."

"Good. Make it so. And good luck."

**17**

---

In the two days since the debris impact and subsequent shuttle explosion, the full extent of the damage to the life support system on Level 57 had become apparent. It had taken almost a full day for Angus Fraser and his engineering crew to weld patches over the damaged outer hull and patch the inner hull with permaplas. Atmosphere had then been restored to that level, finally allowing full access for technicians and various crew to begin sifting through the floating wreckage and carefully check the equipment that remained. The news was not good.

As Angus had predicted, the $CO_2$ scrubbers were a mangled, unsalvageable wreck. Technicians and engineers spent hours pulling apart components of the wreckage and brainstorming ideas but, in the end, they admitted defeat. The massive $CO_2$ scrubbers that serviced the whole ship, were ruined beyond repair. In the normal course of affairs, this would not have been a problem, because Longshot was built with multiple redundancies and spare parts. In the case of $CO_2$ scrubbers, there were two whole replacement units that had been thoughtfully included in the Level 12 storage bay. The only problem was that Level 12 no longer existed, except as a sparkling cloud of debris, billions of kilometres behind them.

But there was worse news to come.

"So, what is the status of our life support systems?" asked Captain Anderson, as he chaired yet another emergency meeting of the mission team.

"The $CO_2$ scrubbers are completely cactus, Captain," said Angus. "We've sifted through the wreckage and there's absolutely nothing we can do to fix them or even rig something temporary. We're going to be rebreathing our own air from now on."

"And how long can we do that before the $CO_2$ builds up to a toxic level?"

"That's not my department, sir. I'm just the monkey who turns the wrench."

Maria Vargas spoke up. "Normal air has about 0.04 percent $CO_2$. Our scrubbers on board Longshot usually keep that level pretty close to stable. But without scrubbers, we will continue to exhale $CO_2$ and it will build up. When it gets to 1 percent, we will start to function less effectively and struggle with tiredness. At 2 percent, we will be getting headaches and feeling ill. At 4 percent, we will experience seizures, coma and, finally, death."

"So how long do we have?" asked Anderson again.

Vargas puffed her cheeks out as she exhaled. "It's hard to say, Captain. There are 40 crew currently awake, but it's a big ship. With the loss of our bottom 17 levels, and loss of atmosphere on Level 18, we have 56 viable levels left. That's an average of nearly 1.5 levels of breathable air per crew member. I've done some calculations and I estimate it will take about 10 to 12 days before $CO_2$ levels become toxic."

Anderson looked at Lieutenant Alvarez. "What was the latest estimate from Tama System Control regarding the estimated time until rescue?"

"The message we received about an hour ago confirmed that they will be rendezvousing with us in 14 days 8 hours."

"Surely our problem is easy to remedy?" said Commander Decker, in his usual arrogant manner. "We'll just put most of the crew back into cryogenic stasis. That will get us out of trouble, won't it?"

Vargas nodded. "It will certainly fix that problem. With less crew breathing out CO2, we will easily survive until we are rescued. But unfortunately, I think Mr Fraser has more bad news for us."

"Aye, ma'am. That I do. The TCS – the thermal control system– is also on the fritz."

A few heads turned to Kelly, who continued to function as official Scottish translator.

"Stuffed," she said.

"What exactly is the problem, Mr Fraser?" asked Anderson.

"As you know, Captain, the TCS keeps warm air circulating throughout the ship, to protect us from the cold of space. Our TCS wasn't directly damaged by the wee rock that tore through us, but it was shredded by multiple pieces of shrapnel from the exploding CO2 scrubbers. The two big RHUs – radioisotope heater units – didn't look too bad on the outside, but the insides are a mangled mess. My men could certainly repair the pipes that were severed, but there are complex electrical components and circuitry that are beyond my ken to fix."

"And I'm guessing that we don't have those replacement parts or replacement whole units."

"Not anymore, Captain. They were all blown to kingdom come when we lost the back part of the ship."

"I see." He turned to his science officer. "Lieutenant Vargas, how quickly will we cool down without the RHUs?"

"Once again, I'm only guessing, sir. It's complicated. The temperature of the vacuum that we are currently flying through is 2.7 degrees Kelvin, which is about minus 455 degrees Fahrenheit, or minus 270 degrees Celsius. Our inside thermostat was set at 22 degrees Celsius. The ship is reasonably well insulated, so it will lose heat slowly. Plus, the electrical systems, our fusion drives, and even our own bodies will all be contributing heat which will slow the cooling process."

"Give me a rough estimate."

"My best guess is that we will lose about three degrees Celsius per day."

There was a moment's silence as they all digested this.

"So, after seven days, we will be at zero degrees Celsius – freezing point?" asked Anderson.

"Yes, Captain."

"And by the time we are rescued, it will be about minus 19 degrees Celsius?"

"Yes, sir."

"Who said space travel wasn't fun?" quipped Jordan, who had become part of the mission team, at the Captain's invitation.

"Let's work the problem, people. Give me solutions," said Anderson, looking around the oval table.

"We could make simple electric radiant heaters and plug them into the ship's power supply," suggested Daniel.

"I was about to suggest the same thing, sir," agreed Angus. "My men could easily whip up a bunch of portable heaters. A simple coiled metal element with a current regulator, inside a safety grill."

Daniel nodded. "Plus, if most of the crew are in cryogenic stasis, the few who remain awake to communicate with the rescuers could sleep in one of the shuttles in Shuttle Bay 1."

The Captain addressed his chief engineer. "Angus, can the heaters inside the shuttle be brought online?"

"No, sir. The entire power output from the shuttle's fusion reactor is required to power Longshot's deflector shields. The shuttle's internal systems have been completely disconnected from the reactor. We need every last electron of power for the laser annihilation field surrounding our deflector dish."

"I see. But with a radiant heater plugged in, we could be reasonably comfortable inside a shuttle."

"Yes, sir," agreed Angus.

"It'll be a bloody cold trip to the toilet though, won't it," offered Jordan.

"What about all the passengers and crew in cryogenic stasis?" asked Anderson. "How will the cold affect them?"

"It won't," replied Vargas. "At least not while they're asleep. But when they wake up, they will be emerging naked into a temperature of minus 19 degrees Celsius. Not exactly what they were expecting to encounter. I suggest that those of us who are awake should station ourselves there with hot drinks and blankets and jackets."

"Will the food dispensers in the dining room still work at below zero temperatures?" asked Jordan, who was always thinking about food.

Vargas answered, "The drink dispensers will still work. They will be able to dispense hot drinks in zero gravity drinking pouches. But most of the food will no longer be available, as the yeast and hydroponics farms will become unviable once we hit zero degrees. It will be energy bars for the last week, I'm afraid."

There were several groans all around, but Captain Anderson put a positive spin on it.

"If having to huddle around makeshift heaters and eat energy bars for week or two is the worst we have to put up with, we should be thankful. It looks like we can survive this, folks! We're nearly there! After everything we've been through, I think we're actually going to make it!"

There were nods all around and several half-smiles.

"Good! Let's get ourselves organised! Commander Decker, I want you to come up with a list of all non-essential personnel – as many as possible who we don't really need awake. Get them into cryogenic stasis as soon as possible. Mr Fraser, get started on those heaters, immediately. Lieutenant Vargas, make sure we have a strong comm patch from there to the command centre, so we can listen in to any signals we receive. Lieutenant Alvarez, draft a morse code message telling our rescuers what our predicament is and what we're planning to do. The rest of us will start moving supplies, bedding and blankets into the shuttles."

He looked around the table. "Have I missed anything?"

"Last time we had a crisis, I missed out on the booze," said Jordan.

Anderson chuckled. "Jordan, I'm placing you in charge of ... let's call it 'internal liquid heating'."

Jordan cracked a smile. "That's the best order an officer has ever given me."

## 18

It had been a whirlwind of a week. Keelor had scurried from one class to the next, trying to absorb the huge amount of information that was being thrown at them by their instructors. There were 28 in the new intake, and Keelor was the oldest by three full years. The others were all 18, straight from school, the cream of the crop. He remembered when he had sat his own finals at the end of school. While others in his class had studied intensely, vying to earn a prestigious invitation to join the ADF, he had been unmotivated, preferring to pursue his own vague interests. Consequently, his final results had been mediocre. His mother had fretted, but his dad had been philosophical.

"Give the boy a chance. He's clearly gifted. He just hasn't worked out where to focus his attention yet."

For three years, he had muddled through a university course, with mixed results, excelling at tasks he found interesting, but barely passing those he found dull or irrelevant. At one point, his mother had forced him to visit a vocational guidance centre. His IQ was estimated to be over 150, and the advisers had told him that he could do anything he wanted.

But that was precisely the problem. He had no idea what he wanted to do.

And now, here he was. Did he really want to be in the military? He must admit, the problem-solving aspects of military intelligence intrigued him, but he wasn't sure how he felt about all the other stuff: ranks and uniforms and saluting and not being your own boss.

The others in his intake class treated him with moderate respect due to his age, but he also sensed a subtle gulf separating him from them. They were just so ... young!

He found the morning PT sessions relatively easy. The daily hard work of helping his parents on the farm had hardened him and broadened his shoulders. He was fit and strong for his age and he breezed through the morning exercises while many of the other recruits wheezed and gasped. After the first PT session on the second day, several of the girls began to take a particular interest in him, which he found mildly annoying as they seemed so immature. Besides, he was comparing them all to Maran Cartwright, the ensign who had shown him around on his first day on base, and whom he hadn't been able to stop thinking about ever since.

Not that he was ever going to have a chance with her. Romantic relationships between the lowly enlisted ranks and officers, even junior commissioned officers such as ensigns, were strictly taboo.

"Mr Trantum! Come back to us! What girl were you dreaming about?"

There was subdued laughter from the class and several heads turned in his direction. The instructor, a barrel-chested sergeant with a gruff voice, had walked from the front and was now standing beside Keelor's desk. For a moment, Keelor was shocked, wondering how the sergeant could possibly have guessed his thoughts. Then he realised it was a joke.

"I was thinking about my mother, sarge, of course."

That brought forth more laughter from the class.

"Then perhaps we should contact your mother and see if she can calculate the orbital velocity!"

More laughter. The class was really enjoying this.

"She's no good with numbers, sarge, but I'll have a go if you like."

"Would you mind? That would be awfully nice of you. As long as it doesn't inconvenience you."

Keelor glanced at the front screen and read the problem that the class had been set. He ran the numbers through his head and calculated the answer.

"4.2 kilometres per second, at that altitude."

The sergeant frowned and glanced down at Keelor's screen, which was completely blank, without any working calculations at all. The rest of the class were silent now and were looking down at their own calculations. Some of them erased what they had typed and began again.

"Very good, Mr Trantum. How did you work that out so quickly?"

"It's only my mother who's no good with numbers, sarge."

"Humph." The sergeant walked silently back to the front, and for the rest of the lesson, Keelor tried to stay focused.

After class, one of the girls started walking beside him as they exited the room.

"Are you coming to the break-out party tonight? It's our last night before we ship out to the Nut."

Atraya's moon, Rios, was affectionately called the Nut, because its slightly irregular shape made it look like a macadamia nut. At the conclusion of this week's induction classes at Angel City, the new recruits would then spend a month at the military base on Rios, to complete their training.

"I suppose so," he said vaguely. "There's nothing much else to do around here at night."

"That's good. Maybe we could have a drink together?"

"Sure."

She smiled at him, hoping to receive something similar in return, but was mildly disappointed in his blasé expression.

Later that night, a little after 20:00, Keelor wandered into the Blue Moon, a popular bar on one of the lower levels of the hub. Deep blue UV light was the pervasive lighting, and the ceiling was speckled with thousands of tiny, reflective mirrors. A juke box was pumping out loud music, lights were flashing and the dance floor was packed with people. The new recruits had grabbed the far corner of the seated area and Lystall, the girl who had spoken to him after class, spotted him and waved him over. The group was in a good mood and were laughing and talking loudly. Their induction week was over and only two of them had not been invited to continue their training at the Nut. They had a week's pay to their credit and some of them looked intent on spending it all on booze tonight. In fact, a couple of them looked like they had already spent half of it.

Keelor ordered a drink but had barely begun to sip it when Lystall grabbed his hand and dragged him onto the dance floor. He knew he was a terrible dancer but did his best. Lystall didn't seem to notice his awkwardness, or if she did, chose to ignore it. Most of the group had ditched their recruits' uniforms and were dressed in 'civvies', and the girls, in particular, had dressed up for their celebration night. Lystall swayed and gyrated in her tight dress and high heels, dancing alluringly all around Keelor who had never been in a situation like this. The song ended and Keelor thought he had done his duty, but several other girls and guys from his class joined them on the floor as the next song started and Keelor was trapped into dancing some more.

For the next two hours, he had very little time to sit and relax, because any time he did, someone else was dragging him back to the dance floor. Often, he couldn't quite tell who he was meant to be dancing with, as he was often surrounded by several girls, swaying closer and then swirling away. All in all, it was very confusing. But he did notice that Lystall, in particular, had developed a somewhat proprietorial attitude toward him.

Eventually, he managed to excuse himself to go to the restroom, and he spent some extra time just standing at the basin, enjoying the relative peace and quiet. He was walking back from the restroom a few minutes later, when a voice said, "I told you that you'd be beating them off with a stick."

Four attractive women in civilian clothes were sitting at a

booth, drinking what appeared to be cocktails. It took a moment for him to realise that the girl with the short blonde hair who had spoken to him was Maran Cartwright. She was wearing a particularly skimpy dress and was looking stunning. He hadn't seen her all week, although he had thought of her more than he cared to admit.

"You're ... not in uniform," he mumbled.

Maran turned to the others at her table. "He's extremely perceptive, don't you think? The future of the military is in good hands with recruits of his calibre."

Keelor was sure he was blushing, but in the blue UV light no one would notice.

"Are you having a good time?" she asked him.

He shrugged. "I'm not much of a dancer. In fact, I'm nothing of a dancer. I have no idea what I'm doing."

"You're doing okay. You just need to relax into it a bit more." She stood up. "Come on, I'll help you."

She grabbed his hand and led him onto the dance floor, which was still packed with people. She leaned forward and spoke loudly, over the music. "Just watch me and do what I do."

She started doing a simple sideways shuffle, from side to side, and Keelor had barely begun to copy her when the song ended and a new song started. Someone had obviously decided that it was time for something mellower, because a soft love song started. There were several groans and half the people left the dance floor while the remaining couples held each other and started dancing more intimately. Keelor just stood there awkwardly for a moment.

"Oh well, that was a short lesson," he said.

He started to walk toward Maran's table, but she grabbed his arm.

"Not so fast, sailor! You don't get out of it that easily! I promised you a lesson and it hasn't finished yet."

"But this is ..."

"Just follow me."

She reached out and drew him in, and they began an intimate slow dance, shuffling slowly in time with the music.

"There. That's not so bad, is it?"

Actually, he had to admit, it was pretty damn good!

"You can hold me closer if you like. I promise I won't bite."

They drew closer together and swayed in time with the ballad. Keelor was incredibly conscious of her body up against his and was feeling a swirl of emotions. He glanced across at the recruits' tables and saw Lystall staring at them. She wasn't wearing her happy face.

"I thought officers weren't meant to fraternise with the lower ranks."

"You aren't any rank, yet. You're just a trainee, technically a civilian, until you graduate. Besides, all we're doing is dancing. We're not getting married or anything."

"That's a shame," he said, and then wondered if he'd overstepped the mark.

Maran laughed. "Cheeky as well as good looking! No wonder the girls are fighting over you."

"No, they're not." Then he began to wonder, and he frowned. "Are they?"

"Trust me. I'm a girl. I know these things. They definitely are."

They danced quietly together for a few moments, and Keelor marvelled at the fact that he was holding this beautiful woman in his arms.

"Who's your favourite so far?" she asked.

Without thinking, he blurted out, "You are."

The song ended at that moment, and they stood still. She looked up at him and he couldn't be sure, but he thought he saw a spark of something in her eyes. Was he only imagining it, or was she actually interested in him?

"In that case, you're in luck. You're going to be spending a whole lot more time with me. You're not going to the Nut with the other recruits. I'm taking you to Corfu tomorrow, for your enhancement."

"My enhancement? I'd forgotten all about it."

"Pack your bags and meet me tomorrow at 08:00 outside Shuttle Bay 2."

She started to walk away, then turned back and said, "And don't overdo it with the booze, tonight. I don't want you throwing up in the shuttle tomorrow."

She started to walk away again but stopped and turned back one final time.

"And don't have anything to eat or drink tomorrow morning, before your surgery."

**19**

---

"How did the rest of last night go?" Maran asked, as the shuttle pulled away from Angel City. "Have you got any scratch marks from those girls fighting over you?"

Keelor shook his head. "I excused myself pretty early and went to bed. Besides, they're all just a little too ..."

"Young?" she suggested.

"Yes."

Maran nodded. "Are looking forward to your enhancement?"

"To be honest, I'd forgotten all about it."

"Major Maxwell wants it done and out of the way before you start work in his department. Plus, you need to be enhanced to be commissioned as a junior officer."

"Commissioned?"

"There are no lower ranks working in military intelligence. The lowest rank is ensign, a junior commissioned officer. So, congratulations, you're going to be an ensign."

"Just like that? No tests or evaluation process?"

"What do you think this whole week has been? The instructors describe you as 'brilliant but bored'. You've demonstrated a high level of intelligence, particularly in the areas of logic, abstract thinking and mathematics. The military uses this initial week of instruction to highlight potential officers. You stood out, head and shoulders above the rest of your class."

"What if I'd been dumb?"

"You'd probably be heading back to your family farm by now, to tend all those cows." She smiled. "Major Maxwell was never going to let you into his department if you didn't have the intellectual cred."

"But how can I be an officer, even a junior one like an ensign, when I hardly know anything about the military?"

"That's why this trip to Corfu is important. Once you're enhanced, they will upload everything you need to know in order to be a competent officer. You'll leave Corfu completely familiar with everything military, as if you've known it all your life."

"Is that how it happened for you?"

"Of course."

She lifted the hair at the back of her neck and showed him the plug: a small round piece of metal at the base of her skull, flush with her skin.

"When did you get enhanced?"

"Three months ago."

"So, you're the same age as me?"

"Of course not! I'm much older than you – by three months."

"Wow! That old? I can't imagine how much extra wisdom you must have, after having lived for all that extra time."

She smiled. "Absolutely! You can learn a lot in three months."

Keelor grew more serious. "Does it hurt?"

"It absolutely kills. It's agonising. You can hear people screaming in pain as far away as the mainland."

"Ha, ha. Okay, I get it. I'll man up and stop worrying."

"Did you call your parents, before you left the base?"

"Yes. I've called them a few times this week."

"They must be surprised at the way things are turning out for you."

"Yes. Especially mum. I think she was worried I was going end up drifting through life with no real direction. I can tell she's pretty pleased."

Half an hour later, they disembarked at Jasper Spaceport and caught a flitter cab to the wharf where they boarded a superfast cat for the island.

"How come you got lumbered with me?" Keelor asked as the fusion powered catamaran pulled away from the wharf and headed for the harbour entrance. "I can't imagine that escort duty is high on the list of things you hoped to do when you joined the military."

"There's a department tradition that the most junior member of the team has to baby sit the newbie."

"Gee, thanks. I feel so special."

"You're welcome. Plus, I'm due for two days' leave, so I get to visit my folks, who live right here, in Jasper."

The catamaran reached the mouth of the harbour and turned to meet a gentle swell rolling in from the east. The throttle opened up, and the vessel surged forward, lifting out of the water on its twin hydrofoils. Keelor had chosen to stand on the viewing deck near the bows, and now the howling wind created by their speed made all conversation impossible. Maran went back into the protected cabin, but Keelor stayed outside, holding the front rail of the viewing deck and revelling in the salty air and occasional sea spray that whipped up from the hydrofoils.

It took 20 minutes for the island to come into view and another 15 before the catamaran throttled back and entered the tranquil inner harbour. Maran re-joined him on the deck and laughed at him.

"What's so funny?"

"Your hair. It's sticking up and flared backward. You look like a clown who's just seen a ghost."

"Don't you know? This is the latest thing here in Jasper. It's called the salty scarecrow. All the coolest people are doing it."

As they walked along the jetty shortly afterward, Keelor said, "Did you know that Corfu is named after an island on Earth?"

She raised her eyebrows in surprise. "Really? No, I didn't know that."

"Not many people do. But Corfu on Earth was a similar shape

to this, although much bigger, and the first settlers here thought the name was appropriate."

"Is that one of the things you learned when you broke into the archives?"

"No. That piece of information isn't hidden. It's just that very few people are interested in history, even our own history."

She tilted her head and regarded him curiously. "You're a unique person, Keelor Trantum."

"Thank you, Maran Cartwright," he smiled. "I'll take that as a compliment."

"Don't get too carried away. 'Unique' can also mean 'weird'."

Ten minutes later, they disembarked from a flitter outside a huge, multistorey building, with a sign saying, 'Corfu Enhancement Facility'. The facility was set in luxurious grounds in the foothills, east of the main township.

Maran and Keelor walked through the main entrance into an impressive, large vestibule. Maran led the way to a reception desk. A woman at the desk saw her approaching and, noting her military intelligence insignia, seemed to straighten up in anticipation.

"Can I help you?"

"I'm Ensign Maran Cartwright, from Military Intelligence. Major Maxwell has booked in this gentleman for expedited enhancement."

"Certainly. Your name, sir?"

"Keelor Trantum."

"Let me see if we can find you on our system," she said, looking at her screen. "Ah, yes. Here you are. Keelor Trantum. You turned 21 last week?"

"That's correct."

"Excellent. Everything is ready for you, sir. You just need to sign this indemnity form, and we can get the process underway."

Keelor was handed a screen with pages of information and waivers. He simply scrolled to the bottom and scribbled his signature with his finger. A porter came and picked up his small bag of spare clothes and personal items. The woman came around from behind the counter.

"Just follow me, please sir, and we'll get you started. The porter will take your bag to your room."

She walked toward a bank of lifts, and Keelor turned to Maran.

"This is where I leave you," she said. "I'll be back to collect you when you're done."

He took a deep breath and exhaled. He was already feeling nervous. Maran reached out and touched his arm.

"You'll be fine." Then she gave him a cheeky smile. "Hardly anyone dies getting this done."

**20**

---

The receptionist took Keelor to a small cinema room, with a seating capacity of about 30 people.

"We reserve this cinema for military personnel, as there is a slightly different, military-specific video presentation you need to watch. You've got the cinema all to yourself today. Just press the call button on your armrest if you need help. Someone will arrive at the end of the presentation to answer any questions and take you on to the next stage. Enjoy!"

As she left, the lights dimmed, and a video presentation began.

*"Neural enhancement, also sometimes referred to as neural augmentation, is a means of allowing humans to interface more smoothly and easily with various technologies. The neural interface transceiver is a small device inserted at the base of the skull. It has monofilaments which interface with the cerebellum, the cerebellar cortex and the rear of the brain stem, under the cerebellum."*

"Once the neural transceiver is in place and has been calibrated to your brain, you will be able to more readily interface with many technologies, such as computers, household appliances, communication devices, and various modes of transportation. For example, your flitter or other transportation device can be calibrated specifically to you, so that no one else may fly or drive it. The front door to your home can be calibrated so that only those within your family may unlock it. Many personal or electronic items can be calibrated to you so that no one else can use them. Families can also easily locate and communicate with each other through private comm calls via their own private enhancement network.

"Military-grade neural transceivers have additional monofilaments that interface with the hippocampus and cerebral cortex. This facilitates a process known as fast-stream cognitive absorption, which allows for rapid uploading of skills and knowledge vital for specific roles. The military-grade neural transceiver also allows you to calibrate your weapon to you alone, so that no one else will be able to fire it.

"The process of having your neural transmitter fitted is completely painless and safe. Minor surgery of about one hour's duration will be required to initially fit your neural transceiver to the base of your skull. The insertion of the monofilaments into the various regions of your brain, however, will take much longer. Over a period of five days, the monofilaments will grow and expand, one molecule at a time, using computer guided nanobot technology. You will be kept sedated throughout these five days. Once the monofilaments are in place, a simple calibration and alignment will take place, and then you will be woken up.

"Because of the effective cocktail of drugs that you will be given, you will wake refreshed and rejuvenated, feeling as though you have only slept for a few minutes. You are about to embark on a whole new, interactive way of life! So, sit back, relax, and let us enhance your life!"

Some corny theme music swelled up and images of happy smiling people appeared, flying flitters operating appliances and calling each other over their personal comms. The presentation culminated in a scene of a smiling couple walking hand in hand down a beach as the words 'Enhance your Life!' expanded to fill the screen.

The video ended and the cinema lights faded up. A nurse in a spotless white uniform entered the cinema room and smiled brightly.

"Do you have any questions, Mr Trantum?"

"No. I was pretty familiar with the whole process already."

"Excellent! If you could follow me now, please, I'll take you to the prep room."

She led him down a wide corridor past another cinema room. The curtain was drawn across the cinema entrance and Keelor could hear another video presentation being shown. Presumably, that was the general public cinema room. They continued down the corridor which ended in a short 'T' section. The nurse turned left and led him through a set of double doors marked, 'Military'. They entered a plush foyer which looked like it belonged in an expensive hotel rather than a medical facility. Keelor noted the plush, softly upholstered lounge chairs, thick pile carpet, dim lighting and gentle music playing softly in the background.

The nurse led him to one of the lounge chairs and invited him to sit. He sank into the chair, and she leant down and scanned the biochip in his wrist. She looked at the results on her hand-held scanner.

"Good. All seems to be in order. You are Keelor Trantum, age 21, and all biological indicators are optimal. You have no allergies and no underlying health conditions." She tapped the screen one more time. "And you are here to receive a military-grade neural transceiver. Is all that correct?"

"That's right."

"Excellent!"

She took a few steps back from him and gave him another bright smile.

"You'll be feeling very sleepy in a moment. Don't fight it. Just relax, and we'll see you on the other side."

"What ... how ...?" The room started to lose focus and his eyelids became heavy. Before he realised what was happening, he was asleep.

**21**

———

Keelor woke up in a comfortable bed in a nicely furnished room. One minute he was asleep, and the next he was wide awake. A medibot on an extendable arm was just retracting into its ceiling cavity and a nurse with a data pad was standing beside his bed. He looked around and noted the wide window overlooking a plush garden, with rolling hills in the distance.

"It's done?" he asked.

The nurse smiled. "I've just summoned the doctor. He can explain."

Keelor sat up and felt the back of his head. It didn't feel any different.

"Where's the ...?"

"Good! You're awake!" said the man who walked into his room. He was wearing surgical scrubs, although he had removed his cap, revealing a completely bald head.

"Is it done?" asked Keelor again.

"No, we didn't carry out the procedure. Not yet, anyway."

"Is there a problem?"

The doctor smiled, reassuringly. "No problem. But we have standing instructions to not proceed with enhancement when we encounter ... certain conditions."

"What does that mean? What conditions? Is my brain somehow incompatible?"

Again, the doctor smiled, and he shook his head. "Your brain is perfectly compatible. And we may still go ahead with the procedure if that is your choice. But there is another option you will be asked to consider."

"What option? What other option is there to enhancement? I've never heard of one."

"That's not for me to say. Major Maxwell, your commanding officer in Military Intelligence, is on his way here as we speak. He will explain it to you."

Keelor frowned. "How long was I asleep?"

"About 90 minutes. We prepped you for surgery but cancelled the procedure after completing the initial scans of your brain."

"So, you did find something ... strange?"

"Perhaps 'strange' is the wrong word. 'Interesting', is more apt. But I'll let others explain all that to you. In the meantime, your clothes are in the wardrobe. Please get changed. We are expecting the major to arrive shortly."

With that, the doctor and nurse left the room, closing the door behind them, leaving Keelor puzzled.

Major Maxwell arrived a short time later and found Keelor sitting patiently in a chair beside the window.

"Well, well, well, young Keelor. You certainly are a bit of a surprise package."

"Am I? What's going on? I don't understand."

"All is about to be revealed. Come with me, there's someone I'd like you to meet."

He turned and walked out the door, leaving Keelor scurrying to catch up. They entered a lift at the end of a wide corridor and the lift began descending, which Keelor found strange because they were already on the ground floor and the lift screen only showed levels from the ground level up. He also noted that Maxwell had not pushed a button or even spoken a command. Clearly, he had used his neural transceiver to issue an instruction to the lift.

The lift door opened and they emerged into a spacious vestibule. As they traversed the vestibule, Maxwell spoke softly,

"We're here. Where would you like to meet us? Okay, see you there."

He had clearly initiated a private comm call, once again using his neural transceiver.

"Good morning, Major," said an ensign stationed at a reception desk. "There's a buggy ready for you."

"Very good."

They approached a panel in the wall which slid aside, revealing a wide tunnel, leading slightly downward and disappearing around a bend. An open-sided buggy was parked nearby, and Keelor noted its beetle-like appearance as he and the major climbed in. Maxwell accelerated the bug down the tunnel, its smooth floor and smooth semicircular domed roof and wall structure racing by. They descended like this for about a minute and the air became increasingly warm. Finally, the tunnel ended. Maxwell parked the bug next to several identical bugs and led Keelor through another sliding door into a brightly lit facility. They entered a round foyer at the intersection of three corridors: one to the left, one to the right and one leading straight ahead. Two armed military personnel saluted the major who ignored them and turned left. There were laboratories opening off the corridor on both sides, with white lab-coated people working at benches filled with scientific equipment.

As they walked, Maxwell explained to Keelor, "This is Tesla Base, a military research facility. There are two more levels underneath us as well. It's quite a large complex."

"I've never heard of it."

"You wouldn't have. Most of the research that goes on here is classified. We don't exactly advertise the base to the wider community."

They came to a door marked, 'Dr Harry Melville', and Maxwell walked in without bothering to knock.

A man rose from behind a desk and smiled warmly.

"Ah! Here he is! The man of the moment!"

Harry Melville was in his early 60s, with long, straggly grey hair, a bushy grey beard and a slight pot belly. He was dressed in crumpled trousers, a casual shirt and a stained cardigan that looked like it needed donating to charity – or burning.

Maxwell did the introductions.

"This is Dr Harry Melville, the head of our research facility."

Melville came around from behind his desk and shook Keelor's hand.

"Very nice to meet you, Keelor. How are you feeling?"

"Very confused, sir."

"No need for the 'sir' nonsense. Just plain old Harry is fine," he said with a twinkle in his eye.

"Harry has resisted all attempts to officially join the military," commented Maxwell. "Goodness knows I've tried, but he's a stubborn old coot."

"You'll never get me wearing a uniform, Major. Please, sit down," he said to them both, indicating four comfortable chairs surrounding a small coffee table. They sat, with Harry on one side of the coffee table facing Keelor and Maxwell on the other.

"Let's cut to the chase," said Maxwell. "We've brought you here because we have an offer to make – one that will change your life."

**22**

Keelor glanced between Major Maxwell and Harry Melville. "What sort of offer?" he asked.

"We want to offer you an upgraded enhancement," answered Maxwell.

"More upgraded than the military one?" asked Keelor.

"Significantly. But it's complicated, so I'll let Harry explain."

Keelor looked to the scruffy, pot-bellied scientist who smiled back at him reassuringly. Harry clasped his hands over his prodigious stomach, leaned back in his chair and began his explanation.

"This research facility is involved in a wide range of ongoing research projects. All sorts of things: more efficient power generation, new propulsion systems for spaceships, communications, weapons, cryogenics, genetics, and so forth. One of the projects, and the one I am most passionate about, is the Newman Project: a research project aimed at helping humans achieve a higher level of cerebral functioning. It involves enhancing the human brain by augmenting it with a biologically-based quantum processing system."

"Biologically based?"

"Yes. You would be aware that our most important and most

powerful computer systems today are quantum-based. They operate at millions of times the speed of the old binary computers of the 24<sup>th</sup> century. Their only drawback is that the quantum qubits – the fundamental computational particles of these computers – can only operate at minus 273 degrees Celsius. This limits them to being housed in facilities that can maintain that degree of extremely low temperature."

"Which is why our portable devices all still use the old binary computers," offered Keelor.

"Precisely. Because of their need to be super-cooled, quantum computers aren't exactly portable. At least, they weren't portable until the Newman Project. As far as we can determine, the project began on Earth, in the years immediately preceding the Great War. A molecule was developed that provided an environment for quantum qubits to operate at normal room temperature. But the molecule could only exist within a living host. It was designed to reside in the human brain."

"A quantum computer inside people's heads?"

"Essentially, yes. Using nanobot technology, it was discovered that the quantum molecule could be coaxed to develop into monofilaments even thinner than the ones we use for connecting our current neural transceivers. The quantum molecule filaments are about as thin as a single micron, but much more invasive. Whereas the filaments we use for standard neural enhancement only attach to several key locations, the quantum filaments grow throughout the entire brain, connecting directly to the billions of neurons."

"And this was developed in the 24<sup>th</sup> century, back on Earth?"

"The essential elements were developed back then by an unscrupulous corporation that illegally experimented on human subjects without their consent. They all died in the process, except for one who escaped and disappeared from the historical records."

"Let me guess. His name was Newman?"

"Yes. Daniel Newman. Sadly, given the unfortunate end that the previous test subjects met with, he probably died from complications from the experiment as well. He was the last test subject prior to the researchers being arrested. The Great War happened within weeks of that, the result of which was catastrophic disruption of Earth's technology. It took more than a century for mankind to claw their way back from their near annihilation.

"When the first starship arrived here 158 years later, in 2474, it brought with it a complete library of mankind's scientific knowledge. Every paper, every lecture, every video, every research protocol, every book ever published, all digitally preserved. And buried in that vast library were the details of the quantum molecule and the records of those early, tragic attempts to install it in the human brain."

"And you've continued to try to develop that idea?"

"We haven't just tried, we've perfected it."

"You've got people walking around with quantum processors in their brains?" asked Keelor, incredulously.

"Yes. But we've discovered that not everyone's brain is equipped to deal with the quantum molecular filaments. In fact, most people's brains will actively reject them. That was a major part of the problem that those early unscrupulous researchers failed to understand. There is an enzyme produced in the brain, called monoamine oxidase A, which seeks out and destroys unwanted neurotransmitters, and in the vast majority of people, this enzyme will attack the quantum molecule filaments. But in a small percentage of people, the MAOA gene responsible for producing the enzyme is either recessive, or inactive. Only people with a recessive or inactive MAOA gene are suitable for quantum enhancement."

"Furthermore, in order for the quantum molecule filaments to form successful connections with the brain's neurons, an unusually excessive amount of another enzyme, called alpha synuclein, is required. The amount produced by most people's brain is insufficient to bind the quantum molecule filaments to the neurons. But a very small percentage of people have a copying error, known as copy number variation, or CNV, in the gene that codes for alpha synuclein. They have two sets of the gene, instead of one, and their brain makes twice the amount of alpha synuclein that most other people do."

Harry looked at Keelor, closely. "Is this making any kind of sense to you?"

"Yes. I think so. You're saying that only people with a lack of one enzyme and too much of another are able to effectively bind with the quantum molecular filaments."

"Yes! Yes! You've got it!" Harry seemed overjoyed that Keelor had latched onto the basic meaning. He looked at Maxwell and said, "You told me the lad is extremely bright. I can see that for myself, now."

"He's also a pain in the arse, when he decides to do his own thing and break the law."

Harry waved that objection away. "Not my problem!" He smiled at Keelor and continued his explanation.

"But there's a third essential factor for someone to be compatible with the quantum filaments: their level of intelligence. In people with an IQ of less than 130, there is a likelihood of developing psychosis, as their brains are not able to cope with the input from the quantum filaments. But in people with a high IQ, there has never been an incidence of psychosis."

"So, you need very intelligent people with defective genes."

"Precisely! To be safe, we only accept people with an IQ over 140. And, of course, they must have both gene mutations."

"And how often do all three factors line up?" Keelor asked.

"I haven't worked out the percentages, but it's an extremely rare combination. Out of the entire human population of this solar system, we currently only have 10 people who have qualified and have been quantum enhanced."

"And I'm assuming that bringing me here means that I meet all three of these qualifications."

"Yes! While you were sedated, we sequenced your DNA, and you have both mutations. Your IQ, as measured in the test you did on day three of your recruitment and also in your first year of university, is between 152 and 154. You are a perfect candidate!"

"Is it a risky procedure?"

"No. Not anymore. It's perfectly safe. But it is a bit longer. You would need to be sedated for a whole week, while the quantum molecule filaments permeate all the regions of your brain."

Keelor shrugged. "What's in it for me? I don't mean to be rude, but I would be perfectly satisfied with standard enhancement. I don't have any desire for anything more."

"There are two parts to that answer, Keelor," said Harry. "Firstly, it will radically improve your brain function. Neither the standard nor the military enhancement improve or augment brain function at all. They merely provide a smooth interface between your brain and the technology around you. But quantum enhancement will exponentially increase the speed and accuracy of your thought processes. You will have literally billions of quantum cubits adding their fire power to your much slower chemical brain processes. And who wouldn't want that?"

"You said there were two parts to the answer. What's the second part?"

"The second part of the answer is that you should do it for the good of our society. You see, there's a reason why I'm so keen to find as many people as possible for quantum enhancement. I'll be honest, I'm not just wanting to do this for your good. We need people with quantum enhancement for a particular line of research which has huge implications, including military ones."

"Which is?" asked Keelor.

Harry looked at Major Maxwell who nodded. "You may as well tell him."

Harry looked back at Keelor and said, "We're developing a means of instantaneous travel to anywhere in the universe, and quantum enhanced humans are essential to that process."

**23**

———

Keelor looked back and forth between Major Maxwell and Dr Harry Melville, trying to determine if they were joking.

"Instantaneous travel? To anywhere in the universe?"

"Well, almost anywhere in the universe," admitted Harry. "The whole thing's still a bit sketchy – still in the very early stages. But we're making definite progress."

"And you need quantum enhanced people to make it possible?"

Harry nodded enthusiastically. "Yes, we do. And you would be a perfect addition to our team."

"It would mean you would be working directly under Harry, working alongside the other quantum enhanced people," said Maxwell. "You'd be based in Angel City, where Harry spends most of his time."

"I'm only down here on Corfu occasionally. Most of the projects in this facility carry on quite effectively without me. My main focus is the Newman Project, which is based in Angel City.

Maxwell continued. "If you agree to join the project, we will need you to sign an NDA – a non-disclosure agreement – as part of the Official Secrets Act. You wouldn't be able to talk about your work with anyone. On the positive side, you would be given an immediate commission as a lieutenant with the commensurate rate of pay. For someone in your position, it's a very good deal."

Keelor sat thinking. "What if I decline your offer? What if I just say no? It seems to me you've already risked a lot by telling me stuff I shouldn't really know."

"That's okay," said Maxwell. "If you choose the usual military enhancement, we will simply erase your memory of the last 24 hours. We have the technology to do that quite easily. You will walk out of the enhancement facility without any memory of this conversation."

Keelor regarded Maxwell carefully, and a thought occurred to him.

"What if you've already done that? What if we've already had this conversation and I said 'no', and you erased my memory and tried again? This could be the second or third time we've had this conversation. You could keep doing this until you finally come up with some way to convince me."

"My word, he's clever!" said Harry.

"I told you he'd suspect," agreed Maxwell.

"Perhaps we should use some kind of physical torture next time?" suggested Harry.

"Or maybe ply him with alcohol and women," added Maxwell.

"If that doesn't work, we'll inject him with my newly invented compliance serum."

They both looked at him, smiling.

"Okay, okay! I get it," said Keelor. "Maybe that whole scenario was a bit far-fetched."

"Just a bit," agreed Maxwell. "You've been watching too many spy movies."

"We would never do that to you, Keelor," said Harry, sincerely. "It really is your decision."

"That's right," agreed Maxwell. "One of the highest values of Atrayan society is the protection of the rights of individuals. We absolutely oppose the kind of totalitarian dictatorship that almost destroyed Earth. Our ancestors fled to this solar system to escape that kind of thing and to set up a free and respectful society. My role, and that of the whole military, is to protect and preserve that freedom, or die trying. This really is completely your choice, Keelor."

Both men gazed at him as he pondered his decision.

He sighed deeply. "The alcohol and women was a pretty tempting offer. I don't suppose you could throw that in as well?"

"You'll have to source those things for yourself," said Maxwell. "Mind you, from what I've heard, you seem to have an impressive line-up of interested women already."

Keelor blushed but laughed at the same time, then he nodded his head.

"Okay. I'll do it."

**24**

—————

Daniel woke with a numb nose. He was floating in a sleeping bag which was zipped up to his chin, but his face was exposed to the cold air that now permeated the entire ship. The radiant heater that had been hastily constructed by Angus and his team provided some warmth within the confines of the shuttle, but it was fighting a losing battle against the pervading cold. With three days to go before their predicted rescue, the air temperature throughout Longshot was now minus 12 degrees Celsius. Inside the shuttle, with the door closed and the heater going, the temperature was hovering around eight degrees above zero, but every time someone went outside to use the amenities or go to the dining room for hot drinks, the cold air snuck in like an unwanted intruder.

There were only four of them left awake now: Captain Anderson, Daniel, Jordan and Angus Fraser. Angus was still awake in case there was something else that went wrong and needed urgent mending. Daniel was there because the Captain trusted his opinion and had come to rely on his quick thinking. Jordan, however, was still awake because she refused to "spend another six hours sitting on the crapper" as she so delightfully put it. Daniel was secretly pleased to have her company, because she added a light-hearted tone to their somewhat dire circumstances.

Most of the crew had entered cryogenic stasis on the first day of the crisis to conserve oxygen within the stricken starship, and Kelly had been one of those. Four days ago, the Captain had ordered most of the mission team to enter stasis as well, as there was no need for them to be awake and suffering.

The shuttle door opened, and Jordan came in, huffing and puffing with cold, her breath clouding in the icy air.

"Holy cow, that's cold enough to freeze the warts off my grandma's chin!" she exclaimed as she closed the door firmly behind her.

"I thought you'd previously told me your grandma had hairs on her chin," commented Daniel.

"She does. But she's got warts as well."

"She's a mess."

"That's nothing. You should see my grandpa."

She handed each of them a zero-grav pouch of hot coffee, and then climbed into her sleeping bag again. Each sleeping bag was tied loosely to a section of wall.

"The good news is that the dispensers in the dining room are still dispensing hot drinks. The bad news is that there's no running water in the toilet facility. The pipes have all frozen."

"I'm surprised they lasted this long," commented Anderson.

"I assume the toilet suction system is still working, lassie?" asked Angus.

"Yeah. But when you hold that icy suction cap against your private parts you'll be yodelling in a higher octave. It's a wonder you didn't hear me from here."

"I did hear some faint yodelling," Daniel commented. "I just thought it was the pipes constricting."

"It was. My pipes!"

They sucked appreciatively on their coffees, drawing warmth from the hot liquid.

"I'm disappointed," quipped Daniel. "I specifically ordered a double shot caramel soy latte with a mocha twist. You must have got my order mixed up."

"Give it here, then. I'll drink it for you," answered Jordan.

"I'll put up with it, I guess," conceded Daniel with feigned reluctance.

A soft chime indicated an incoming transmission. A moment later, a voice came over the shuttle's comm system.

"Longshot, this is Captain Bronson from the Atrayan cruiser, Ulysses. We are continuing to decelerate and will be alongside you in three days from now. We note, however, that your trajectory has altered slightly, and we are having to alter our own trajectory to match yours. Can you please advise your situation? Are you outgassing, or is there any other cause for your trajectory change? Please advise. Ulysses out."

"Altered trajectory?" asked Daniel. "That doesn't sound good. What could be causing it?"

Anderson addressed their artificial intelligence. "Eric, you heard the transmission. Are we experiencing any kind of outgassing or anything else that would be adding an unwanted velocity vector to our trajectory?"

"No, Captain. There are no hull breaches and there is no outgassing. I can find nothing to indicate that Longshot is actively altering its trajectory."

"That leaves only one possibility," said Daniel.

"Yes," agreed Anderson. "Eric, examine all data from our long-range scanners. Is there anything to indicate a source of increased gravity?"

"I can detect no stars or planets within the range of my scanners, Captain, but I can now confirm our change of trajectory. Our course has altered by 0.12 of a degree over the last 24 hours."

"Something is dragging us aside," said Anderson.

"Eric, do you have the ability to detect black holes?" asked Daniel.

"Only by measuring the bending of light around them. At this stage I can detect no distortion of starlight within the range of my scanners. However, I do note an increase in X-ray radiation."

"Keep scanning and advise us of any change," said Anderson.

"Aye, sir," responded the AI.

Anderson scratched his trim grey beard. "That's very puzzling."

"X-rays?" said Daniel. "That's not something that you expect to find in the middle of interstellar space. They don't just pop into existence from nowhere. They have to have a source."

"Yes, but what?" asked Anderson.

"I've got an idea," said Daniel. "Let me check the science archives."

He pulled his neural interface transceiver out of his pocked and placed the clear cap on his head.

"I love it when you put that shower cap on, Professor," commented Jordan. "I only wish I had a rubber ducky to give you as well."

Daniel, however, wasn't listening. He was already searching the science archives, and what he discovered gave him deep concern. If his suspicions were true, they were heading into grave danger.

# UNTITLED

25

Keelor woke up feeling rested and refreshed. It was the same bed and same room where he had woken previously. The retractable medibot arm was hovering over him with a syringe in its 'hand' and, as he watched, it quickly retreated to its cavity in the ceiling. A nurse was standing on one side of his bed and a doctor in a white coat was on the other.

"How are you feeling?" asked the doctor.

"Fine," he said. "Actually, more than fine. Wonderful!"

"Good!" the bald-headed physician replied. "That's just how we want you to feel."

"So, it's all done?" Keelor asked.

"Yes. All done."

He reached around the back of his head and felt the smooth metal surface of a circular plug, flush with his skin at the base of his skull.

"It feels the same as a normal plug," he commented.

"Yes, the transceiver unit is the same, no matter what grade of neural enhancement you receive."

"So, I've received the quantum enhancement?"

"Yes, you have. It's all in place. While you were sleeping, we temporarily activated it, in order to calibrate it to your brain. It's now in sleep mode, awaiting full conscious activation. That will take place in the Newman labs."

"When?"

"As soon as you've eaten. I'm sure you're hungry."

"I'm starving!"

The doctor smiled. "We'll send in your breakfast. Once you've finished eating, get dressed and then someone will escort you to the research facility. Harry is very keen to finalise the process for you."

Shortly afterward, Keelor was given a small breakfast of fruit and cereal, which he quickly devoured. It left him still feeling hungry, but the nurse who took away his empty tray assured him that a small meal was best after seven days without food in his stomach. She left, and Keelor got out of bed and opened the wardrobe door. His old clothes were gone and, in their place, was a lieutenant's uniform. He held the shirt up and looked at the insignia and the epaulettes. He shook his head. It was all so difficult to believe. Just a few days ago, he had been helping his father milk the cows, and now he was a lieutenant in military intelligence. He hoped Major Maxwell knew what he was doing, because he, Keelor, didn't have a clue.

He donned the uniform and then emerged from his room, feeling like an imposter in a fancy-dress outfit. An ensign who was waiting outside his room snapped to attention as he emerged. Keelor was nonplussed and awkwardly returned a salute.

"This way, sir. Dr Melville is waiting for you."

A few minutes later, Keelor walked into Harry's office and was greeted warmly by the friendly scientist. If anything, he looked more dishevelled than previously. His grey beard and straggly grey hair looked as if they hadn't come within lightyears of a brush, and Keelor was fairly sure there was a fresh stain on the front of his cardigan.

"Keelor! How are you feeling?"

"Very well, thank you, sir."

"That's enough of that 'sir' nonsense. It's Harry!"

"Okay. Thanks, Harry."

"Now, lets' get your quantum system activated. Are you ready?"

"I guess so."

"You'll be fine," said Harry, placing a friendly hand on his shoulder as he guided Keelor out the door. "The lab is just down the hall."

A moment later, they entered a relatively small room. There were only two things of note in the room. The first was a console station, consisting of a large desk with a built-in screen. A technician was sitting at the desk, fine tuning some settings on the screen.

It was the second thing in the room, however, that captured Keelor's attention. It looked like a huge, white soccer ball, hollowed out in the middle, with a chair in its centre.

"Take a seat," said Harry, indicating the soccer ball encased chair.

Keelor did so, his heart rate rising as his nerves kicked in.

"Let me explain what is about to happen," said Harry. "The quantum filaments throughout your brain are all in place and ready for activation. They were temporarily switched on while you were asleep so that we could calibrate them, but we are now going to switch them on while you are conscious. An operating system is already in place and once the system is activated you will sense it and have full access to it. It will be like a whole new dimension opening up within your consciousness.

"It can be a bit disconcerting at first, particularly as you adjust to interacting with the system while still engaging with the world around you. The reason why we've got you sitting down, is that we don't want you to be so overwhelmed with your new system that you forget to balance yourself and fall over."

"So, it won't hurt?"

"Not at all. It will be a bit like sitting in a dark cinema and suddenly the screen bursts to life with music and visuals. You'll quickly learn to dial it down and even ignore it. You can put it to sleep anytime you want, which most of our Newbies tend to do when they're not using it."

"Newbies, as in, new to the whole thing?"

"No. Newbies, as in, the Newman project. You will be our 11th Newbie."

Harry turned to the technician and asked, "Are you all set, Raylee?"

"Ready when you are, Harry."

"Ready, Keelor?"

Keelor took a deep breath and exhaled slowly. "Okay."

Harry nodded. "Let's do it!"

Keelor was expecting the soccer ball around him to start glowing or pulsing or whirring. But it didn't. Nothing seemed to happen at all.

And then everything happened. He felt a huge shift in his consciousness, and his thought processes accelerated as if he had been injected with a megadose of adrenaline. His mind literally raced now, at a speed that was astonishingly fast. In less than a second, he had explored the billions of new neural pathways provided by the quantum molecule filaments and had learned to turn the system on and off again. He blinked in astonishment as a whole new world of computational power lay at his mental fingertips.

He blinked in amazement.

"Wow."

"How does it feel?" asked Harry.

"Amazing! I feel like I could do a thousand computations in my head in a single second."

"You can! That's the whole point." Harry smiled at him, in obvious delight. "Take a few moments to familiarise yourself with it. When you feel ready, you can step out of the neural inducer."

Harry continued, "We'll spend a few hours today getting you used to your enhancement, including the standard neural transceiver plug connected to your brain stem. It always takes a little while to learn how to operate that and interact with technology. Even super-enhanced Newbies have to learn how to open a lift door or place a private call with their new interface. But before we do all that, there's an old tradition that we like to do for each new Newbie. It supposedly dates back to the original Newbie, Daniel Newman himself. At least that's what the archives suggest."

"A tradition?" asked Keelor, as he stood and stepped out of the device.

Harry nodded. "Yes. A simple question, really." He came to stand face to face with Keelor and looked directly into his eyes. "What's the square root of 1,081?"

Without a pause, Keelor responded, "32.8785644455471. And some change."

Harry smiled and shook Keelor's hand.

"Welcome to the team, Newbie."

D aniel took off his neural interface transceiver cap.
"I think there is a neutron star in our vicinity. Those X-ray emissions are the giveaway."

"That's a concern," said Anderson. "Because if there is one, it will be too small to see until we are dangerously close."

"Exactly."

"Pardon my ignorance," interrupted Jordan, "but what's a neutron star? I don't know whether you've noticed, but I'm not a cosmologist."

"It's basically the remnant of a supernova that hasn't managed to collapse to a black hole," explained Daniel.

"Back it up a few steps, Professor. Explain it in layperson's terms."

"Stars are basically huge fusion reactors. The huge gravity of a star's mass creates enormous pressure in the star's core. The pressure is so great that hydrogen atoms are compressed together in a fusion reaction to form helium. This releases enormous amounts of energy in the form of heat and light which pushes out from the core. That outward push of energy balances the huge inward drag of gravity, keeping the star from collapsing inward upon itself.

"But all stars all have a limited lifespan. Eventually they run out of fuel at their core and the nuclear fusion reaction ceases. With no energy pushing outward to counteract the star's own massive gravity, the star collapses inward, its atoms becoming compacted denser and denser. The larger stars have so much gravity that they collapse into black holes – the densest material in the universe A black hole's gravity is so strong that nothing can escape from it, not even light."

"But some stars don't have quite enough mass to become black holes. They compress into neutron stars. They're called neutron stars because the electrons and protons of the star are compressed to form neutrons and neutrinos. The neutrinos quickly escape, leaving a solid core of unimaginably dense neutrons."

"Wow. I'm sorry I asked," commented Jordan, sarcastically. "Will this lecture last much longer?"

"Just a bit longer," Daniel replied. "The average diameter of a neutron star, once it has finished collapsing, is between 10 and 20 kilometres."

"That doesn't sound too bad," said Jordan.

Daniel shook his head. "It's not the size that's the problem. It's the mass. A 20-kilometre neutron star can have 10 times the mass of our old sun, Sol."

"So, it weighs 10 times as much?"

"Yes. A neutron star is so dense that just a teaspoon of its matter weighs about 1 billion tons. That's the weight of a large mountain."

"In that case, I'm not going anywhere near a neutron star with a teaspoon," quipped Jordan.

"Anyway," continued Daniel, ignoring her flippancy, "The gravity of a neutron star is about 200 billion times the gravity on Earth, and about 250 billion times the gravity on Atraya, which we've now discovered is the name they've given to Tama-B. The gravity is so great that the escape velocity on the surface of a neutron star is 70% of the speed of light."

"All I'm hearing is 'blah, blah, blah', Professor. What's the big deal for us?"

"The big deal is that neutron stars are silent assassins,

wandering around the universe, devouring planets and even other stars. Their gravity is so great that they can rip planets out of their orbits and drag them in, collapsing a whole planet to a lump of matter the size of a baseball. And if we get too close to its gravitational field, it will drag us in and collapse our whole starship to a lump of matter the size of a pinhead."

"That's certainly one way to lose weight."

"Actually, you don't lose weight, you just lose size, squished to a teeny-weeny lump of dense matter."

"Okay, but how do you know we are nearing a neutron star. It hasn't shown up on our scans. Shouldn't we be able to see it shining?" she asked.

"Neutron stars don't shine. Some are completely black – at least in the visual spectrum. That's why they are known as silent assassins. You can't see them with normal telescopes or cameras. But you can determine their presence in other ways. Three to be precise. Firstly, an unexplained increase in gravity with no visual source."

"Tick," said Jordan, helpfully.

"Secondly, the presence of X-ray radiation. Neutrons stars give off large amounts of radiation in the non-visible X-ray spectrum."

"Okay. Double tick."

"Thirdly, neutron stars emit a super strong magnetic field. That's because they spin incredibly fast, up to 600 revolutions per second."

"Why so fast?" asked Angus, who until now, had listened quietly.

"Because of the conservation of angular momentum."

"Dumb it down please, Professor," said Jordan.

"Okay. Have you ever seen an ice skater spinning? When they spin with their arms out wide, they spin slowly. But when they tuck their arms in close to their body, they suddenly accelerate and spin much faster."

"Yeah, I've always wondered how that works," said Angus.

"Well, when an ice skater tucks her arms in close, she still weighs the same, but her mass is much more compact and is therefore easier to spin. The conservation of angular momentum means that the same amount of angular momentum can now work on a more compact mass, so it spins faster. The same thing happens when an ordinary star collapses into a neutron star. As it shrinks and becomes denser, it spins faster and faster, and that increased rotation increases the magnetic field that it produces."

Captain Anderson, who had been listening quietly to Daniel's explanation, now spoke up.

"Eric, are you detecting any increase in magnetic radiation?"

"Yes, Captain. There is a definite spike in unexplained magnetic radiation."

"So, what does all this mean?" asked Jordan.

"I think it means we're in trouble," said Daniel.

"Great. I might get to do my table dance after all."

Captain Anderson addressed the ship's artificial intelligence. "Eric, send a morse code message to Ulysses. '*Suspected neutron star ahead. We appear to be coming under its influence. No visual confirmation yet.*' Send it immediately please."

"Yes, Captain."

Now that they were occupying a shuttle, there was one less shuttle bay that was open to space and therefore one less set of lights to flash on and off. But the cruiser, Ulysses, was closing on their position quickly and would have no trouble detecting the diminished light source.

They didn't have long to wait for a reply.

*"Longshot, we have received your message. Our long-range scans have confirmed your suspicions. We detect a neutron star of approximately 22 kilometres in diameter bearing 60 degrees off your starboard bow, at a distance of 8.2 billion kilometres. We detect that the star is beginning to capture you in its gravity well, and your trajectory is beginning to curve toward it. At our current rate of closure, we will be alongside you in less than three days. By then, we calculate that you will be only 150 million kilometres from the neutron star and experiencing significant gravitational acceleration. It's going to be touch and go whether we can get to you in time before we are also caught in the star's*

*grip. We have ceased deceleration in an attempt to reach you sooner, meaning that we will have to decelerate violently when we reach you. We're going to do our very best to rescue you. Ulysses out.*

"Can they do it, Captain?" asked Angus. "Will they reach us in time?"

"I don't know, Angus. All we can do is hope and pray."

"No. That's not all," said Jordan. "I could teach you my dance moves."

---

## 27

After lunch in the subterranean research facility's cafeteria – a meal that Keelor was very pleased to see was more substantial than the measly breakfast he had been given in the enhancement centre's cafeteria – Harry collected him and brought him back to what Keelor now referred to as the 'soccer ball room.'

"Major Maxwell has asked me to upload the military competency augmentation to your cerebral cortex," he said, as he settled Keelor into the chair again.

"The what?"

"It's an augmentation that is given to every newly commissioned officer. It basically gives you an instant and complete understanding of military protocols, procedures, rules and regulations. You could spend 6 months learning it all in the old-fashioned way, but that's so inefficient and costly. The military would much rather upload all that information directly to your brain and save a whole lot of time and money in the process."

"So, everyone gets this, not just Newbies?"

"Yes. This is part of the military enhancement that every military officer receives. As part of the basic military augmentation, you will also receive proficiency in weapon handling and in some theoretical areas of orbital physics and propulsion."

"Why do I need that?"

"Because, as an officer, you may need to one day serve on a military vessel, and the military would like to be assured that every officer has the ability to oversee the navigators and other technical staff. The military can't have its officers being less educated than the lower ranks."

Harry looked to his assistant who was seated at the console and got the thumbs up. He turned back to Keelor.

"All set?"

"I guess so."

Harry nodded to his assistant. A moment later, he said to Keelor, "You can step down now."

"Why? What's wrong? Didn't it work?"

Harry smiled and asked, "What does Section III Sub-section 4b, paragraph two of the Atrayan Military Handbook say?"

"*In the event of a senior officer being incapacitated, by way of injury, loss of physical functioning or diminished mental capacity, confirmed and corroborated by two officers of at least senior commissioned rank, ...* My goodness! I know it!"

"Yes, you do."

Keelor probed his mind and saw that it was true. He knew and understood the whole military handbook. He was as familiar with military practices and procedures as if he had been in the military all his life. Furthermore, he could sense the muscle memory of handling and firing a laser rifle and he knew he could strip a projectile pistol down and reassemble it in less than thirty seconds.

"Wow! That's amazing."

"Yes, it is rather impressive, isn't it?" Harry glanced at the time on the digital readout on the desk console. "You have an appointment now, with a military intelligence lawyer. He needs to clear you for release. You'll need to sign a non-disclosure agreement. You won't be allowed to discuss your quantum enhancement with anyone. As far as anyone outside this facility is concerned, you've received the normal military enhancement. After you've signed the legal documents, you're free to go."

"Go where?"

"You've got a two day leave pass and two weeks' pay credited to you. I believe your family has a farm nearby."

"Yes. Just outside of Emerald, about 20 minutes south of Jasper."

"You might like to visit them. I'm sure they'd like to see you."

"When do I start work?"

"Report to Level 1, in Angel City in three days, and we'll get you started. Your neural implant will give you instant security clearance to military transport and to the appropriate levels in Angel City."

Thirty minutes later, the newly minted Lieutenant Keelor Trantum walked out the front doors of the Corfu Enhancement Facility, dressed in his new uniform and carrying a small bag with his old civilian clothes. He stood blinking in the bright orange light and pulled a pair of military issue sunglasses out of his pocket and put them on. It was a strange feeling. One part of him felt as though he had been in the military all his life, so familiar was he with its machinations. But the other part of him still felt like the 21-year-old who had only recently been browsing T-Net in his bedroom, unsure about what to do with his life.

He stood in the early afternoon sunshine, taking in his surroundings. He had been planning to grab one of the ubiquitous beetles that were provided free of charge in most cities and towns on Atraya. He saw several of the small, clear-domed, driverless vehicles parked nearby, but the day was so nice that he decided to walk into the main town centre. He would catch the ferry to the mainland and then get the bullet tube to Emerald. He started walking down the path, past the line of parked beetles.

"My, my! Don't you look the part?"

He turned around and saw Maran Cartwright sitting in the small interior of the nearest beetle. She climbed out and stretched.

"You're late," she said.

"Late for what?"

"For me, dummy. I've been waiting here for nearly an hour. I was told you'd be coming out around lunchtime."

"Sorry, I didn't know you would be here."

"Major Maxwell asked me to give you a lift back to your farm. I don't know how you've managed it, but you've got him rolling out the red carpet for you. I didn't get picked up after my enhancement. Nice uniform, by the way. I'm not even going to ask why they commissioned you as a lieutenant."

"Good. Because I'm not sure I could explain it to you."

"Not sure you could? Or not sure you're allowed to?"

"A bit of both."

"Fair enough. We won't talk about it then. Come on, jump in. I'm starving."

"You haven't had lunch?" he asked as he climbed in beside her.

"No, dummy. I've been waiting here for you."

"Are you technically supposed to call lieutenants 'dummy'?" Of course, he knew the answer, but he was being deliberately obtuse.

"Yes. There's an exemption clause in the updated military manual that says that an ensign can call a lieutenant 'dummy' if she has been kept waiting in the hot sun for an hour, starving her guts out."

"Really. That must be a new edition that's only just come out. I'll have to read up on that clause."

"The next clause says that in such a scenario, the time-challenged lieutenant must buy the hungry ensign lunch."

"Is that so?" he said, enjoying their light-hearted repartee.

"Yep," she assured him.

"Well, I'd better not disobey the military manual on my first day as a commissioned officer."

The beetle had already started moving, and Keelor guessed that Maran had given it instructions via her neural interface.

They ate lunch at a café overlooking the sheltered harbour. It was seafood and it was delicious. Keelor had already eaten, so he picked at a small entrée of gobies, a local shellfish, while Maran devoured a seafood mornay. They washed it down with a glass of local Corfu wine, after Maran insisted that there was another clause in the military manual stating that a newly commissioned officer's epaulettes had to be 'wet'.

They talked and laughed all through lunch, and continued to do so on the ferry and on the flitter flight to his family's farm. As the flitter circled above his house and prepared to land, Keelor experienced a wave of sadness. He didn't want his afternoon with Maran to end. The flitter landed and they both sat silently for a moment, reluctant to end their afternoon together.

"This has been nice," Keelor said.

"Yes, it has."

"Do you want to come in?"

"No. Your folks will want to make a fuss over you. Besides I've got to head home myself. I've got two days off, and I promised mum I'd be home for an early dinner."

"What are you doing tomorrow night?" he asked, blurting it out before he lost the courage.

She smiled. "That depends on who's asking. Is this an official request from a lieutenant in the ADF?"

"No. It's just a question from a boy who wants to spend more time with a pretty girl."

She smiled again. "That's exactly the right answer."

## 28

The day of their proposed rescue had arrived, but it was far
from certain. Over the last two days, their crippled starship
had spiralled in toward the neutron star, gradually accelerating as
it did so. The Atrayan military cruiser, Ulysses, had needed to
initiate a series of complex course corrections in order to remain
on target for its rendezvous with Longshot, and the cruiser was
now less than two hours away, undergoing extreme deceleration.

The last message from Ulysses had stressed the urgency of the
transfer process. Once they had established a hard dock, everyone
on board Longshot was to proceed through the docking tube with
the utmost speed, as every minute now counted. The gravitational
pull of the neutron star was accelerating both vessels toward it and
there was an increasingly narrow window of time before escape
from its clutches would be impossible. It was going to be a very
close thing.

The temperature on board Longshot had plummeted to a
frigid minus 21 degrees Celsius, even colder than the science officer, Maria Vargas, had predicted. But right now, the four awake
crew members had no time to worry about the cold, because
things were about to get very hectic. During the previous hour,
they had scoured the sleeping cabins, collecting every available

blanket and item of clothing, taking them down to the cryogenics levels. The crew and passengers who were about to wake up were in for a big shock and would need every bit of clothing they could find.

Now the four of them were standing on the top cryogenics level waiting for the first crew to awaken. Eric had begun the gradual waking process two days ago, removing nanobot infused blood and restarting vital organs. The crew were due to wake first, followed by the passengers.

Anderson looked at the time. "That's it. Their pods will be opening any second now." The four of them had spent several minutes scraping ice from around the seams of the crew's pod lids, ensuring that the lids would open properly.

Even as Anderson spoke, the sounds of lids opening could be heard, creaking and groaning in the icy conditions.

"Okay, let's get to work," said Anderson. "This is no time for modesty. Get in there and help them get dressed as quickly as possible."

They began working, helping newly woken crew members to dress quickly in the sub-freezing conditions. The cryogenics deck came alive with groans and cries of icy shock as the crew stumbled out into the arctic conditions. Frosty clouds of breath floated in the air, and more than a few people used colorful language to describe their feelings. Those who were successfully dressed helped others who were struggling and in less than ten minutes it was all over. A shivering group of 39 crew members huddled around Captain Anderson near the lifts, and zero-gravity pouches of hot coffee were handed around and shared.

Anderson addressed his crew.

"I'm sorry for the temperature, folks. Nothing we can do about it. The good news is that a rescue ship is due to dock with us in a bit over an hour. But this next hour is going to be very challenging. We have 200 colonists about to wake up, and they have no idea of the conditions they are about to face. When these people went into stasis, Longshot was functioning normally and we were on track to arrive at the Tama system. These people will be expecting to wake up in a warm ship circling a beautiful planet. They are going to face extreme shock, the most obvious being the sub-zero temperatures. In short, they are going to need your help."

He pointed to a huge pile of clothing and blankets on the floor.

"We've accumulated all the additional warm clothing and blankets we could find. Distribute these to the waking colonists, because the clothes they have waiting for them beside their pods won't be sufficient. Eric is going to stagger the opening of the pods so that we aren't having to deal with all 200 colonists simultaneously. We've already opened all the curtains, so that we can see each pod as it opens. This isn't a time for modesty and privacy. Every second counts. When you see a pod opening, get in there and get some clothes on them. The last thing we want is for people to have travelled trillions of kilometres across space, only to die of hyperthermia."

"Once each colonist is dressed, send them to the dining room for a hot drink, then instruct them to congregate in Shuttle Bay 1. That is where the rescue ship will dock with us."

Anderson glanced at the time.

"We have about ten minutes before the first pods start opening. In that time, we need to scrape the ice from the seals around the lids of every pod, so that they can open properly. I know you're all cold, but hopefully it's not for much longer. Let's get to work people!"

The crew dispersed throughout the two cryogenics levels, and the sounds of ice being scraped off lids could be heard on both decks as the crew prepared to welcome the unsuspecting colonists to the icy conditions.

The pods soon began opening, and the crew spent the next hour scurrying from one pod to the next, half dragging the waking colonists from their pods in the zero gravity and rushing to get them clothed and booted before their core temperatures plummeted to dangerous levels. Moans and groans abounded, and rushed explanations were given to the ever-growing stream of confused colonists who made their way toward the lifts. Several lids failed to open properly because of a build-up of ice on the hinges, and Eric had to direct crew members to prise them open manually.

The Captain had stationed Jordan at the lifts to direct people to the dining room for hot drinks, but she inevitably brought her own unique style to the task.

"This way folks! Go up to Level 71 for hot drinks then back down to Shuttle Bay 1 where there will be a bikini contest and hula dancing. Everyone is welcome to participate."

"Will you be showing us your special dance?" asked Kelly who was now standing beside her, a cloud of foggy breath hanging in the air as she spoke. She was huffing and puffing, stamping her feet and rubbing her hands together in a vain attempt to keep warm.

"Nope. It looks like that's going to be postponed yet again. I'm thinking we might actually get out of this alive. Besides, I don't think the general population is ready for my special dance."

Kelly smiled. "You're probably right. It would be too much for some of them."

"Keep coming folks!" Jordan yelled, again. "Grab a hot drink from the dining room then get down to Shuttle Bay 1 for ice sculpting classes."

A little more than an hour after the first colonists emerged from their pods, the entire population of Longshot was finally assembled in the shuttle bay, near the passenger airlock. They were a bedraggled and forlorn looking bunch, dressed in an eclectic mix of jackets and wrapped in blankets. News that their rescue ship had arrived alongside them and was preparing to connect via an emergency docking tube was greeted with muted cheers from the freezing colonists. The image of the newly arrived cruiser was being shown on the large video screen in the shuttle bay, captured by Longshot's external cameras.

Ulysses was an impressive looking vessel, roughly the same length as Longshot in its original form, but much more complex in design. The colonists and crew of Longshot gazed at the image in awe, marvelling at the obvious advances in technology that 370 years had wrought. Of particular note, was the fact that it did not have deflector dishes. Instead, it was streamlined, coming to a sharp point at the front and rear but opening to a wide diameter across the mid-section. Instead of the drive nozzles being mounted at the rear, two large engines were positioned amidships, at the widest point of the vessel, and looked as if they could pivot to produce thrust in almost any direction.

Captain Anderson and several members of the mission team withdrew to the shuttle to open verbal communications with the Atrayan vessel, now that they were within distance of the shuttle's comms.

"Commodore Bronson, it's good to finally communicate face to face," said Anderson, looking at Bronson's image on the shuttle's video comm. The short, nuggety bald man had a tough military bearing that made Captain Anderson look like a benign grandfather by comparison.

"Likewise, Captain Anderson. How are your people doing?"

"As well as can be expected. The main problem is the cold. It's minus 21 degrees in here and we didn't come equipped with sub-zero clothing."

"We're going to get you out of there as soon as we can. We're closing to within 50 metres as we speak. Once we are in position, we'll secure an emergency docking tube between the two vessels. The tube is designed to create a seal against the side of your hull by means of an acid-based polymer adhesive that will partially melt the outer metal of your hull and set in seconds. The docking tube will be in place within a few minutes."

"We are incredibly grateful for what you are doing for us, Commodore. We owe you our lives."

Bronson ignored the warm sentiment. "You're going to really need to hustle your people across that tube as quickly as possible, Captain. Both our vessels are being drawn toward the neutron star at an alarming rate. We've calculated that we have a maximum of 40 minutes before the pull of the neutron star will be too strong for us to break free from it. So, I need to warn you that in exactly 35 minutes we will be closing the hatch at our end, disengaging from the tube and firing our main drive – even if there are people still crossing. In the end, it is better to save some lives than to stay too long and all perish."

"Understood."

"I hope you do, Captain. I will save as many of your people as I can, but if there is not enough time to save everyone, I will make that hard decision."

"I understand. I would do the same if I was in your position."

Bronson nodded. "Good luck, Captain. Hopefully I'll see you on the other side."

The screen went blank, and Anderson addressed his mission team with the sternest expression Daniel had ever seen on his face.

"I don't care how we do it, I don't care how much you have to poke and prod and yell and push, but I want every single one of our people through that tube in 35 minutes! Let's get them ready!"

**29**

---

It took longer than anticipated – 11 minutes – for the emergency docking tube to be secured in place Finally, they got confirmation from Ulysses that atmospheric pressure had been achieved. Commander Decker was the first to open the outer hatch, with the inner hatch of the airlock closed just in case there was a problem. As the outer hatch opened, a cloud of fog formed as the warm air from Ulysses met the sub-zero air within Longshot's airlock. Decker could no longer be seen in the fog, but his voice came over the external speaker.

"All clear, Captain. It's safe to open the inner door."

They didn't need any further encouragement, as the countdown timer above the inner door ticked over to just 23 minutes remaining until Commodore Bronson's deadline. The inner door was opened, and a cloud of fog poured out of the airlock into the shuttle bay.

Decker stuck his head out of the airlock and yelled, "Go, go, go! As fast as you can! One behind the other. Your magnetic boots won't work in the tube, so you'll need to pull yourself through using the handrail on the side."

People began moving into the airlock and then pulling themselves through the tube, hand over hand. The officers stood watching and Decker yelled again, "That's not fast enough, people! We have 239 people to get through in less than 23 minutes! Hurry!"

Daniel was standing beside the Captain, and after watching the proceedings for a few minutes, he agreed with Decker's estimation.

"We aren't going to make it in time, Captain. We need to be averaging 24 people across per minute and we're only managing 22. At this rate, there will be 46 people still left on board Longshot when our time is up."

Anderson turned to Decker. "Can you get them moving any faster, Commander?"

Decker stepped closer to the captain and said, in a lowered voice, "I don't think so, sir. We're cramming them in as fast as we can. This is as good as it's going to get."

Anderson nodded calmly and said, "I will advise Commodore Bronson." He turned and entered the shuttle once more and placed a call to the bridge of the Ulysses. Bronson's face appeared on the screen.

"How is it going, Captain?" asked Bronson.

"Unfortunately, we're not going to make your deadline. At the current rate of transfer, we estimate there will be about 46 people still to cross when your deadline of 35 minutes elapses."

Bronson's features were resolute. "I'm truly sorry to hear that, Captain. But I won't stay a minute longer than 35 minutes. To stay any longer would be irresponsible. We will be disengaging and leaving in ...," he glanced aside, presumably to his own countdown timer, "exactly 18 minutes 46 seconds."

Anderson nodded. "Understood. I'm sorry I won't have the chance to meet you in person, Commodore. I would have liked to have shaken your hand and personally thanked you for what you and your crew have done for my people. You have saved many lives today, and for that I am grateful."

The two commanding officers looked at each other in silence, no further words being necessary. Finally, Bronson broke the silence.

"Godspeed. Ulysses out."

The screen went dead, and then there was silence. Daniel had come into the shuttle and overheard the conversation.

"There's got to be some other way, Captain." he said. He looked around the interior of the shuttle, and an idea began to form. "Angus!" he yelled out the shuttle door. Angus Fraser was standing nearby.

"Aye. What do you want, sir?"

"Angus, how soon can you get this shuttle ready to fly?"

"Half an hour to disconnect it from the power grid, and maybe another twenty minutes to reconnect fusion drive to the main engine and bring it online."

"We don't have that long. Besides, we won't be needing the main engine. We'll just be using maneuvering thrusters."

"Even so, sir, disconnecting it from the power grid properly will take ..."

"Bugger 'properly'! There's no need to do it properly, is there? Just rip the damn power conduits out. As long as it's airtight and the thrusters are working, that's all we need."

"Yes, I suppose so, sir. Give me 10 minutes and I can get it done. But without everything hooked up properly to the fusion reactor, the thrusters will only work for about a minute or two. It'll be a one-way trip, sir."

"That's fine. We aren't planning on coming back. Do it!"

Angus looked at Anderson, who confirmed Daniel's order, "Get it done, Mr Fraser."

"Aye, sir." He spun on his heels and began working furiously.

Daniel asked Anderson, "Sir, can you call the Ulysses again?"

The captain made the call and when Bronson's face appeared on the screen, Anderson said, "Commodore, we have a plan. I'll let Lieutenant Newman explain." He nodded at Daniel.

"Commodore Bronson, I'm assuming that those wide bay doors toward the rear of Ulysses are shuttle bays?"

"That's correct."

"Have you got room in one of those bays for an additional shuttle?"

Bronson muted his channel for a moment and spoke to

someone off-screen. He nodded to the person and then unmuted. "Yes, Lieutenant. We'll have to undock a shuttle from its retaining clamps and move it to the side. It will be a tight squeeze, but I can see from the specs we downloaded from Longshot that your shuttle will fit."

"In that case, we are going to pack as many people into a shuttle as we can, maybe 80. That means that the last person we send across via the tube will be about 90 seconds ahead of your deadline. We'll get the last person who enters the tube to seal the outer door of our airlock, then we'll do an emergency air evacuation of the shuttle bay and blow the bay door. While those last people are still transiting the tube, we will bring the shuttle across and slip into your shuttle bay. I think we can do all that in about 90 seconds."

"You'll be cutting it very fine."

"It's our only chance at saving everyone, Commodore."

Bronson pursed his lips and nodded. "Very well. We'll get things ready on our side." He glanced again at his own countdown timer. "14 minutes 38 seconds remaining. Good luck!"

The screen went blank again, and everyone sprang into action. Daniel commandeered several crew members to completely clear out the shuttle. It had already been stripped of chairs. Now they stripped it of the sleeping bags and rubbish that had accumulated over the last two weeks. Daniel grabbed Jordan and explained the plan and she jumped into the pilot's chair and began checking the systems, getting the shuttle ready for flight.

Angus and two of his team continued to furiously work, pulling cables out and banging around amid a stream of curses. As the timer went under 5 minutes, Angus announced that the shuttle was as ready as he could make it at short notice, and "don't blame me if it all goes to shite and we all go up the lum!"

Olivia Alvarez began herding people from the back of the line, into the shuttle. In the space of two minutes, they managed to squeeze 82 people into the shuttle, with standing room only. Commander Decker was to be the last person through the tube, and as the line in front of him dwindled, Captain Anderson shook his hand and wished him luck, then entered the shuttle and closed the door.

Daniel was in the co-pilot's seat, as anyone else with shuttle training had already gone through the tube. He and Jordan sat watching the line of people going through the airlock and disappearing along the docking tube. As Commander Decker finally made it into the tube and pulled the outer airlock door closed, the timer dropped under 2 minutes.

"Eric! Emergency purge of air in Shuttle Bay 1, now!" called Jordan.

They waited, watching the timer count down, and watching for the green light over the large shuttle bay door. Finally, it came on, and the door slid silently open.

The timer on the shuttle bay wall showed 66 seconds.

The shuttle had previously been unclamped from the floor and had floated up during the emergency atmosphere purge. Now Jordan activated the thrusters and skewed the shuttle quickly around, causing some surprised noises from the passengers in the main compartment. She thrust her control column forward and the shuttle staggered clumsily out of the shuttle bay into clear space.

"No time for finesse," she said as she furiously worked the controls. The open shuttle bay on Ulysses was clearly visible, to their right and down. As Jordan continued to work the control column, the thrusters spurted a continuous series of compressed gas jets from all around the shuttle. The open shuttle bay began to loom larger, although they were coming in fast and partly side on.

"No time to line it up, properly," she said, biting her lip in concentration.

They approached the large open bay door and Daniel could see a sleek, black shuttle, parked hard up against the right-hand wall. Jordan had them coming in on an angle from above and to the left, angling down into the shuttle bay, partially side on. At the last moment she activated some thrusters to slow them down and swing them around, and their velocity dropped off.

"Bugger!" Jordan said.

"What?" asked Daniel.

"The thrusters have stopped working. We're out of juice." She turned around and yelled into the compartment. "Hang on everyone! We're going to scrape some paint off!"

She had barely finished speaking when they struck the floor of the bay. A terrible metallic grinding could be heard through the hull, then they were spinning. The shuttle struck the corner of the back wall and spun around some more, colliding with Ulysses' own shuttle and finally coming to a grinding halt, partially wedged against it.

"Ulysses, we're in!" called Daniel over the comms.

"Copy."

There were groans from several people in the shuttle, mainly from head clashes as they had been thrown against each other. Very few people had fallen because there was literally no room to fall.

"My guess is we just lost a few layers of paint," commented Daniel to Jordan.

"Paint's over-rated in my opinion," Jordan replied.

A voice came over the cockpit comm. "Longshot shuttle, this is Ulysses flight control. The shuttle bay is now closed and secured. That was a very interesting landing manoeuvre."

Jordan replied, "Interesting? Not sure what you mean, flight control. That's how we always park our shuttles."

**30**

———

The occupants of the shuttle emerged into the warm air of Ulysses' shuttle bay. Several crew members of the Atrayan cruiser were greeted with hugs and handshakes by the grateful Longshot colonists and there was a spirit of rejoicing among them all.

The joyous mood did not extend to inside the shuttle cockpit, however. The face of Commodore Bronson, the commanding officer of Ulysses, was on the video screen as he spoke with Captain Anderson who was now standing in the cockpit entrance between Daniel in the co-pilot's seat and Jordan to his left.

"We've been firing our engines for the last minute, attempting to decelerate," he explained. "As you know, our plan was to decelerate in order to cancel our relative velocity away from Atraya and then to accelerate back toward it. But the neutron star is proving too strong for us. We are not slowing at all. In fact, we are continuing to spiral in toward it. We had originally estimated that at the point of rescue, both vessels would be approximately 150 million kilometres from the star, but we underestimated its mass and its gravity. We are now only 80 million kilometres from it."

"What's your plan, Commodore?"

"We have one chance at avoiding disaster. We are going to

accelerate at full power toward it; or I should say, at an angle of 27.5 degrees from its centre."

"You're going to attempt a slingshot manoeuvre?" asked Anderson.

"That's correct. We're going to attempt to use the star's gravity to our advantage. With our engines at full power, we believe we can reach escape velocity and slingshot around the star. The only problem is that full power means an acceleration of 12G. Our inertial dampeners usually only work up to 5G, but by disabling the gravity generators and diverting power, we can boost that to 7G dampening. But that still means that everyone on board is going to experience the remaining 5G acceleration. It's not going to be fun."

"How long?"

"About one and a half hours."

"In what direction?"

"Because our decks run longitudinally, as opposed to Longshot's, which run latitudinally, in order to experience acceleration toward the floor, we have already swung the ship around so that we will be accelerating toward the top of Ulysses, toward the roof of each level. It's not optimal in terms of potential impact with debris, but it's our only chance."

"Understood, Commodore."

"Prepare your people, Captain. Acceleration will commence in two minutes. Bronson out."

A few moments later, a general announcement came over the ship's comms.

*"Attention all personnel. We are about to undergo extreme acceleration for a period of approximately one and a half hours. You have two minutes to get to an acceleration couch or make yourself as comfortable as possible. Lying down will be your best option. Bronson out."*

Daniel and Jordan unstrapped themselves and moved into the rear of the shuttle, where they lay down on the floor, alongside Captain Anderson. Kelly came in and joined them, while all through the shuttle bay, people began making temporary beds with their blankets and jackets. All too quickly, an announcement came over the comms.

*"Acceleration commencing in 5, 4, 3, 2, 1, mark."*

The floor seemed to rise up violently under them and they were forced downward, as if a huge weight had been placed on top of them. Groans and gasps filled the air. Every breath was hard work, as lungs were compressed. Hearts began to labour as they struggled to pump blood evenly throughout the body. Each person now weighed five times their normal weight, as if four more of each person were lying on top of them.

"We're starting to make a habit of this," gasped Daniel.

"Yeah," agreed Jordan. "It's the gift that just keeps on giving."

"Are you okay, Captain?" Daniel asked.

"Barely," he groaned.

"Be encouraged, folks," said Jordan. "Only another 89 minutes to go."

In the end, it was another 92 minutes, as the ship's artificial intelligence calculated that an additional three minutes was required to assure that they achieved escape velocity. Finally, the highly anticipated message came over the comms.

*"Acceleration ceasing in 5, 4, 3, 2, 1, mark."*

Instantly, the pressure was gone, and the relief was instantaneous as they experienced zero gravity and floated on the surface of the floor. A few seconds later a second message was broadcast.

*"Restoring artificial gravity in 5, 4, 3, 2, 1, mark."*

Their bodies resumed solid contact with the floor and there was the occasional "ouch!" as people who had not tensed bumped the backs of their heads. It had been a gruelling hour and a half, and no one was sitting up yet, let alone getting to their feet.

"Captain, are you okay?" asked Kelly, who was closest to him. Captain Anderson remained unresponsive, his eyes closed and his breathing a little laboured. "I think he's unconscious!" she said.

Jordan rolled onto her hands and knees and crawled across to him, placing her fingers against his carotid artery.

"His pulse is a bit thready. We need to get him to the med bay."

As she spoke, a message was broadcast over the ship's comms.

*"Deck supervisors, please assess for injuries. Med team, please*

*mobilise and disperse. Those without acceleration couches are most likely to require medical assistance."*

The announcement proved to be accurate. Over a dozen people on the floor of the shuttle bay remained unconscious, having struggled to maintain normal blood pressure. Sadly, that was not the worst of the injuries. Two people had died: one from a stroke and one from a massive heart attack.

The heart attack victim was Pixie Rainbow.

**31**

---

The funeral services were conducted in the dining room, which was the only space large enough to accommodate all 237 of Longshot's survivors and Ulysses' skeleton crew of 18. Both Commodore Bronson and Captain Anderson spoke briefly, while a large screen on one of the walls showed a live video feed of two shroud-wrapped figures lying in an airlock.

Several muted sobs could be heard, including from Kelly who was standing to the left of Daniel. He reached out and held her hand and she clung to his grip, squeezing his hand tightly as tears rolled down her cheeks. Daniel looked to his right, at Jordan, and saw that her usual blasé façade had crumbled. Tears were streaming down her face and her bottom lip was trembling with uncontrolled emotion. Seeing both of his friends so distraught undid him as well, and his eyes welled up.

When the two commanding officers had finished their brief speeches, the ship's chaplain stepped forward and spoke. Daniel was surprised, in fact shocked, that such a technologically advanced society still had a religious element, but no one among the Ulysses crew seemed to find this unusual. On the contrary, as the Chaplain read from sacred scriptures, several among the Ulysses crew could be seen nodding their heads in agreement.

"The Lord is my shepherd; I shall not want. He makes me lie down in green pastures. He leads me beside still waters. He restores my soul. He leads me in paths of righteousness for his name's sake. Even though I walk through the valley of the shadow of death, I will fear no evil, for you are with me; your rod and your staff, they comfort me. You prepare a table before me in the presence of my enemies; you anoint my head with oil; my cup overflows. Surely goodness and mercy shall follow me all the days of my life and I shall dwell in the house of the Lord forever."

The chaplain looked up from his reading and gazed at the audience with compassion.

"These scriptures assure us of two things; that God is with us, through all of life's trials, and that death is not the end. Though from this side, death may seem like a full stop, from the other side it is merely the transition into something more permanent. Just like a mountain, the looming presence of death may seem to cast a shadow on those who approach it, but that is only because, on the other side, there is the light of a new dawn. You cannot have a shadow without a light. We say goodbye to these dear friends as we stand in death's shadow, but we cling to the faith and hope that they, even now, exist in unimaginable light that will never end."

He paused and looked at the screen.

"And so, we commit these two friends into the hands of God, trusting in his goodness and holding onto the promise of eternal life. Amen."

As he concluded, the screen showed the external door of the airlock opening suddenly. The two shrouded bodies shot out into the blackness of space, tumbling end over end as they quickly faded from sight and were lost among the stars. There were several moments of silence and then the gathering broke up, with muted conversations starting as people moved off in different directions. Many people moved toward the food and beverage dispensers that lined the walls, grabbing drinks and refreshments. Many of the Longshot survivors were still recovering from the physical strain of the recent acceleration and also the emotional toll of all that they had been through.

As Daniel, Kelly and Jordan stood together wiping tears from their eyes, the chaplain approached them.

"Oh, oh. Here comes the religious dude," whispered Jordan.

"Jerem Grant," the chaplain said, holding out his hand. He shook hands with all three, saying, "I'm very sorry for your loss."

"Thank you," replied Daniel. He looked closely at Jerem. He looked to be in his early 30s, with blonde wavy hair, blue eyes and striking good looks. He looked more like a male model or a surfer than a religious chaplain.

"I believe you three were very close to Pixie."

"Yes. She was a dear friend," agreed Daniel.

"And quite a character, too, I believe?"

"Oh yes. She was definitely one of a kind."

"I wish I'd known her. She sounds like the kind of irreverent character that would have been fun to be around."

"Oh, she was certainly that," agreed Daniel. "Although I'm surprised that a religious chaplain would find irreverence appealing."

Jerem laughed, and his eyes sparkled as he did so. "On the contrary, I think people who challenge the status quo and refuse to fit into the usual mold are God's special gift to us. They make us think. They inject spontaneity and unpredictability into our lives. They make life interesting."

"In that case, you'll love getting to know Jordan," said Kelly. "Irreverence is her specialty."

Jerem smiled at Jordan, but she gave him a blank stare in return.

"No offense, Reverend, but I'm not religious."

"Excellent! Neither am I. It sounds like you and I have a lot in common."

Jordan frowned in confusion. "But I thought you just read from the Bible?"

Jerem smiled. "Religion is an artificially constructed system of institutional rituals and observances, design by misguided people who are attempting to reach out toward the divine. A set of dos and don'ts and superficial religious practices that are aimed at impressing God and somehow earning his favour. What man-made religion fails to recognise is that God couldn't give a crap about that external stuff. He already loves us and simply wants us to open our hearts to him and be transformed from the inside out."

Jordan blinked in surprise. "You're a Reverend, and you just said 'crap'."

"Firstly, I'm not a Reverend in the sense that you are implying. I'm a molecular biologist who also serves as the ship's chaplain. And secondly, God couldn't give a crap that I just said crap." He smiled politely, and Daniel couldn't help thinking that Jordan may well have just met her match.

**32**

---

The meeting came to order as Commander Bronson and Captain Anderson entered the room. Anderson and Bronson made a mismatched pair. Anderson was tall, with a full head of grey hair and a trim grey beard. Bronson was a small, nuggety man, with a bald head and a strong military bearing. One looked like a benign grandfather, the other a tough soldier.

As far as meeting rooms went, it was spectacular. The large circular glass-like conference table, big enough to seat at least twenty people, was situated in a circular room with a clear domed roof that gave a magnificent view of the vast universe beyond their comparatively tiny lifeboat. Daniel wasn't sure what the transparent dome was made of but was sure it had to be of a substance that was tough enough to endure the stresses of space travel. He guessed it had to be impregnated with a reflective substance or magnetic field that repelled the harmful radiation of space.

The two newly met commanding officers sat together at the clear conference table which obviously had inbuilt biopolymer circuitry, so that each seated position had access to a built-in screen that could be activated when needed or rendered transparent, so that it disappeared altogether.

Present at the meeting were two of Commodore Bronson's

senior officers, his executive officer, Commander Gayer Steetsel, a middle-aged woman who exuded confidence, and the science officer, Grul Thorbid, a man with greying sideburns and a very precise way of speaking. Daniel guessed he was an archetypical science nerd who was completely engrossed in his field of endeavour, to the exclusion of almost all else.

The full complement of Captain Anderson's mission team had been invited to the meeting, so that the newcomers could be officially welcomed and brought up to speed in several areas.

The meeting opened with each person briefly introducing themselves, followed by a warm welcome from Commodore Bronson and an equally warm and effusive expression of gratitude from Captain Anderson, who finished by saying, "We owe you and your crew our lives, Commodore. We are forever in your debt."

Bronson responded, "Not at all, Captain. What we did was what any decent people would have done for anyone in such desperate need. I consider it to be the greatest privilege of my career to have played a part in the saving of so many lives. Which brings me to our current situation. As you know, our slingshot manoeuvre around the neutron star was successful, in the sense that we are now clear of its overwhelming influence, although it will be several days before we no longer feel the pull of its gravity at all. We weren't able to exit the slingshot manoeuvre on a perfect trajectory to Atraya, which would have been too much to ask for, but the necessary adjustment is only minor and over the next week, our ongoing burn will gradually bring us back on course. We are also now aligned properly for long haul space flight, with our 'pointy end first'," he said with a smile, deliberately engaging in a light-hearted use of non-technical jargon.

He took a sip of water from what looked like a glass tumbler, then continued.

"One positive thing to come out of our encounter with the neutron star is that our slingshot manoeuvre has significantly reduced the time required for our return journey. We were originally planning to spend a week decelerating to zero, relative to Atraya, and then another 15 days gradually accelerating up to a decent velocity. When you factor in the deceleration at the other end, we were looking at a return journey of 51 days in total. Our slingshot around the neutron star, however, has significantly reduced that time. The star's gravity well has flung us back toward our home, accelerating us to a velocity of nearly 30% of lightspeed. Instead of 51 days, we will be home in just 30."

"Home," said Anderson, wistfully. "Some of us had begun to wonder whether we would ever make it to our new home."

"You have certainly been through a lot, Captain. Be assured that the Atrayan Senate will do everything in its power to provide for your people, and I am confident that the general populace will welcome you with open arms. You fled here from tyranny even before our ancestors did. We have a lot in common. We all came here seeking peace and freedom from oppression, and I am sure you will soon discover that these are unassailable principles that we have built into the very bedrock of our society."

Without appearing to touch a screen or manipulate anything with his hands, a 3D holographic of Atraya appeared, hovering over the centre of the conference table.

"Let me provide you with a brief overview of your new home," said Bronson. "Atraya is 89 percent of Earth's mass, consequently gravity will be 89 percent of Earth's as well. Atraya also orbits Tama closer than Earth orbits its star, completing a full orbit of Tama in only nine Earth months. So, our year is three months shorter. That means when someone tells you they are 40 years old, those are Atrayan years. In Earth years, they are only 30. Atraya has a rotational period of 22 Earth hours, but we still use a 24-hour clock, so each hour is the equivalent of 55 Earth minutes. In other words, you will have to throw all your time devices away and start using ours."

He smiled at the newcomers.

"Because Atraya's axial tilt is two degrees less than Earth's, the planet's yearly climate is more even throughout the year. Our proximity to Tama, as well as the planet's slightly higher percentage of ocean compared to Earth, means that we also enjoy a much more temperate climate. In many ways, Atraya is a sub-tropical paradise."

He paused to let the Terrans admire the slowly rotating holographic of the planet.

"Why Atraya?" asked Olivia Alvarez. "What's the origin of the name?"

"Atraya is an ancient Hindi word, meaning, 'those who live on three worlds'. The first settlers here saw the three-planet system and thought the name was appropriate. As it turns out, the name has come true. While Atraya remains our home world and the planet upon which the vast percentage of our population live, we have significant human settlements on Jumea, the third planet, as well as bases in orbit around Helios the first planet. We also have bases on Atraya's moon, Rios, and Jumea's moon, Kronos. Jumea, by the way, is the French word for twin. Jumea is almost exactly the same size as Atraya but is barren of liquid water and does not have a breathable atmosphere."

"I could bore you with more details, but I think that is enough for the moment. The data screens in your cabins will have much more information for you to peruse at your leisure over the next 30 days of our return voyage."

He paused and considered his next words carefully.

"One significant difference you will notice in most Atrayans, is that most adults have had neural enhancement. Perhaps the best way to explain it is to play you a brief excerpt from an explanatory video that is shown to people who are about to undergo the procedure."

Again, without moving his hands, the holograph of the planet disappeared, and a 3D video appeared in its place, with a pleasant female voice over.

*"Neural enhancement, also sometimes referred to as neural augmentation, is a means of allowing humans to interface more smoothly and easily with various technologies. The neural interface transceiver is a small device inserted at the base of the skull and which has monofilaments which interface with the cerebellum, the cerebellar cortex and the rear of the brain stem, under the cerebellum."*

*"Once the neural transceiver is in place and has been calibrated to your brain, you will be able to more readily interface with many technologies, such as computers, household appliances, communication devices, and various modes of transportation. For example, your flitter or other transportation device can be calibrated specifically to you, so that no one else may fly or drive it. The front door to your home can be calibrated so that only those within your family may unlock it. Many personal or electronic items can be calibrated to you so that no one else can use them. Families can also easily locate and communicate with each other through private comm calls via their own private enhancement network."*

Commodore Bronson pointed to the back of his head. "You have probably already noticed my neural enhancement transceiver, or 'plug' as we commonly refer to them. I draw this technology to your attention, not in any way to put pressure on you to have the procedure done for yourself, but simply so that you can be fully informed. Of course, you are very welcome to have it done, but you will not be ostracised if you choose not to. Indeed, there is a small percentage of Atrayans who, for a variety of reasons, choose to remain 'unenhanced'. It is totally your decision."

"Commodore, would I be right in assuming that you have been operating the holographic system via your neural interface?" asked Daniel.

"That is correct. It is a simple and seamless means of interacting with technology. Enhancement certainly makes life a little easier."

The commodore looked around the table at the newcomers.

"In terms of the next 30 days, let me make a few concluding comments. Firstly, in order to have room for all of you on board Ulysses, we voyaged here with a skeleton crew whose shifts were longer and more frequent than normal. I realise that our technology is 370 years more advanced than your own, but the next month would be an excellent opportunity for your own crew to work alongside ours in the hope that it might prove to be mutually beneficial. It is an opportunity for your crew to learn on the job, and it may also result in some of the burden being lifted from my crew. In fact, in some areas, it may be possible for some of your crew to take over a full shift once sufficient learning has taken place."

"Secondly, I wonder if some regular social events might foster good relationships between my people and yours, as well as providing a welcome boost to morale among your people after all you have been through."

"That is a truly wonderful idea!" said Dara Bernstein, Longshot's welfare officer. "Thank you, Commodore."

"Perhaps you, Lieutenant Bernstein, could co-ordinate with my executive officer in organising some suitable social events?"

"I would love to," she replied, smiling at Gayer Steetsel, who nodded in return.

"Good!" said Bronson, enthusiastically. "Captain Anderson, is there anything you would like to add?"

"No, Commodore. You have been most accommodating."

Bronson nodded. "In that case, meeting adjourned."

## 33

"This food is amazing!" said Jordan with her mouth nearly full. "I don't know what half of it is, but I love it!" She piled another forkful in and sighed contentedly.

"Those small purple things are a native fruit called brindleberry," said Jerem Grant who had just arrived at their table with a plate full of food. "May I join you?"

"Sure," said Daniel.

"Yeah," added Jordan, "pull up a pew, Reverend."

Jerem smiled but said nothing in response to her semi-facetious comment. He sat in the seat next to her and took an appreciative mouthful of food from his own plate.

"Don't mind her," said Daniel. "She calls me Professor when she knows I'm not really. It's a token of endearment."

"So, you're a microbiologist and a chaplain?" asked Jordan, still chewing on a mouthful of food. "No offense, dude, but you look more like a surfer to me."

"I am."

She looked up in surprise. "Really?"

"Absolutely! I was born on the island of Nalu, about 30 minutes north-west of Jasper city by flitter. It's renowned for its consistent surf. I could ride a board almost before I could walk. It's still my go-to way of escaping and destressing. I have a small cottage on the island that I retreat to at every available opportunity."

Jordan shook her head. "Wow! You are a walking contradiction, dude."

"How so?"

"I can't see how all three of those things fit together; faith, science and surfing."

"Surely surfing and faith are a good fit?" he suggested.

"Yeah, I get that, I suppose. But it's the science and faith combo that seems so contradictory."

Jerem nodded. "Coming from your perspective in the 24$^{th}$ century, I suppose it must seem that way."

"Are you saying it's not a contradiction 370 years later?" Daniel asked, joining in the conversation.

"To be perfectly blunt, it never was a contradiction, even back in your time. The concept of an inherent contradiction between faith and science was propagated by a small but very vocal atheistic element within the scientific community, and most people in the general population just assumed it was the case. But throughout the ages, some of our most profound intellects and most influential scientists have been people of great faith."

"I suppose there have been a few," conceded Daniel.

"More than just a few. Albert Einstein, Isaac Newton, Galileo Galilei, Nicholas Copernicus, William Kelvin, Johannes Kepler, Louis Pasteur, Robert Boyle, Max Planck and Nikola Tesla, were all people of profound faith."

"Look, I don't want to pour water on your worship candle, dude," said Jordan, "but didn't they all live in an age when faith was just accepted unquestioningly? Surely, as mankind's scientific knowledge grew, it led us further away from those outdated beliefs."

Jerem shook his head. "There's that bias I was talking about: the idea that the more we understand science, the less reasonable faith becomes. But it's actually the exact opposite. Albert Einstein once famously said, 'The more I study science, the more I believe in God', and William Kelvin said, 'If you study science long enough and deep enough, it will force you to believe in God'."

Jordan shook her head. "But they all lived before the advent of the kind of evidence we have today."

"Like what?" he asked, genuinely interested in her response.

"I don't know. Genetics and cells and stuff."

"But that's what actually led me to believe in God! I was converted in the course of my university studies when I began to study the unimaginably complex microbiological world. It was once thought that simple cells could have evolved by chance processes. Some scientists were still saying it in your era, in the 24th century. But you won't find any serious microbiologists today who claim that the living cell evolved by chance. Even the simplest living cell is now understood to be a complex factory of millions of biological machines, all interdependent and all needing to be in place and fully functional for the first viable cell to have formed. The chances of millions of complex bio-machines coming into existence at the same time, each one comprised of millions of precise combinations of proteins and amino acids, and containing a full set of genetic instructions, is beyond the realm of possibility. The simple cell cries out that there is an intelligent designer at work."

"Wow! Sorry I raised the topic," said Jordan. "Let's talk about surfing."

He smiled. "Sorry. I get a bit passionate sometimes."

"Do you? That's interesting. With anyone in particular?" she said, raising her eyebrows suggestively.

Jerem laughed. "I like you," he said.

"That's only because you haven't got to know her yet," Daniel said. "Give it time. It will wear off."

"Ha, ha, Professor. Very funny."

"So, let's talk about surfing," Jerem said. "Do you?"

"Do I what?"

"Surf."

She shook her head. "Nope. Never had a chance to try."

"Would you like to give it a go?"

She nodded as she stuffed another mouthful of food in. "I guess."

Jerem looked at Daniel and Kelly. "How would you guys like to come and stay with me on Nalu for a few days when we get back? It's a pretty basic bungalow, but the island is the closest thing to paradise I've ever found."

Jordan raised her eyebrows in surprise. "Are you serious?"

"Absolutely! I'm due for furlough, and you guys seem like you could do with some relaxation."

"But you hardly know us, dude! For all you know, I could be a psychotic murderer."

He tilted his head as he looked at her circumspectly. "No. You're not even close to that."

"Is that so? What am I really like, then?" she challenged him.

He regarded her closely for a moment, choosing his words with care.

"You're intelligent. You're funny and irreverent, but in a delightful way. You are courageous and extremely competent. You are distrustful of authority and have a strong aversion to superficial pomp and ceremony. You have strong opinions and don't mind expressing them. I'm guessing you don't form friendships quickly or lightly, but when you do, you are incredibly faithful. You have an undercurrent of insecurity, and you sometimes use humour and gruffness to shock others and to keep people from seeing the real you. I'm not sure whether you have ever been loved completely and unconditionally, and maybe that's the reason for your insecurity, but I suspect that not far below the surface there is a beautiful, tender, caring heart and a passionate woman who is just waiting to blossom when true love comes along."

There was stunned silence at the table. Daniel glanced at Jordan and was amazed to discover that she had tears glistening in her eyes. She stood up suddenly, pushing her chair back, then she turned and began walking away. After a few steps, she paused and turned back. She stood behind the chair that she had just vacated, her eyes still glistening.

"Yes," she said, looking at Jerem.

"Yes, what?" he asked.

"Yes, I'd like to come surfing."

"Good. Because I'd really love to teach you."

She nodded, as if that was an acceptable response, and then she turned and walked away again, leaving a half-finished plate of food.

"Bloody hell!" Kelly said to Jerem. "Remind me never to ask you what you think of me!"

**34**

---

Daniel rose at 05:00 the following morning, after their first night on board Ulysses. He crept out of the room without waking Kelly and made his way to the gym on the lowest level of the ship. He was still recovering from the physical ordeal of the previous two weeks and was feeling dull and listless after a broken night's sleep. In fact, he had lain awake for long periods throughout the night, reflecting on the series of life-threatening calamities that he and the rest of Longshot's crew had had to deal with and overcome. At times, it had seemed that their chance of survival was tenuously slim, and many, including himself, had almost resigned themselves to the idea that they were not going to make it to the new world. It was difficult to suddenly adjust to the sense that they were now safe and were headed to a life that promised peace and security.

At 05:45, after a moderate workout, he was still feeling restless, so he made his way to the dining room, on the top level, planning to sit quietly and enjoy a cup of coffee before the day began. To his surprise the dining room was not empty. The two commanding officers were sitting together, sharing an early breakfast. He paused after stepping out of the lift, thinking that he would leave them to chat together in peace, but Captain Anderson spotted him, having heard the lift door open.

"Daniel! Come and join us."

Daniel walked in their direction.

"I don't want to intrude, sirs. I'm just here to grab a cup of coffee."

"Nonsense," insisted Anderson. "It's not an intrusion at all. Come and sit with us."

Daniel got a coffee from a nearby dispenser and reluctantly joined them, still feeling that he was a third wheel.

Bronson turned toward Daniel. "Captain Anderson has been bringing me up to date on the many challenges you have all had to overcome to get here."

"Yes," agreed, Daniel. "I was doing a bit of reflecting on that during the night as well. It's been quite a journey. There were times when it looked as though we weren't going to make it."

"From what your captain has told me, it sounds like you played a key part in the survival of everyone. You are to be commended."

Daniel shook his head. "I was just trying to stay alive. There's nothing particularly commendable about that. It's the basic instinct that we all have: to fight and claw and cling to life with our fingernails if necessary. I came across a poem recently by someone from the 20th century, which I think expresses it well: *'Do not go gentle into that good night, Old age should burn and rave at close of day; Rage, rage against the dying of the light.'* We survived our ordeal, not because we are heroes, or special in any way, but simply because of that basic instinct to fight for life until our dying breath."

"True," agreed Bronson. "But people bring differing levels of ingenuity and resourcefulness to that fight. You appear to have those qualities in abundance."

Daniel shrugged. "Maybe I'm just more afraid of dying that most other people."

The commodore smiled politely and shook his head. "I think not. I'm a good judge of character and you certainly aren't a coward. It sounds like you played a pivotal role in bringing your people safely through the life-threatening challenges you faced."

"Speaking of life-threatening challenges," Daniel said, changing the topic, "why were your people threatening to destroy us when we first entered your solar system? There's obviously a backstory there."

Bronson nodded. "Yes. A very sad one, unfortunately. The nuclear conflict that you fled from when you left Earth 370 years ago ended very badly. The dictatorship that was known as the Republic of Independent States won the war, but only just. Earth was a mess. Large areas were a wasteland and almost certainly still are. A small remnant from the Alliance of Nations retreated to the Moon, which became the last outpost of democracy in the solar system. They built a starship and came here, abandoning their base on the Moon. They were looking for a new beginning, free from tyranny and oppression. The Republic wasn't satisfied with controlling Earth and its solar system. On three occasions the Terrans, as we now call them, came here, not to negotiate or trade, which our ancestors were willing to do, but to attack us and seek to take control of Atraya as well. The last attack was 120 years ago, which we only just managed to repel. Since then, we have had sentinel satellites in place to warn us of further invasion attempts. It's incredibly sad that we have to do that, but we refuse to let them do here what they did to Earth."

"And you thought we might have been a new threat from the Terrans?"

"Yes. And your silence didn't help. There were a lot of fearful Atrayans calling for your destruction long before you reached the outer edge of our solar system."

Daniel was about to say something else, when the lift opened and Ulysses' science officer, Grul Thorbid, approached their table.

"I'm sorry to interrupt, Commodore, but I thought you would want to be told personally."

"What is it, Lieutenant?"

Thorbid glanced uncertainly toward Daniel.

"He's alright," assured the commodore. "You can speak freely."

Thorbid nodded. "Well, sir, it's a bit of disturbing news, I'm afraid. I've taken the opportunity to study the neutron star as closely as possible. As far as I'm aware, it's mankind's first close encounter with one. I've made many fascinating discoveries, but one very disturbing one." He paused and considered his words carefully. "It's not stationary. In fact, it has considerable velocity. It was moving toward us as we approached Longshot, which is why we didn't have a lot of warning. Our combined velocities amounted to nearly half the speed of light."

"Go on," said Bronson, "but I have a nasty feeling about what you're leading up to."

Thorbid nodded. "I think you've guessed it, sir. The neutron star is following us. It's on almost the same trajectory."

"Define 'almost'."

"That's the problem, sir. It's very difficult for me to accurately determine its velocity and precise trajectory, as we are in a constant state of acceleration ourselves. It's made even more complicated by the fact that we were initially not on a perfect trajectory for our solar system after our slingshot manoeuvre. We have had to make a course adjustment, which means that we are approaching the Tama system from a slightly different angle now, compared to the neutron star."

"But you're saying the star is heading for our solar system."

"Yes, sir. It definitely is. I just can't determine what part of our solar system it will pass through or exactly how long it will take to get there."

"What's your best guess?"

"My calculations indicate it will arrive in our system in about six months."

"And what's your best guess about what part of our system it will pass through?"

"I can't say at all, sir. The only reliable way of determining that, will be from our observatories at our $L1$ and $L2$ Lagrange points. From their fixed positions in space, they should be able to determine a pretty accurate trajectory."

"What level of danger does it pose?"

"That is completely dependent upon its distance from Atraya, sir. If it passes us at a distance of more than 1 billion kilometres, it will have very little effect. If it passes at half that distance, it will shift the orbits of all three planets, drawing them further from our sun and creating a colder climate. Any closer than 200 million kilometres would be catastrophic. The severe changes to Atraya's orbit could turn our planet into an ice world."

There was silence for several moments, as the seriousness of the situation sank in.

"Will your observatories be able to see it this far out?" asked Daniel.

Thorbid answered, "Because it's only 22 kilometres in diameter, they wouldn't have detected it this early, except by pure chance. But now that we can give them the specific coordinates to search for it, they should be able to pick it up from its strong X-ray emissions."

"In that case, get a message to them immediately," said the commodore. "And let's hope it's going to miss Atraya by a very long way."

**35**

___

On the morning after his two-day break, Keelor reported back to Angel City. The upload to his neural implant had provided him with a complete working knowledge of where to go and how to get there. As he rode the shuttle up to the city in high geosynchronous orbit, it felt as if he had done this a thousand times before.

After the shuttle docked, he rode a lift up to Level 1 and navigated his way to Harry's office. The sign on the door simply said, 'Dr Harry Melville'. He walked into the office and the dishevelled scientist welcomed him with a warm smile.

"Welcome, Keelor! How was your break?" he asked.

Keelor thought back to his date with Maran the previous night and smiled. "Better than I could have hoped." Maran still had an extra day in Jasper and was returning to Angel City later that afternoon.

"Good! Good! Glad to hear it," said Harry as he came around his desk and ushered Keelor to one of his comfortable chairs. He sat opposite and said,

"I suppose you're keen to find out what your job will actually be?"

"Very. You said something about instantaneous space travel. But I'm not sure how that could be possible."

"All will be revealed in due course. But first let me give you some background information. I have found, from past encounters with new Newbies, that doing this in a conversation is more effective than via a neural memory dump."

"Okay," said Keelor, settling himself more comfortably into his chair.

"Let me start at the beginning," said Harry. "Our greatest challenge in travelling to the stars has always been distance. Even travelling at the speed of light, at 300,000 kilometres per second, it would take years to reach our closest neighbours, hundreds of thousands of years to travel across our galaxy, and millions and billions of years to reach other galaxies. So, realistically, we are limited to visiting only the very closest stars, and even that is an extremely difficult journey to make."

Keelor nodded. So far, there was nothing new in what Harry had said.

"But one of the theories that has been floated for many centuries, beginning in the 20th century on Earth, is the idea of folding space-time. It was theorised that the whole of our three-dimensional universe is embedded onto or into a quantum fabric – an underlying reality of dark energy and dark matter that binds the physical universe together and gives it its form. In a sense, the space-time fabric is a bit like the soil of a garden and the physical universe is like the plants. The universe grows out of the space-time fabric, but its roots are unseen to those on the surface. This is why we refer to the concept of sub-space: the underlying reality that gives substance to the physical space of our stars and galaxies."

"Yes," said Keelor. "I'm familiar with the concept of sub-space."

"Good! Well, for centuries it has been argued that it may be possible to bend or fold subspace, so that two points that are separated by a vast distance in the physical world can be brought together in the subspace world and a much shorter trip between those two points could become possible."

Harry took a piece of paper and drew two dots on it, at opposite ends of the paper. "These two dots represent two stars in normal space, separated by a vast distance. The paper represents the sub-space continuum. If we fold subspace, we can bring these two points together." He folded the paper so that it was now folded in half, with the two dots on the outside, opposite each other. "Then all we need to do is create a tunnel through subspace, often referred to as a wormhole, to travel from one point to the other." He drilled a small hole through the folded paper with his pen, at the point where the two dots opposed each other.

"In this scenario, the physical, three-dimensional universe hasn't changed. No one in the physical universe is aware that anything has moved. The folding occurs in the sub-space fabric of the space-time continuum, that underlies the physical universe. The theory is that by folding sub-space and opening up a wormhole, a journey of thousands or even millions of lightyears could occur in just moments."

"So, the wormhole becomes a subspace shortcut between two distant points in the physical universe?" suggested Keelor.

"Precisely. At least, that is the theory."

"And that's the technology you are developing here?"

"No. The theory is completely wrong. Mankind has been barking up the wrong tree for centuries."

"It's wrong?" Keelor was puzzled, now. Why had Harry just taken the time to describe a theory that was wrong? "Why is it wrong?"

"It's wrong for two reasons. Firstly, wormholes that are big enough for a starship to travel through are simply not possible. We now understand that wormholes in subspace are forming all the time, millions of times per second, but they are only possible at the sub-atomic quantum level. To open and maintain a wormhole big enough for a peanut to travel through would require unthinkable amounts of dark energy – about as much energy as is present in our sun, Tama. It's just not feasible."

Harry continued. "But the second flaw in the theory is even more serious. The theory of wormhole travel is based upon the idea that we can manipulate the fabric of space-time itself; that we can fold space time in the first place. But that also is not possible. Nor is it necessary. Because over the last few years, my team and I have made a remarkable discovery. We don't need to fold space time. It's already folded."

He looked at Keelor closely, watching to see if he was following.

"Okay," he said tentatively.

Harry nodded. "Consider a ball, let's say a basketball, and there are two points on opposite sides of the ball. What is the shorted route between those two points?"

"A direct line through the middle."

"Correct. In this scenario the physical universe exists on the surface of the ball and the subspace fabric of space-time is inside the ball. Everything in our physical universe, from an atom to a galaxy, only has a physical existence because it has roots that extend down into the sub-space continuum, like plants in a garden. But what we have discovered is that instead of the subspace soil of the garden being a flat garden bed, it is more like the inside of the basketball. Subspace is already twisted and folded in upon itself – so much so, that every point in our physical universe is already folded over every other physical point in the universe at the subspace level. It's as if every point on the surface of the basketball has a root that reaches into the heart of the ball and meets at a single point, where all the roots are tangled or joined up together. Unfortunately, where this analogy breaks down, is that the distance from the surface of the basketball to the centre of the subspace realm is no distance at all, because there is no such thing as distance in sub-space. Everything is folded over everything else, so travelling through subspace from one point in the physical universe to another takes no time at all because there is no distance at all."

"Okay ..." said Keelor, hesitantly, grasping what he was saying but struggling to picture it in a way that made sense. "But you are still talking about travelling through subspace, similar to a worm-hole, aren't you?"

"No. And this is where it gets complicated."

"It's not complicated already?"

"Trust me, this is going to blow your mind." Harry paused, then said, "We aren't planning on travelling through subspace at all. We are simply going to change our subspace address and instantly relocate ourselves to another point in the physical universe."

Keelor frowned. "Do you want to run that by me again?"

"Do you have a personal T-Net site?"

Keelor blinked and gave a puzzled frown. "Yes."

"What is it? 'TN://keelor' or something similar?"

"TN://keelortrantum."

"Okay. So, when someone enters that T-Net address into their computer, your page comes up, and there it is, on their screen in their study or bedroom. But that image on their screen is simply the external image, the remote image if you like, of the actual page or site that resides in the T-Net quantum computer in Angel City. That is the source, the origin."

Keelor nodded, beginning to see where this was leading. "So, in this scenario, the image of my site on people's screens around the solar system, represents the physical universe, which is rooted in the subspace reality, represented by the central T-Net computer?"

"Correct. But let's suppose you decide to change your T-Net address to TN://superkeelor."

"That sounds like a good idea," Keelor smiled.

Harry continued. "You wouldn't make any physical changes to your site at all. All the information and all the videos and photos you have placed on your site remain exactly the same. All you would do is change the address bar, where people can find you. A moment after you do that – a fraction of a micro-second – someone entering your old address would discover that your site has completely disappeared. Someone who had your old site already on their screen, if they hit 'refresh', would find that it had disappeared. The reality is that your page hasn't travelled any distance at all inside the T-Net computer, but in the outside world it no longer exists at its previous location and is now in a brand new, completely different location."

"And you're saying that this corresponds to the relationship between the physical universe and subspace."

"Precisely! We have discovered that everything in the physical universe has a specific subspace address in the form of a complex set of frequencies in what we call the subspace foam. Far from being stable, like a piece of fabric, subspace is a seething foam of quantum fluctuations where every part of subspace is constantly talking to every other part of subspace, effectively saying, 'I'm here! I'm here!' And everything in our physical universe has a slightly different set of subspace frequencies, which defines and determines its position in the three-dimensional universe. We refer to this as an object's subspace address."

"And you believe that by changing an object's subspace address, you can instantly change its position in the physical universe?" asked Keelor.

"We don't just believe it." Harry gave Keelor a sly smile. "We've actually done it."

**36**

___

Keelor's eyes opened wide in surprise. "You're saying, you've instantaneously moved an object from one place to another, simply by changing its subspace address?"

"I wouldn't use the word 'simply'. There's nothing simple about it. But, yes, that is precisely what we've done."

"What have you moved?"

"So far we've moved several pieces of fruit."

Keelor laughed and shook his head. "You've translocated fruit? How far? How far have you moved them?"

"That's the problem at the moment. We have no idea where they went. We changed their subspace address and they simply vanished."

Keelor laughed again. "So, it's possible that an orange suddenly appeared somewhere else – perhaps in someone's kitchen, or at the bottom of a swimming pool, or in orbit around a distant star – and you have no idea where it is now."

"Pretty much."

Keelor shook his head in astonishment. "And you're trying to develop this as a method of translocating an entire starship?"

"Yes. But, as you can gather, it's rather important that we learn to control the subspace destination address so that we can control where we send the ship. It would be rather unfortunate if we sent a starship full of people into the heart of a star, for instance."

"It would ruin their whole day," agreed Keelor.

"Indeed." Harry stood up. "Come and let me introduce you to the team. They are all here this morning and keen to meet you."

Harry led Keelor out of his office and down a short corridor which ended with a sliding door with no signage. As they approached the door, Harry said, "The door will recognise you and open. No one outside the Newman Project can gain entry.

As he spoke, the door slid open, and they stepped into a stunning circular room. It was stunning primarily because of its clear, domed ceiling which gave a magnificent view of the stars. There was a bench around the entire circumference of the room, against the circular wall, with chairs facing screens built into the wall. At one point on the bench there was a food and drink station. In the centre of the room was a large circular sunken pit with a circular lounge around its perimeter, broken only by two gaps at opposite sides, where two steps led down to the cosy seating area. A group of people were currently seated there, and they looked up with anticipation as Keelor and Harry entered the room.

"Keelor, meet your fellow Newbies," said Harry. He led Keelor down the steps into the sunken lounge area and introductions were made: Storv, Bree, Kira, Dahl, Andy, Ryder, Bryl, Carmen and Josie. Keelor filed the names away, his enhanced neural ability making them easy to remember. The group seemed warm and friendly, and eager to embrace a new member to their team.

"It looks like I caught you having a break," said Keelor said to the group.

"Nope," said Kira. "This was us hard at work."

Keelor laughed, but Harry confirmed what she had said. "Your quantum neural interface provides a direct link to the quantum mainframe computer here on base. Most of the time, you have no need to sit at a workstation. You will find this lounge area the most comfortable place to work, particularly as you form a linked neural network."

"I see." Keelor counted them and noted that there were only

nine. "You said there were ten currently on the team. Is someone missing?"

"No. I'm the tenth," said Harry, smiling. "And you are number eleven."

Keelor looked at Harry in surprise. "You have the necessary genetic mutations?"

"Yes. I was enlisted to the quantum enhancement program as a young man by my predecessor, and I eventually took over. This has been a long-term project, spanning centuries."

Keelor nodded, absorbing this information quietly.

"Why don't we make a start," said Harry. "There's no simple way of explaining this. It has to be experienced to be understood. Let's all take a seat."

Everyone sat back down, and Harry said to Keelor, "Don't stress if you don't end up connecting properly at first. It takes a bit of practice. For your first time, it's easier if we cancel the lights."

As he said this, the lights switched off and they were plunged into darkness. The only light now came from the spectacular array of stars that shone through the transparent domed ceiling.

"It might also help if you close your eyes." Harry said.

Keelor did so and listened carefully to Harry's instructions.

"For your first session, we are going to lead you. You just need to connect to us and tag along. We'll make a group connection first and then ping you."

A moment later, Keelor's neural interface registered an incoming communication request and he accepted it. Immediately he sensed the presence of the others.

"Good. Very good," said Harry, impressed. "Can you sense the distinctive differences between each person's neural patterns?"

"Yes, I can," agreed Keelor, surprised. It was hard describe, like trying to explain color to a blind person, but each person's neural presence had a distinctive ... something! Shape, color, smell, texture; none of these things adequately described the distinctiveness. Perhaps 'pattern', was the best approximation. Storv was sharp and pointy, Bree was soft and complex. Kira was jumbled and unpredictable. Immediately he could identify each one.

"Now we are going to access the quantum mainframe."

Keelor sensed or saw a new presence, the enormously powerful quantum mainframe that ran the solar system's T-Net. He watched as Harry navigated a labyrinth of pathways until he opened a connection inside an encoded folder marked 'Newman Project'. It was as if a doorway opened, and the group stepped through into a sea of seething foam or froth. It was like looking at the ocean when it was being pelted with heavy rain or hail. The surface of the ocean was constantly erupting into vertical splashes, but the surface wasn't flat either. It was a three dimensional landscape that was constantly shifting and folding upon itself, even as each individual part was foaming in a myriad of vertical eruptions.

"What you are seeing is the flux of subspace. It has taken us centuries to develop sensors capable of detecting and interacting with subspace at the quantum level: the subspace reality that underpins everything in the physical universe. Each physical object in our universe has a unique set of frequencies in the flux: a complex subspace address that defines its location in the physical universe. I am going to stand up now and move around the room. Keep your eyes closed, Keelor, so you don't get distracted by my physical presence. Follow the others and they will help you to focus on my subspace frequencies."

He felt the others draw him toward a set of small eruptions in the foam. They zoomed in and he followed. There were eruptions within the eruptions and still they zoomed in further. Finally, they settled on a set of particular frequencies and as Harry apparently walked around the room, he watched those frequencies in the quantum foam change slightly.

"The subtle changes you see, are a reflection of my changing position in three-dimensional space." Harry explained. "If I physically change my position, my subspace 'address' changes slightly. But it's also a two-way thing. Change the subspace address, and an object's physical location changes with it. I am now placing an apple on the coffee table. Can you see its frequencies? Its subspace address?"

"Yes! I can!" said Keelor, excitedly, as he noticed a small set of frequencies separated from the ones that represented Harry.

"Excellent! Focus on that apple, while I return to my seat. Open your eyes and look at it on the table, while still holding your focus on its subspace address."

Keelor focused.

"Now concentrate on the frequency fluctuations and watch while I reach out and join it to another set of frequencies."

Keelor watched while a set of frequencies were dragged across and joined to those of the apple. Instantly the apple on the table disappeared and the frequency patterns that represented it within subspace disappeared also.

"When we are in the Flux, we are not only watching; we are also interacting with it," Harry explained. "Attached to this facility is a dark energy generator that has been developed over the last two hundred years. It harnesses dark energy from subspace which we direct via this interface. It is that dark energy that enables us to interact directly with the subspace flux and alter the subspace address of an object."

Harry, brought the demonstration to an end, saying, "I think that's enough for your first introduction." Everyone in the group opened their eyes. Everyone, except Keelor, whose eyes were now firmly closed.

"Keelor?" said Harry. "You can open your eyes now."

"Just a moment," said Keelor, frowning.

A moment later the apple appeared on the table. There were gasps of astonishment from several in the group.

"How did you do that?" asked Kira. "We've ... we've never been able to get anything back to its original location."

"I followed it and I saw the part of the frequency that had changed, and I changed it back again."

Harry was agog. "You followed it? What do you mean?"

"While Harry was walking with the apple, I analysed the frequency shift and saw the part that was changing and the part that wasn't. I figured the part that was changing corresponded to its position."

"Yes, that much we understand," said Harry.

"I did the same thing when you combined it with the frequency of another location. That's when the apple disappeared."

"Yes, but we've never been able to track where things have disappeared to, from that point."

"It's simple math," explained Keelor, surprised that they hadn't worked it out for themselves. "You didn't replace the location frequency of the apple with the new location, you added them together. I calculated the addition of the two frequencies and searched for that. When I found it, I simply completely replaced that frequency with the original one, and it came back to its starting point."

The group were stunned.

"Did I do something wrong?" Keelor asked, looking at their astonished expressions.

Harry's voice was shaking with excitement.

"I think you might have just solved a big part of our problem."

Keelor reached out and picked up the apple.

"Do you guys mind if I eat this? I'm starving."

**37**

---

U lysses' message regarding the approaching neutron star was received by Tama System Control. Commander Shila Hansen immediately flagged it as Priority 1 and forwarded it to the head of the science department, Dr Harry Melville. Harry took one look at the recorded video message and called an emergency meeting of his astronomy team, which consisted of himself, his wife of 38 years, Dr Andrea Melville, and Sari, a research assistant doing her doctorate in astronomy. The coordinates of the rogue neutron star were noted, and they dropped all other research in order to locate and track it.

Because the offending celestial body was so small and such a vast distance away, it took three days of careful observations until they had clearly located it, mainly via its X-ray emissions. For the next two weeks tracking the position of the approaching star became the sole focus of Andrea and her assistant, with Harry dropping in regularly to check the results. As each day passed, hope slowly faded and a grim new reality asserted itself.

After the first week of measurements, they knew without a doubt. The second week was spent simply fine tuning their calculation of its trajectory and confirming their estimation of the star's impending influence. When it could no longer be denied, and further delay would have been irresponsible, Harry and Andrea met with General Claymore and Commander Hansen from Tama System Control.

"I'm assuming this isn't good news," General Claymore said.

Harry and Andrea's faces spoke volumes. Neither had slept much during the last week, as they considered the extent of the impending disaster.

"It's the worst possible news, General," Harry said. "We were initially hoping that the neutron star would pass through our solar system somewhere beyond the orbit of Jumea. But that is not to be." He took a deep breath. "The star is travelling at considerable velocity and will intersect our solar system in seven months."

"Where will it intersect us?" asked Claymore, already anticipating that he was not going to like the answer.

"We have had to calculate where each of our three planets will be in seven months' time. We've checked, double checked and triple checked our calculations, and we are now in no doubt at all."

"And?" prompted Claymore.

Harry let out a long sigh. "The neutron star is going to pass directly between us and Tama, our sun."

"And I'm guessing that's very bad."

Harry nodded. "I'll let Andrea explain just how bad it is."

Andrea swept an errant strand of grey hair from her eyes and looked directly at the general. In many ways, she was the strong one of their marriage. Harry was the excitable dreamer, gregarious and affable, friendly and lovable, but often lacking in organisation and in follow-through with specific strategies. She, on the other hand, was disciplined and organised, able to focus on one thing to the exclusion of almost all else, following the facts through to their logical conclusion irrespective of the inconvenience to people's feelings or preferences.

"I'm not sure how much you know about neutron stars, General, but let me give you a few pertinent facts. Although this star only measures 22 kilometres, don't let its small size fool you. It is a gravitational monster. Its gravity is 11.3 billion times stronger than our sun, and a whopping 250 billion times stronger than the gravity we experience on Atraya. When it reaches our solar system, even before it gets anywhere near to passing between us and our sun, it is going to drag all three of our planets and their moons, as well as Tama itself, into its gravity well."

"What does that mean in layman's terms?"

"It means it's going to suck our sun and our planets into itself. We will implode into the neutron star, and that implosion will transform the neutron star into a blackhole that will happily continue on its way and eventually gobble other solar systems in its path. In short, General, our entire solar system is going to be destroyed in seven months."

Claymore's face showed no emotion. He glanced at Harry who was shaking his head with his eyes downcast, as if he still couldn't believe it. Claymore looked back at Andrea who continued to return his gaze with her steely green eyes.

"Is there anything that can be done to avert it or alter its trajectory?"

"Nothing at all. It's simply too massive. We could throw a projectile the size of our whole planet at it, and the neutron star would simply gobble it up, lick its lips, and keep on coming. The only thing we can do is abandon our solar system: get as many people as we can onto starships and away from here before it arrives."

Shila Hansen spoke up. "General, I've been getting messages from Ulysses, asking whether we've confirmed its trajectory yet. How do you want me to respond?"

"When are they due to arrive?"

"In 16 days, sir."

"Let them have 16 days of peace. They've been through a hell of a lot, especially the passengers from Longshot. Just tell them that our scientists are still calculating. They'll have plenty of time to get used to the bad news when they arrive. We'll limit comms to and from the ship until they get here. I think this is news that needs to be conveyed in person."

He looked at Harry and Andrea again. "I'll need you to present this information to the Senate. Obviously, this is urgent, so you can expect to be called to appear before them within the next day or so."

He thanked them both and dismissed them. As they left the room, he activated an emergency comm call. "President Jonas, this is General Claymore. I'm afraid I have some very bad news."

## 38

The emergency meeting of the Atrayan Senate was in session. Its twelve members, elected from various regions of Atraya and Jumea, sat with shocked expressions after listening to the devastating news presented by Drs Harry and Andrea Melville.

"And you have no doubt about your projections?" asked President Jonas.

"None, whatsoever," confirmed Andrea, who had done most of the talking.

The President frowned. "Can't we change its trajectory, somehow? Hit it with missiles or launch an asteroid at it? Surely we could divert its trajectory?"

Harry spoke up. "I'm sorry, Mr President. The neutron star is so massive that even if we launched a whole planet at it, there would be no change to its trajectory at all. It would be like throwing a feather at an iron ball." He looked around the circle of faces with resignation in his eyes. "Make no mistake about it; this neutron star is going to destroy this whole solar system, and there is absolutely nothing we can do about it."

There was stunned silence after this final pronouncement. Any hope of reprieve they might have had was squashed. Several people shook their heads in disbelief, and one counsellor, a woman in her late 50s, had tears rolling down her cheeks.

The President addressed General Claymore. "General, what is our current capability regarding interstellar starships?"

"We have none."

There was a shocked murmuring around the senate chamber, situated on the top floor of Jasper's tallest building. The magnificent 360-degree views to the ocean to the east and the mountains to the west only heightened the sense of impending tragedy for their beautiful planet.

"Let me explain," continued Claymore. "We have three military cruisers, capable of carrying a crew of 250 each. But these are military vessels, designed to patrol our solar system and protect us from possible further attacks from Earth. But we have no starships, designed to travel the void between the stars."

"Why not?" asked one of the senators, aggressively. "What have you done with the budget we so generously provide for the science and development arm of the military each year?"

The general bristled. "Your so-called 'generous' budget, senator, barely keeps our current programs ticking over! We have repeatedly asked for a significant increase in funding, but every year our request is declined." He glared at the senator, daring him to deny the claim, but the senator could not meet his eyes.

"Furthermore," continued Claymore, calming down a little, "we haven't really had any reason to build starships. There are two reasons for that. Firstly, we are very settled here, and no one has any desire to go elsewhere. Until now, there has been no pressing reason for us to even consider leaving. There are no environmental or population pressures forcing us to leave our planet and look elsewhere. Secondly, our exploration of the galaxy via our long-range scanners and telescopes has failed to find another habitable planet: not a single one anywhere. So, there has been absolutely no reason for us to build a starship."

He let his explanation hang in the air. It made logical sense, but it didn't make it any easier to accept.

"If we did have a starship, the only place for us to seek refuge would be Earth," said the president. It was a statement, not a question.

"That would be awkward," commented a senator, dryly.

"How long would it take us to build a starship from scratch?" asked someone.

"I'll defer that question to Dr Melville," said Claymore.

"At least five years," said Harry. "And that would be pushing it. It would be utterly impossible in just seven months."

"What about refitting our military cruisers?" asked the same senator. "Could we convert them into starships for a longer voyage?"

Harry scratched his straggly beard. "They would need to be fitted with cryogenics pods, and that, in turn, would require a complete refitting of the ship's power systems, computer systems and life support systems. You would still be talking about at least 18 months to two years for every ship."

"And if we didn't fit them with cryogenics pods?" asked another senator. "What if we just packed them full of people and sent them to Earth?"

Harry answered, "That is certainly possible. The journey would take 38 years, travelling at lightspeed. The current food production facilities on board our cruisers – the hydroponics and yeast facilities – could certainly be upgraded in time. But that would take up more space and reduce the number of passengers to more like 150 per vessel."

The general jumped in and added a further reflection. "Bear in mind, senators, that would mean 38 years living in a spaceship. It's not something that many people could cope with. But in terms of our options, it's the only one we've got."

"What is our current population?" asked President Jonas.

Several senators interacted with their screens, and someone called out, "4.6 million. That's total population throughout the entire solar system."

Jonas nodded. "So, out of 4.6 million people, we can possibly save only 450: that's 150 in each of the three cruisers. And they would have to live in a cramped spaceship for 38 years, and then face an uncertain reception by the Terrans."

He looked around the circular chamber.

"It's not a great option, is it? But it's all we've got. I'm sure some people will be keen to make the trip. The question is, how do we decide who gets to go?"

An hour-long discussion ensued, discussing how and when they would inform the general population and how they would conduct the ballot to determine who would get a chance to leave for Earth. Security measures were discussed, including the possibility of society degenerating into violence and chaos as the time of their destruction drew near. It was a grim and depressing discussion, and one that no one in the room ever thought they would be having. In the end, their meagre plans were set in place and the meeting was concluded.

They each left the chamber and returned to their homes, to be with their loved ones and to share the terrible news that they had a little more than 6 months left to live.

**39**

---

The mood among the passengers and crew of Ulysses was one of elation as they finally docked with Angel City. For 30 days they had streaked through the void at astronomical speed after their close encounter with the neutron star. Now, after 15 days of extreme deceleration, they were home. The crew and colonists of Longshot marvelled at the size and complexity of the orbiting city and were intrigued by the glimpses of the orange-hued world that spread out below them.

Longshot's 38 crew members were given temporary accommodation in the rooms normally assigned to recruits during their induction week in Angel City. The 200 colonists were transferred to Jasper City, where a temporary camp had been set up a few kilometres west of the spaceport. The plan was to provide them with several days of orientation talks, aimed at assimilating them into Atrayan society, before then moving them to more comfortable billets. The plight of these newly-arrived ancient Terrans had been made public throughout the long rescue mission and there had been an overwhelming response. There were more offers of homes than there were colonists. Atrayan families were ready to welcome the newcomers into their homes and into their lives – despite the devastating news that those lives would now be cut drastically short.

The Atrayan Senate had decided that complete transparency was their only option. The population had been told of their impending doom, and so far, society had not begun to disintegrate, although it was still early days. There was a deep sadness and an understandable fear among the general population. Death is never a welcome visitor. An overwhelming sense of grief pervaded society. Families were coming to terms with the fact that their children would never grow into adulthood. Young lovers were mourning the loss of a future that had seemed so promising.

But there was also a widespread public movement that sought to uphold the ordered and civilised nature of their lives until the very end. A public media campaign, begun anonymously, gained traction and coined a slogan that became a rallying cry for many: 'live with honour, die with honour'. T-Net stories of people reaching out to the poor and sharing their possessions, abounded. Things that were once important no longer seemed to matter. Values changed and priorities shifted. Relationships were reconciled and broken families sought healing, as if they wanted to put things right before they met their end.

It was in the midst of this spirit of compassion and generosity that the colonists would be welcomed into the homes of the Atrayans. They would be treated as long lost relatives from their planet of origin and have their needs provided for, in the short time that remained.

In Angel City, high above the Jasper City, a meeting was held with the combined leadership teams of Longshot and Ulysses, informing them of the terrible fate that awaited them all. The news was a devastatingly cruel blow, particularly to the Longshot crew members. They had come through so much and overcome seemingly impossible odds, to now be dealt a final, inescapable, crushing hand. It was almost too much to take in. As Harry Melville finished his explanation of the grim news, there were the expected questions about possible courses of action, but as each suggestion or question was countered by the harsh facts of their predicament, the inevitability of their situation sank in. There was nothing to be done. Nothing except to make the best use of their remaining time: to give and receive love, to embrace the beauty and joy of life and to treasure each precious second that remained.

General Claymore concluded the grim meeting. "Ladies and gentlemen, I'm so terribly sorry that your homecoming isn't what you were expecting. Captain Anderson, we will endeavour to place all your crew and colonists in homes on Atraya where they will be treated with kindness and generosity. A lottery is being drawn shortly from among those who have indicated a desire to undertake the 38-year journey to Earth. The crew and colonists from Longshot are welcome to participate in that ballot, along with all Atrayans. Every resource is now being directed toward preparing our three cruisers for that long voyage. But for the vast majority of us, all that is left is to treasure the time that remains to us and share it with those we love. I hope that each one of you manages to find a measure of peace and purpose in the months that remain. God bless you all."

As the meeting broke up, Jerem Grant approached the stunned trio of Daniel, Kelly and Jordan.

"How are you folks coping?"

Kelly shook her head. "It's ... I don't know. I don't have words to adequately express it."

"I do," said Jordan. "It's shit."

Jerem nodded. "That's certainly one word for it."

"How do you reconcile this with your belief in God?" asked Daniel.

"That's probably a conversation for another time and another place. I think we are all hurting and in shock. What we need most, right now, is comfort and support. Which brings me to ask whether you are still interested in coming and staying with me on Nalu."

"Haven't you got family you would rather be with at this time?" Daniel asked.

"My mother and brother live on the island, so I will see plenty of them. But I would love to have you folks come and stay as well."

"Well ...," began Daniel, looking at Kelly for confirmation.

"We'd love to," interjected Jordan, with more enthusiasm than she had intended. Then she blushed slightly and looked away.

"Wonderful!" Jerem replied. "I'll arrange a shuttle transfer for us for tomorrow morning." He smiled at them, glancing particularly at Jordan, then left.

"That's very kind of him," said Kelly, glancing at Jordan.

"Yes," agreed Daniel, also looking at Jordan with eyebrows slightly raised. "I'm sure it's completely altruistic. There can't possibly be an ulterior motive in it."

Jordan completely ignored their comments. "I'm going to the gym. If I'm going to spend the last few months of my life learning how to surf, I want to be at least reasonably fit." She left without another word.

"I don't think I've ever seen her like this," commented Daniel.

"Neither have I," agreed Kelly. "She's like a schoolgirl with a crush. Who would have thought?"

At that moment, Captain Anderson approached them, accompanied by Harry Melville.

"Daniel!" said Anderson, enthusiastically. "Dr Melville and I were just chatting. He heard me introduce you at the meeting as Lieutenant Newman, and he was curious as to your first name."

"You're Daniel Newman?" Harry asked, without polite preamble.

Daniel smiled. "Last time I checked."

"And you left Earth in 2316?"

"Yes." Daniel was slightly puzzled by the line of questioning.

"And I'm guessing you had a nasty encounter with a research organisation called, Senticorp. They did things to you without your consent."

Now Daniel was perplexed now. "How ... how do you know that?"

They stared at each other, Daniel with a frown, and Harry with a look of growing incredulity.

"What's the square root of 1081?" he asked, his eyes drilling into Daniel.

"No idea," Daniel replied, feeling threatened and completely confused about what was happening.

Harry continued to stare at him, then he shook his head and smiled. "I seriously doubt that. I think you know the answer to 100 decimal places."

There was strained silence for a few moments, then Kelly spoke up. "Tell him, Daniel. What's the harm? We're all about to die, anyway."

Daniel nodded in resignation. "32.878564445547l9"

Harry shook his head in wonderment. He reached out and grabbed Daniel's right hand in both of his and said, "It really is you!"

"Yep. I'm definitely me. I tried being someone else, but it didn't work out."

"I need to show you something! Something my team and I have been working on. Because I think we can save a lot more people!"

## 40

---

"You've managed to translocate some pieces of fruit?"

The lights had come back up again after the demonstration, and Daniel was perplexed. He removed his cap, his version of the neural interface transceiver, which seemed antiquated to the Atrayans, but they were too polite to comment.

"I understand the theory, and I can see how you are doing it, but how does this save more people?" he asked, looking around the group. The others all stared back at him, still coming to terms with the fact that that the person who had been the inspiration for the whole Newman Project centuries ago was sitting in the same room with them.

Harry smiled. "Because that's not all we've moved."

"What have you moved? Don't tell me, you've moved a loaf of bread as well."

Keelor laughed out loud. He liked this guy. He was unconventional and mildly disrespectful of authority, just like Keelor himself.

"No," responded Harry patiently. "We've moved some space probes. And got them back again. Although we don't call it moving or translocating. We've coined the term, 'warping'."

"Really? Okay. Go on, I'm listening."

"Three weeks ago, we had a breakthrough. We finally worked out how to read the quantum frequencies in the subspace foam. Keelor worked it out. Planets have a distinctive set of bass frequencies. Stars have an even deeper set of sub-bass frequencies. We began warping probes to planets, leaving them there for a few minutes and then returning them and analysing the data that they had collected. The first couple of probes crashed into the planets and were destroyed, until we worked out how to modify the frequency slightly to place the probe near enough to the planet to gather data but far enough away so that it was safe."

"You've been sending probes to planets orbiting other stars? And bringing them back again in a matter of minutes?"

"Yeah! Pretty cool, hey?" said Keelor.

"How many probes have you sent?" asked Daniel.

"We only have four left after we destroyed the first two," began Harry.

"I told you we should have tweaked the frequencies a little before sending them!" complained Keelor.

Harry ignored him and continued with his explanation. "So, we divided into four teams, and each team has been warping their probe out and back again up to thirty times each day for three weeks."

"So, you've checked out about 2,500 planets?"

"Nearly," said Harry. "We stopped looking a few days ago when we found another planet just like Atraya. It's orbiting a Type-G, yellow dwarf, just like Earth's sun."

"Really? Where is it?" asked Daniel.

"No idea," said Keelor, cheerily. "We haven't worked that part out yet."

"Yes," agreed Harry. "We don't know where it is, and the star constellations aren't recognisable. But that's not really important. The point is, we can warp there, and we can warp back again."

"Well, you can warp a probe there and back. But how does that help your population? How do we get people there?"

"We're planning to warp a spaceship there!" Keelor said, enthusiastically.

"You can do that?" asked Daniel.

There was silence for a moment, and everyone looked at Harry.

"Not quite yet," he admitted. "But we're trying to figure it out."

"What's the problem?"

"Size and energy," replied Harry. "The bigger the object to be warped, the more dark energy is required to change that object's subspace address frequency. Dark energy is the negative energy that permeates subspace. We believe that if we can manufacture a larger, more powerful dark energy generator and place it on board a cruiser, a team of us could be stationed on the ship and warp the ship to the new planet."

"I see," said Daniel. "And I suppose the idea is that you could warp the ship back and forth to the planet and drop people there, presumably using the ship's shuttles to get them down to the surface of the planet once you're there."

"Yes! Exactly!" said Harry excitedly. "We could probably do four trips a day, with a full load of 250 passengers. That's 1,000 people each day! We've got six months until the neutron star gets here, and even allowing for the fact that it might take us another month to get the ship ready, in the remaining five months we could warp a total of 150,000 people to the new world!"

Daniel nodded. "It's a bold plan, Harry."

"It's the best plan we've got," said the dishevelled scientist. "General Claymore is giving us unlimited resources, and we've already started working on the manufacture of the new dark energy generator. We'll be installing it in the cruiser, Scorpion. We're hoping to start testing it within a month."

Harry concluded his explanation with a simple request, "We'd like you to be involved, if you're willing to help."

Daniel looked at the circle of expectant faces. "I'm not sure whether you need my help at all. But when you're ready to start trialling it, if you need an extra presence, I'll be happy to be here."

**41**

———

Nalu island was like stepping back in time. After the impressive technology of the orbiting Angel City and the towering skyscrapers and congested airways in Jasper City, the small tropical island was simply delightful. They disembarked from the ferry and walked along the jetty to the small group of shops and cafes spread along the foreshore of the harbour. A sou-easter had blown up during the crossing and the sailing boats and motor launches that were tied up at the marina were rocking in the wind chop, their rigging clanging and banging musically. Scattered cloud was scudding low and fast across the island, and the wind was gradually increasing in intensity.

"The colors are all ... weird," said Jordan looking around. "The orange light changes everything."

"Yes. You'll get used to it," Jerem said. "It seems natural to me. The upside is that there's not much harmful UV radiation to cause sunburn and skin cancers."

They stood in front of the small selection of shops, and Jerem glanced up at the fast-moving clouds.

"It looks like we're in for a bit of a blow. I just need to get a few supplies and then we'll get going."

He walked into a small fruit and grocery store and left them on the sidewalk, gazing around the town. No one seemed to be in a hurry. People were sitting at tables and chairs on the sidewalk, or on park benches along the harbour front, drinking coffee and eating. Heads turned languidly in their direction, mildly curious about the strangers in military uniform, but they soon lost interest and returned to their lazy conversations.

Jerem returned shortly after, loaded with bags of groceries and fruit.

"You guys are going to need some swimmers and some island clothes. Let's get you kitted out while we're here." He led them to a store that boldly declared itself to be 'The Style Palace'. They walked in and a lady at the counter looked up.

"Boobsy, darling! How lovely!"

She came around and enveloped Jerem in an affectionate embrace, kissing him on the cheek. She was in her mid to late 50s and had long greying hair arranged into dozens of tiny braids, each one filled with shells and beads. Her clothes consisted of sandals, baggy trousers and a loose flowing top, made of a thin material that was dyed in odd colorful patterns. She wore several necklaces of shells around her neck and had large swirly earrings dangling from her ears.

"Mum, these are the friends I was telling you about," Jerem said.

"How lovely! Welcome to our island."

Introductions were made and she told them to call her Lulu.

"They're going to need some clothes," Jerem explained.

"Of course! Let's get you out of those ghastly uniforms! How dreadful."

"We have no way of paying you for clothes," said Daniel.

"Don't be silly! We're all about to die in six months," Lulu said, brightly. "Money doesn't mean much anymore. Besides, it will be nice to see all my hard work being put to good use."

"Mum makes all these clothes," Jerem explained.

"Wow!" said Kelly, looking at the racks of colorful clothing.

Half an hour later, they emerged from the Style Palace wearing an eclectic mix of island clothes and carrying more in bags.

Jerem led them around the corner to a stand of bicycles, each with a wire basket in front.

"Grab a bike each," he said, placing his groceries in the wire basket attached to the front handlebars of the nearest bike.

"You've got to be kidding!" said Jordan.

"No. It's the only form of transport on the island. There are share bikes everywhere. It's a decision that the locals made long ago. The people here want to live as close to nature as possible."

"Well, I've got news for them," said Jordan. "There's nothing natural about bicycles, unless you've managed to genetically engineer a bicycle tree in the last 370 years."

"Perhaps I should have said 'they want to live as simply as possible'." He looked at Jordan. "You do know how to ride a bike, don't you?"

She shook her head. "Nope. I was too busy going to polo lessons and ballet practice and horse riding when I was a kid. That was usually after my violin practice."

"Is she always this sarcastic?" Jerem asked Daniel and Kelly.

"Only when she's breathing," replied Daniel

"Grab one of the trikes," Jerem suggested. "You can't fall off those."

"Oh yeah? Just watch me," she said walking up to one and regarding it sceptically, as if it was about to bite her. They loaded their carry bags of clothes into the baskets and set off up the road, with Jordan huffing and puffing in the rear. The paved road surface disappeared after 100 metres, and so did the buildings. The road became a hard-packed dirt track that wandered along the south-eastern coast of the island, with the beach on their right, occasionally glimpsed through the lush vegetation. Every 200 metres a sandy path led off to the right, into the thick vegetation between them and the beach, and they caught glimpses of simple houses nestled among the tropical trees and bushes.

"How far is it to your house," gasped Jordan.

"I'm two kilometres out of town. Not far."

"Not far if you're an Olympic athlete," she replied, puffing.

"We're nearly there. It's on the top of this next hill."

"Oh great. A hill."

They soon turned off the main track and followed a narrower path that rose steeply through a grove of overhanging palm trees. As the track rose more steeply, they all had to dismount and push their bikes up the last section until they emerged into a clearing at the top. A simple bungalow was sitting serenely on the top of the grassy hill that was at least 100 metres above sea level and which sloped steeply down to the sand. The sea was being whipped into a frenzy now, and the wind was howling. They parked their bikes against the side of the bungalow and carried their bags of clothes and provisions around to the verandah that faced the spectacular view out to sea. Jerem opened the large double sliding glass doors in the centre of the of the bungalow and led them inside.

It was a simple design. A central living area with a kitchen, small dining table and a couple of lounges. To the right was a small bedroom and a bathroom. To the left was a second, identical bedroom and a small laundry.

"Jordan, you take the bedroom on the left. Daniel and Kelly, you guys take the one on the right. There's a double bed in both rooms."

"But where will you sleep?" asked Kelly.

"Here on the sofa. I often sleep here, even when I'm alone. I like to leave the sliding doors open and listen to the surf."

"We can't kick you out of your own bedroom," Kelly said.

"I insist. Besides, as I said, I often prefer to sleep here."

They unpacked and Jerem made cups of tea. "It looks like I'm out of coffee," he said. "But this is a local tea made from the leaves of the lava bush."

They sat on chairs on the verandah, drinking their lava tea and watching the wild surf. The wind coming in from the ocean seemed to hit the grassy slope and bounce over the top of the house, leaving them strangely wind-free.

"This tea makes my lips tingle," said Kelly.

"Yes. It very has mild sedative properties. It's the opposite of normal tea. Instead of a stimulant, it's a relaxant."

"A sedative?" asked Kelly, looking at her cup with suspicion.

"Don't worry. You'd have to drink about 15 mugs before you started to fall asleep."

Kelly took another tentative sip and nodded her head, appreciatively.

Jordan put her mug down on the verandah deck and said, "Okay, I've got to ask. It's been killing me. 'Boobsy'?"

Jerem laughed. "Yeah. It's my nickname. My family started calling me that when I was a toddler. There's a local flightless bird called a Booby. Apparently, I was fascinated with them. I would spend hours chasing them around."

"So, it's not because you've got saggy man boobs?" asked Jordan.

"No," he laughed again. "I try to keep in shape. Surfing helps."

"So, when's my first lesson?"

"First thing tomorrow morning."

"Define 'first thing'."

"The best surf is soon after dawn, before the wind picks up."

"I don't get up at dawn for anyone, dude," she said.

## 42

Daniel left Kelly sleeping, made a cup of lava tea in the kitchen and wandered out onto the verandah to sit drinking it. It was their first morning waking up on the island, and Daniel was intrigued by the orange-colored mist and the apricot sky as the strange sun peaked over the horizon. Jordan and Jerem were already out in the early morning surf. He hadn't heard them leave, but he marvelled at the fact that Jerem had managed to coax her out of bed so early. During their trip to Atraya on board Ulysses, Daniel had watched the blossoming romance between Jerem and Jordan with interest. They had spent long hours together, talking and laughing, and when there was a more formal social event organised, they were almost inseparable. There was still nothing overt yet, but Jordan was obviously smitten with him, and the interest seemed to be reciprocated.

There was no breeze this morning, and the sea was glassy, with a small swell running that seemed just right for learning to surf. Daniel sat sipping his tea, watching the surfing lesson taking place directly in front of the hill-top bungalow. Jerem was standing waist deep in the rolling whitewash, holding a large wooden board while Jordan lay on it, wearing her newly acquired one piece swimming costume. He pushed her forward as the next broken wave came through and she attempted to get to her feet, only to wobble and fall straight off. They laughed and had several more attempts, and Daniel noticed that a lot of touching seemed to be involved.

Finally, Jerem got on the board with her, moving her toward the front while he paddled from the rear. He paddled out through the small break to the unbroken water and swung them around. A slightly larger set came through and Jerem paddled onto the second wave of the line-up. He leapt to his feet and dug the rail in, sending the board shooting along the small glassy wall. He leant down and dragged Jordan to her feet and wrapped his arms around her, and even from this distance, Daniel could hear her hoot with delight. They rode like that until the face of the wave was about to close out, and then Jerem flipped them off the back.

Daniel lost sight of them over the back of the wave, but as the whitewash subsided, he glimpsed them standing face to face in the shoulder deep water, laughing. A moment later they kissed, and Jordan's arms circled his neck as she clung to him. They stayed like that for some time, the board forgotten. Daniel smiled and looked away. He was glad for Jordan. In fact, he was happy for them both. He hoped that they might find a measure of comfort and happiness together to lighten the darkness of these final months.

The rest of the day unfolded at a leisurely pace. Following a healthy breakfast of fruit and cereal, the four of them swam, walked, talked and snoozed at various points throughout the day. There was no program to follow, no schedule to be adhered to. The slow, steady rhythm of the waves was a salve for their souls and the incremental movement of the warm orange sun across the arc of the apricot sky was their only clock. At one point in the afternoon, Jerem and Jordan went for a walk along the beach and were gone for a long time. When they returned, they were unashamedly holding hands and there was a spark in Jordan's eyes that Daniel had not seen before.

As the sun lowered toward the horizon, Jerem's family arrived for a barbeque dinner. Cam and Lori, Jerem's brother and his wife, along with their two young children, were the first to arrive, lugging a basket of food and drink. They greeted him with cries of "Boobsy!" and "Uncle Jerem!", amid hugs and kisses. Jerem's mother, Lulu, arrived a little later, having closed her shop for the day, and the noise and laughter increased further with the addition of her flamboyant personality. Freshly caught fish, purchased from the town market that morning, was cooked over a pit fire, and damper bread was baked in the coals. They began eating as the sun finally set and external lights were switched on. The simple meal was supplemented with fresh salad and a locally produced wine, and the family sat in chairs around the fire, laughing and teasing one another with the kind of easy familiarity that spoke of their deep love for one another.

The new-found romance between Jerem and Jordan didn't go unnoticed by the family, who picked up on the subtle looks and touches that betrayed their growing intimacy. Nothing specific was said, but the family paid particular attention to Jordan, asking about her interests and making sure to include her in their conversation. Jordan, in turn, was curious to find out about Jerem's childhood, and was enthusiastically regaled with tales designed to embarrass him.

Eventually, the fire died down, Jerem's family went home, and the two girls went to bed, leaving Daniel and Jerem sitting on the edge of the verandah with the lights off. Daniel had a beer in hand and Jerem was sipping a wine.

"It's been a wonderful day. I can't remember the last time I felt this relaxed," Daniel said, taking another sip of beer.

"I'm glad," said Jerem. "That's why I invited you here. There's a special magic to this place. It never fails to calm my spirit."

Looking up at the spectacular spread of stars in the moonless sky, Daniel felt mellow and philosophical.

"This whole situation is so ... surreal. I can't quite come to terms with it. Everything we see, everyone we meet, will be gone in six months, swallowed up in a cruel cosmic accident. It's all so utterly meaningless!"

"It's only meaningless if you think that this life is all there is," Jerem said.

Daniel turned toward him and shook his head, a look of incredulity on his face.

"How can you possibly still believe in God or an afterlife, in the light of such a cruel twist of fate? What sort of God would allow this to happen? Surely this, along with everything else that's happened to us on our ill-fated voyage, proves that there really is no one in control."

"On the contrary, I think that the incredible story of your survival against seemingly hopeless odds, not just once but on several occasions, is strong evidence that Someone was watching out for you."

"Well, the big feller sure isn't watching out for us now, is he?"

"You don't know that. It's not over until it's over."

"Really? You think we're all going to get out of this alive, somehow?"

"I'll admit, it's certainly not looking like it. But even if we are all about to die, it's not the end of the world; it's just the end of this world."

"I wish I had your faith."

"Let me ask you something," said Jerem. "What do you see when you look up at the stars? What's the overall impression that you get?"

Daniel looked up into the night sky. The moon had not yet risen, and the stars were as thick as dust. The Milky Way galaxy was revealed in all its glory, its central hub a glowing ball of light.

"It's big," Daniel said, simply.

"For me it's different," Jerem said. "I get an overwhelming sense that the universe isn't just some cosmic accident. I can't believe that the billions of galaxies and trillions of stars and planets all came from nothing, by nothing and for nothing. Something doesn't come from nothing. To me, the stars cry out that there is a Creator and that there is a purpose to the universe."

Daniel took another sip of beer. "Well, I sure as hell would like to know what the purpose of our current predicament is."

"We don't always get to see the purpose behind every event. That's not how this life works. But sometimes we can glimpse some of the good things that flow from our trials. At the moment, all over Atraya, families are reconciling, people are reaching out in love, strangers are being welcomed and the poor are being cared for. People are re-assessing their values and altering their priorities. For the first time in many people's lives, they are turning from frivolous pursuits and embracing things that truly matter. I've never seen a time like it. There is great good happening in our world right now, and it would never have happened without this imminent disaster."

Daniel nodded. "I can agree with that. This is certainly a time for focusing on what truly matters."

Jerem had a sip of wine. "It's a time to give and receive love."

"I notice there's a bit of giving and receiving going on between you and Jordan."

"She's a very special person. I only wish I'd met her before now."

"She seems very happy. I wish you both the best."

"You'll be able to do that in a few days' time. I just asked her to marry me."

"You what?" Daniel was stunned. "But ... you hardly know her!"

"That's not exactly true. We were together constantly for 30 days on Ulysses. You can get to know a person pretty well when you're effectively living in each other's pockets for a month."

"Yeah ... but it's still only a month."

"And we've only got six months left to live," Jerem said, bluntly. "I think that changes everything. If that's really all that we have left, don't you think we should make the most of every single day? Why put off being with the person you love, when there's so little time left to love?"

"You love her?"

"Of course. She's exactly the kind of girl I've been waiting for my whole life."

"Wow!" said Daniel, still coming to terms with the sudden development. "What about her lack of faith? Doesn't that bother you?"

"I'm not convinced she's as faithless as she likes to make out.

We've talked a lot about it, and I think she does believe, deep down. Besides, it's God's department to change her heart, not mine."

Daniel shook his head. "I'm ... surprised ... but very happy for you both."

"Thank you." Jerem stood up. "Time for bed." He walked toward the sliding door that led into the bungalow, then paused and looked back at Daniel. "A lot of people are getting married at the moment. It's a way of affirming the love that you already have with someone and saying, 'I'll be with you to the end'. I think it means a lot, even when the world is about to end."

He went inside, leaving Daniel deep in thought.

**43**

———

Kelly was told of the impending wedding at breakfast the next morning, and her reaction differed from Daniel's. There was no surprise or shock, just excitement and joy. She could see how suited they were to each other and couldn't miss the new light in Jordan's eyes.

For her part, Jordan played it cool and still displayed some of the feisty bluntness that was part of her nature.

"Just don't expect me to get dressed up like a fairy princess. I'm not into any of that crap."

"Of course not," said Jerem. "I'm marrying the real you, not some idealised, make-believe version."

"Well, with Jordan, you can guarantee you'll always get the real her," quipped Daniel.

"That's why I love her," Jerem said, squeezing her hand.

"Where will the wedding be?" asked Kelly.

"Right here, on the grass overlooking the beach," answered Jerem.

"Who will do the ceremony?" asked Daniel.

"No one. On Atraya, we don't need a celebrant. There just needs to be a public pledge witnessed by two people. The wedding couple and the witnesses then send a declaration to the Atrayan Records Office, and it's official."

"We're getting married, too," Kelly said, abruptly, looking at Daniel.

It wasn't a question.

"We are?" Daniel asked in surprise.

"Yep."

"Umm ... okay. If that's what you want. Are you sure?"

"Oh, gee, let me see. I love you, and you love me, and the world's ending in six months. Of course I want to marry you, dummy!" She gave Daniel a peck on the cheek. "When you finally find the person you want to spend the rest of your life with, however short that might be, there's no reason not to get married." She took a sip of her lava tea. "Besides, all the other guys I asked are busy and couldn't commit."

The weddings took place on the third day after the barbeque and gave rise to another barbeque of significantly greater proportions. Jerem's mother and brother witnessed the simple pledges and a crowd of about 30 other guests turned up. Most were Jerem's friends from around the island, but Nash Anderson and Olivia Alvarez, from Longshot's crew, also came as surprise guests.

The ceremony took place in the middle of the day, and the barbeque that followed extended lazily into the late afternoon. By 18:00, guests had begun departing and Jerem's family were cleaning up. Nash Anderson and Daniel sat on the edge of the verandah together, catching up.

"These are strange times, Captain," Daniel said.

"It's Nash, Daniel. I'm without a ship now. And, yes, these are strange times, indeed. Sadly, they're going to get a lot stranger, too. I was in a meeting yesterday in Angel City with some Atrayan officials and scientists. They painted a grim picture of what we can expect."

"What did they say?"

"Two weeks from the end, Tama, our sun, will start to grow larger in the sky, as we are both drawn toward the neutron star on a converging trajectory. There will be heat waves and major weather events. During the final week, there will be an escalating series of huge earthquakes and volcanic eruptions as the neutron star's massive gravity causes the planet's tectonic plates to shift and warp. On the last day, Atraya will simply be ripped apart. It will be cataclysmic."

"I don't think I want to be around to see all that," said Daniel.

"A lot of people feel the same. The Senate have authorised the mass production of what they are calling the 'Goodnight Pill', a simple and painless way for people to end their life. It's expected that the majority of the population will avail themselves of that during the final week or so."

Daniel shook his head. "It's so sad. So terribly sad."

"Yes. But even in the midst of this sadness, there is still cause for celebration." Nash placed his hand on Daniel's shoulder. "I'm so glad for you and Kelly, that you have found each other and will have the comfort of your mutual love over these last months. That's incredibly special."

By 18:30, all the guests had departed. The two couples were left sitting on the verandah watching a pair of sea hawks hovering over the wind-blown surf and diving into a school of fish. They finished their glasses of wine and then Daniel and Kelly said goodbye.

"Are you sure you can find your way there okay?" asked Jordan facetiously.

Daniel and Kelly had moved into a cabin 200 metres further along the beach. The cabin had been vacated by Jerem's neighbour, an elderly woman who had decided to move back to the mainland to spend the remaining months with her married daughter and her grandchildren. The lady had been overjoyed to know that her simple cabin would be used by a newly married couple.

Jordan and Jerem watched Kelly and Daniel walk hand in hand down the sandy track toward their new home.

"Alone at last," said Jerem, turning toward his new bride.

"So, what are you going to do about it, big boy?" asked Jordan as she wrapped her arms around his neck.

"This," he said, bending down, lifting her into his arms and carrying her toward the sliding glass door.

"You're not serious, are you? This is such a cliché! I thought they only did this in movies."

He smiled and kissed her tenderly. "That's me. An old-fashioned cliché."

He carried her inside but left the door open. The sound of the crashing waves and the cries of the sea hawks filled the bungalow.

## 44

I t had taken nearly a month to fit a larger, more powerful dark
energy generator to the Scorpion. Scientists and engineers had
worked around the clock, using all the resources and manpower
that General Claymore could make available. Finally, the day of
the trial arrived, and Daniel was invited to be part of the process.
He sat with six other Newbies in the 'quantum pit', which was how
they were now referring to the circular sunken lounge under the
clear domed roof in Angel City. The other six quantum enhanced
Newbies were onboard Scorpion, connected to the ship's own
quantum mainframe and to the newly installed dark energy
generator.

Nothing like this had been attempted before. Over the
previous four weeks, they had continued to warp satellites to and
from the new planet, collecting data. But now they were
attempting to warp a whole spaceship. Its mass was the compli-
cating factor. An enormous amount of dark or negative energy
would be required to alter its subspace address and ,for something
that massive, it needed to carry its own dark energy generator.
Harry believed he had calculated the energy requirements
correctly and had designed the new generator accordingly, but
nothing was certain.

For the trial, they would attempt to warp the ship within their own solar system. A point approximately a million kilometres beyond the third planet, Jumea, had been decided upon. To determine the subspace frequency address of that point in space, a military vessel had been flown there and back again, while the Newbies tracked it in subspace. The frequency address, a very specific set of overlapping quantum frequencies, had been noted.

Everything was now ready. The 'warp team' – the six Newbies on board Scorpion – were now in place, and the ship had been moved 200 kilometres clear of Angel City. The 'home team' – the remaining six Newbies in the quantum pit in Angel City – were connected to the others via standard comms, and General Claymore and Commander Hansen, in Tama System Control were also linked in. Scorpion was manned by a skeleton crew, the absolute minimum who would be required to fly the ship home if something went wrong. The ship was fully stocked with enough food to last them a year if they found themselves stranded far from home, and the crew had been fully briefed on the risks and had willingly agreed to take part.

Daniel and the other five in the quantum pit heard Harry's voice come over the comms.

"We're in place and entering the Flux now."

"Roger," said Keelor, who was sitting beside Daniel in the pit. "We see you, Harry."

Daniel was wearing his cap and had his eyes closed in the darkened room to help him concentrate on the complex frequency eruptions of the seething quantum foam. He saw the patterns of the six Newbies on board Scorpion and the stronger frequency of the ship itself. All the home team could do was watch and track the ship. The warp team would have to do all the heavy lifting, directing the dark energy of their generator to bring about the required change in the ship's subspace address.

"Permission to warp, General?" asked Harry.

"Permission granted. Good luck, Harry," came the general's reply.

"Okay. Here goes," said Harry. His voice was trembling slightly, although it was unclear whether it was from nerves or excitement or a bit of both. "Making the frequency change in three, two one, mark!"

The home team watched the ship's subspace frequency signature disappear from its current location and reappear in the targeted location with a new subspace frequency.

"I think they've done it!" said Bree, one of the home team Newbies.

"Harry, do you copy?" said Keelor.

There was nothing.

"Harry? Can you hear us? Over."

Again, nothing.

"Something's wrong," said one of the others.

"No. I don't think so," answered Daniel. "If they are where we think they are, they are 380 million kilometres from us. At that distance they won't receive our message for another 21 minutes. We're just dealing with normal communication delay. They'll probably be back before ..."

"We're back!" exclaimed Harry's voice, as the Scorpion appeared again in its original subspace frequency location. "We did it! It worked!"

There was a spirit of elation among the team, who had all worked so long and hard for this moment. It was the breakthrough they had all hoped and planned for. Now there would be the opportunity of saving tens of thousands more people before the dreadful day of their annihilation arrived.

The final stage of the trial was to warp the ship to the new planet. They had originally planned to conduct that final trial on the following day, but now that they were all in place, there seemed no obvious reason to delay. General Claymore gave the green light, and the most important part of the trial took place shortly after. Anyone tracking Scorpion with scanners would have witnessed the cruiser disappear from their screens a second time, only to reappear in the exact some position several minutes later.

The way to the new world was open.

## 45

The logistics of evacuating people to the new world was not simple. You couldn't just plonk them on the planet and hope they survived. A viable colony required extensive resources: power generators, prefab materials for construction of dwellings, farm machinery, seeds, basic food supplies, medical equipment, engineering equipment, construction equipment, scientific equipment.

But the problem was that the more equipment that was transported, the fewer people they could evacuate in the limited time available. This was not going to be a well-planned, well-resourced colonisation program from a world that was simply looking to expand its presence into another solar system. It was an emergency evacuation from a dying world. Those who didn't go, would die.

Because of this, the obvious decision had to be made; they had to send people in preference to resources. There would still need to be essential supplies and equipment provided for the new colony, as the evacuees would need to be assured of survival in the short term. But there would be very little in the way of large machinery or bulky scientifically advanced equipment. Every box of supplies that was sent, would mean one less person who could be saved. Consequently, it was decided that it was better to save more people with less equipment, than fewer people who might live in greater comfort.

The evacuees would be reverting to a very basic way of life. They would be digging with shovels, rather than with machinery. They would be sowing seeds by hand, rather than with tractors. And instead of prefab materials for constructing dwellings, they would be living in tents while they felled trees to make log cabins.

News of the instantaneous warp capability of the Scorpion was made public and those willing to leave for the new world were asked to enrol in a lottery. Most of the population of Atraya registered for the lottery, and names were drawn randomly on a daily basis. People who were selected had to report to a clearing camp at Jasper spaceport within six hours of being advised, or their place was forfeited. Immediate families were not separated. If a person's name was drawn, their partner and children were selected simultaneously.

Within 36 hours of the successful trial, Scorpion made its first fully laden warp to the new world. A site for the new settlement had been selected on the west coast of a major landmass, near the equator. Scorpion carried five shuttles, each capable of carrying 50 people. It had been decided that one shuttle would be laden with supplies and the other four with people. The shuttles flew from Jasper City, fully laden with people or supplies, and entered Scorpion's shuttle bays. The warp then took place with everyone still packed into the shuttles. The shuttles then emerged from the shuttle bays to fly down to the new world. It was an efficient process, and it meant that Scorpion could make four trips each day, the major time factor being the shuttle flights to and from the ship at both planets.

After the first two warps, the warp team on board Scorpion was trimmed down to two Newbies, and the home team to the same number. A warp team served a 24-hour shift of four warps on board Scorpion before being replaced, and the same roster occurred with the home team. This meant that Daniel, who had become part of the home team, was on Angel City for one day and then home with Kelly for two.

Days turned into weeks, and the exodus continued. 800 people were evacuated each day, and the new settlement slowly expanded into a city of tents.

Meanwhile, engineers and scientists were furiously working on constructing and installing a second dark energy generator, this time on board Ulysses. By week six of the evacuation Ulysses began warping, thereby doubling the number of people being evacuated each day. It was decided to establish a second settlement, about 30 kilometres south of Melville, the existing settlement that the locals had named in honour of Harry. The planet had been named Elpida, which is the ancient Greek word for hope, and as the second settlement slowly began to take shape, it was given the name Bayview because of its position on the northern tip of an expansive bay.

With two vessels continually warping, the away team now consisted of one Newbie on each of the vessels. Two would have been preferable, but they simply didn't have the resources to spread themselves any further. The whole team were tired after five weeks of working a 24 hour shift every three days.

It was during the sixth week of the evacuation that the first subspace radio was successfully trialled. The theory behind subspace communication had been under development since the beginning of the evacuation. If physical objects could be transported instantaneously through subspace, why not radio waves? It had taken scientists and engineers six weeks to come up with a means of converting normal radio frequencies into subspace ones that could be transmitted through the underlying quantum foam of subspace. Once that had been accomplished, instant communication between Atraya and Elpida was possible. Requests for specific items of equipment or supplies was now much more efficient.

By week 12, portable subspace communicators had been produced and made available to each of the Newbies. The portable units were simple relay units that facilitated connection to the main subspace radio transceiver at Angel City and, via that, to the ones now on Elpida and on the two cruisers. This meant that even when Daniel was at home on the island of Nalu, he could communicate not only with the rest of the team on Angel City, but also with whoever was rostered on the warp teams on the two vessels.

A third dark energy generator was fitted to the ADF's third cruiser, Stingray, but during a preliminary test activation of the generator, it exploded, destroying the cruiser and wiping out the manufacturing facility on Rios, Atraya's moon. Shortcuts in the manufacturing process were blamed. Whatever the cause, however, there would now not be a third warp-capable ship.

The days and weeks continued to roll by. 1,600 people were being evacuated to the Elpida every day. The clearing camp on the outskirts of Jasper City was in a constant state of barely controlled chaos as crowds of people were processed and transferred to one of the warp ships via shuttles. The lotteries continued to roll out, and there were daily tears of joy and sadness around the globe as people farewelled their extended families and friends. For the people who were chosen, it was bitter/sweet, because they knew that those whom they were leaving behind were facing certain death.

Meanwhile, the deadly neutron star moved inexorably closer day by day, its path unwavering as it hurtled through space toward them. Scientists could now calculate with great accuracy the time remaining until Atraya broke apart, and almost every home had a countdown timer running on at least one screen. As the time remaining turned from months to just weeks, people stopped referring to days of the week. They simply referred to each day as a number, representing how many days were left. "On D 42 we visited my mother and her new partner." "We are planning a party for Kara's birthday on D 28." Technically, 'D' stood for 'day', referring to the number of days left, but many people came to regard it as standing for 'destruction'. Either way, it was a grim, daily reminder of how little time remained until their lives came to an end.

**46**

---

On D 19 the last lottery draw was held, selecting all those who would be evacuated over the next 19 days. For the few who were chosen, there was relief and elation, although those who were scheduled to depart over the last few days would have to wait to see whether evacuation was still physically possible by then. For the vast majority who did not see their names on the official list, there was despair and resignation. As the last names were revealed on screens all over Atraya, those who were not chosen now knew with certainty that they were about to die.

If all the evacuations currently scheduled were successful, a little over 250,000 people will have been relocated to Elpida. While this was a great achievement, considering how few they had originally thought they would be able to save, the sobering truth was that it represented a mere five percent of the population.

For those who were not chosen, the last vestige of hope was now gone, and all that remained was to prepare for the dreadful approach of the neutron star. Daniel only knew of two people from the crew of Longshot who had been chosen: Olivia Alvarez and Angus Fraser. One of the Newbies had also been chosen: Bree. The last warp jumps would, of course, contain at least one Newbie on board each vessel, so at least another two would be saved. But for the rest of them, they would remain behind and accept the same fate as the rest of the population.

On the morning of D 18, Daniel and Jerem returned to the hilltop bungalow from a mid-afternoon surf to find Kelly and Jordan both in tears. The men stood uncertainly in the doorway watching as the two women cried and consoled each other.

"Um ... what's happened?" asked Daniel.

Kelly looked up at him and burst into a fresh bout of tears, and Jordan looked as if she was about to join in, her bottom lip trembling and tears running down her cheeks.

"Is everything okay?" asked Daniel, which, he realised as soon as he said it, was a particularly stupid thing to say, as everything was clearly *not* okay.

Kelly dried her eyes and looked at Jordan. "Will you tell them, or will I?"

Jordan's bottom lip started trembling again and she shook her head, looking away. Kelly looked at Daniel and said in a soft voice, "We're both pregnant."

"What?" said Daniel, with an incredulous expression.

"Both at the same time?" asked Jerem.

Kelly shook her head. "Jordan is nearly three months. I'm only just pregnant."

The two men were stunned.

"Three months?" said Jerem, looking at Jordan. "Why didn't you tell me?"

She shrugged. "What would be the point? We're all going to die soon anyway. You didn't need to know."

Jerem knelt beside her and put his arms around her. "You're not meant to bear this kind of burden alone. That's what marriage is for: to share the heartaches as well as the joys."

Fresh tears streamed down Jordan's face. "It's not fair! It's not bloody fair! This little baby deserves a chance at life! We deserve a chance to be a family!" She buried her face in her hands and sobs racked her body.

Daniel sat beside Kelly and hugged her and was about to say

something when a deep rumbling shook the bungalow for several seconds. A mug tumbled over on the sink and several items fell off shelves. The four friends looked at each other in alarm. It was the first tremor, and it was days earlier than had been forecast.

The end had begun.

**47**

———————

The countdown timer on the screen in Daniel and Kelly's tiny cabin read D 09:14:20. Nine days, fourteen hours and twenty minutes until the predicted end of the world. The hours and minutes meant nothing, of course. They were merely referencing the arbitrary estimate that had been made months earlier. The steady deterioration of the world over the last week, however, led many to believe that even the predicted number of days that they had left was optimistic. Many now believed that Atraya would not last beyond D 06.

Another earthquake shook the cabin, this one lasting more than a minute.

"That's the biggest one so far," said Kelly.

As she spoke a comm call came through and Daniel accepted it. Jerem's face appeared on the screen in their tiny living room.

"Hi, Jerem," said Daniel.

"Okay guys, that's it! We won't take 'no' for an answer. You need to move up here with us. It's not safe down there."

"Yeah. I think you're right. Thanks. We'll pack a few things and ..."

"Daniel! Look!" cried Kelly, fear now woven into her voice. She was staring out the sliding glass door toward the ocean – or rather, to where the ocean used to be. "The ocean! It's gone!"

Daniel ran to the door and looked out. It was true! The ocean had disappeared. Where it had once been there was just wet sand, rocks and beds of seaweed that had never seen direct sunlight before. It was an eerie sight. The air was suddenly filled with birds circling higher and squawking in alarm.

"Daniel, what's happening?"

"Tsunami! We've got to go!"

Jerem had seen the same thing from his vantage point on top of the hill and was yelling over the comm call.

"Guys! Get out of there, now! There's a tsunami coming! I can see it on the horizon."

Kelly started to run toward the bedroom to grab some things, but Daniel grabbed her arm and turned her around.

"No time! We're leaving now!" He propelled her through the open door and followed her out, grabbing the portable subspace transceiver from the dining table as he left. Kelly had paused on the verandah, looking out to the east where the ocean used to be.

"There's something on the horizon," she said, perplexed. "A wall."

"It's a wall of water," said Daniel. "Run, Kelly!"

They ran. Across the verandah. Across their patch of grassy lawn. They reached the sandy track leading up the side of the hill and started to ascend. The track was steep, and it wound up the side of the hill, cutting back on itself several times to create a more moderate pitch. The wall of water was racing toward them now, looming larger by the second. Suddenly they were hit by a different wall – a wall of wind. One second the air around them was still and languid in the tropical heat, the next it was a howling gale. Kelly was knocked off her feet and Daniel had to grab her to stop her rolling back down the hillside. The wave was frighteningly close now, possibly 400 metres out, and they could hear the roaring sound of its approach even through the screaming of the wind. Daniel gauged that the peak of the wave was above their current height of only a third of the way up the hill.

"We've got to go straight up!" he yelled, leaning closer so that she could hear.

He grabbed Kelly's hand, and they abandoned the path and headed straight up the grassy hill. It was steep and uneven, and their feet slipped occasionally on the wind-swept grass. Daniel was bent over stumbling upward, holding Kelly's hand and dragging her with him, not daring to look up. Another set of feet suddenly appeared in front of him. Jerem had seen them struggling and had run down to help. He grabbed Kelly's other arm and helped to propel her up the steep slope. Their pace quickened and they stumbled forward as the roaring of the wave reached a crescendo.

They were knocked to the ground by a particularly intense gust of wind and Daniel turned to see the huge wave roar past them, just a few metres below. An almost solid wall of sea spray was being blown back off its crest and the three of them were suddenly drenched in its spray. They lay there panting, watching the wall of water continue on its devastating path inland. It gradually lost its momentum and, instead of a wave, it became a churning maelstrom of floodwater, filled with the flotsam of uprooted trees and debris of all kinds. For many minutes they watched the swirling floodwater. Its invasion of the island slowed, eventually losing impetus and reaching some kind of equilibrium before the draw of the ocean began to reclaim it. Gradually the flood waters receded, pouring back through the paths of destruction it had already wreaked, and draining back into the ocean.

Finally, they were able to see where their cabin had been. It had been swept away, plucked from its meagre foundations and almost certainly broken into pieces. Large swathes of vegetation had been flattened and trees uprooted, and the ground was now stained a muddy brown.

Kelly was sobbing, and they were all cold and wet.

"Let's get you guys inside," said Jerem. "There will probably be a second, rebound Tsunami."

Jordan came down to help them and, together, they staggered

up the remaining section of slope and entered the grateful sanctuary of the hilltop bungalow.

"What do we do now?" asked Kelly

There was silence from the others for several moments. Then Jerem said, "All we can do is wait."

"Wait for what?" asked Kelly, although they all knew the answer.

Jordan looked at her friend with sadness.

"Wait for the end."

**48**

—————

The wind ceased and the grey clouds that had accompanied the tsunami cleared. The heat became unbearable. Over the last 24 hours, Tama had grown larger in the sky. The dark orange sun now appeared 50 percent bigger, as the neutron star drew Atraya and Tama toward itself on a converging vector. Atraya was now being subjected to opposing gravitational forces from the sun, on the one hand, and the neutron star, on the other. Newsfeeds were broadcasting the grim prediction that their planet would be ripped apart within another 72 hours.

"So much for the nine days we were supposed to have left," said Jordan. "I want a refund." She pointed to the countdown timer on the screen, which now read D 09:13:54. "We may as well turn that bloody thing off. It's not going to do us any good now."

Jerem agreed and disabled the timer. The screen continued to show newsfeeds from around Atraya, although Jerem had muted the audio. No verbal explanation was required. Images of tsunamis and earthquake devastation filled the screen. Skyscrapers were beginning to topple. Large fissures were opening up and swallowing houses and vehicles. Long-extinct volcanoes were erupting again, their lava flowing through towns and villages to be extinguished in billowing white clouds in the sea.

Jerem's family – his mother and his brother and sister-in-law – had sought shelter in a friend's house on the crest of an inland hill, and so they were safe for the moment. But everyone realised that no one was going to be safe, ultimately. There would be no escaping from this.

The ADF had announced that today would be the last day of evacuations. Those who had been scheduled for evacuation over the coming days would miss out, even though their names had been selected. They would die here, on Atraya.

The newsfeeds were reporting a growing number of people who were availing themselves of the 'goodnight pill'. As earthquakes worsened and buildings started to crumble, some people were choosing a quick end rather than continuing to watch as the world they loved fell apart. Online discussion groups debated the best time to take the pill, with most people arguing that it was still too soon. While life was still possible, they preferred to cling to it, tenaciously, cherishing every possible moment of time spent with loved ones.

The news from Angel City wasn't good. Its orbit was being stretched into an elliptical one by the competing gravitational forces. There was conjecture as to whether it would crash into the planet or be flung out into space, toward the sun or the neutron star. The forces were complex and constantly shifting now, and no one could predict what would happen.

Daniel grabbed his neural interface transceiver and the subspace communicator and walked out onto the verandah to make a call. The heat was stifling outside, and he immediately broke into a sweat. The intense, dark orange light from the much closer sun cast an eery apocalyptic glow across the landscape.

Another earthquake rocked the bungalow as he placed the cap on his head and activated the subspace communicator. He closed his eyes and connected to the quantum mainframe at Angel City. The Newbies had begun using a particular subspace frequency for their own private communication network. Immediately, Daniel could see who was currently connected, their distinctive quantum presences were easy to recognise. Storv and Bree were on board

Stingray as the final away team, and Kira and Dahl were on board Scorpion. It was to be the last evacuation warp. The vessels would not be returning, as the gravitational forces around Angel City were becoming too dangerous to navigate. Daniel was pleased that at least four more Newbies would make it to the new world.

Harry was in the quantum pit, as the sole member of today's home team. The rest of the Newbies had been dismissed, sent home to spend the last precious days and hours with their loved ones. Keelor was now on his family farm with his new wife, Maran, along with her mother who had been invited to stay there as well.

Harry was giving final instructions to the four warp team members and wishing them well for their new lives on Elpida.

"Why don't you go with them, Harry?" asked Daniel, butting into their conversation.

"Oh, hello, Daniel," said Harry who had not noticed his presence. "Me? No. Isn't the captain supposed to go down with his ship? Besides, there isn't room for both Andrea and me. If she can't go, I'm not going."

"I see," said Daniel.

"Till death do us part, and so on," said Harry, philosophically.

"I understand."

"We're so sorry you can't come with us," said Bree, addressing both Harry and Daniel.

"Don't be sorry," said Daniel. "I wish you four well. Live a good life."

They each thanked him, awkwardly. After all, what do you say to someone who is about to die a violent death? There was a strained silence.

"Who is that?" asked Daniel, indicating a frequency peak that he didn't recognise.

"We don't know," said Harry. "It's none of us. We've noticed it over the last 24 hours. We don't think it's an object or a person. It's most likely an artifact from the confluence of competing gravities in this region of space-time. Once the neutron star has finished devouring our solar system it will probably disappear."

"That's so comforting to know," said Daniel, facetiously.

They chatted for a few more minutes and then said their final goodbyes. It was a sad moment, but in the end, there was not much to say. Daniel signed off and walked back into the bungalow and closed the door on the stifling heat from the looming sun.

The afternoon dragged on and the sun eventually set, but the night was no longer completely dark. There was an orange glow to the darkness now, caused by their growing proximity to Tama. It was as if someone had smeared dark orange luminescent paint across the black canvas of the sky.

The four friends opened a bottle of good wine and huddled together on the lounges, looking out at the strange, glowing night sky. They had turned the inside lights off to better see the glowing night sky.

The bungalow still had power, but only because of their backup graviton generator. The wave-powered generators located one kilometre offshore which supplied wireless power to this side of the island had apparently been destroyed by the tsunami.

"I can't believe this," said Kelly. "People use the word 'surreal', but this time it really fits. It's like a psychedelic dream."

"No. I've had a psychedelic dream," said Jordan. "They're a lot more fun than this."

A violent earthquake shook the bungalow, stronger than anything that had gone before. Kelly screamed, unintentionally, and the bottle of wine and several glasses toppled over. The quake lasted for over a minute, and pieces of plaster from the ceiling crashed down onto the coffee table. A final violent shudder caused the window in the kitchen to shatter, sending glass exploding across the floor. Finally, the shaking stopped.

Kelly was crying again, softly and silently. Daniel drew her closer to him, putting his arm around her shoulders as if he could somehow protect her from what was about to happen.

"Would you guys mind if I lead us in a prayer?" asked Jerem.

"That would be nice," said Daniel.

"It can't hurt," agreed Jordan.

They joined hands and Jerem prayed a simple prayer, asking for courage and peace, and entrusting them into God's hands.

"That was nice," said Kelly, when he had finished.

"More wine, anyone?" said Jordan, calmly walking to the kitchen, her sandals crunching on the broken glass. Another earthquake, this one an aftershock, rumbled underneath them as she opened the cupboard door. "I'm thinking a nice red might do the trick this time."

"Perfect," said Daniel, entering into the spirit of things. "And while you're at it, let's have some music."

"Excellent idea," said Jerem. "How about some soft jazz?" He switched off the newsfeeds that were continuing to show scenes of devastation around the world. He opened a music program and found the files he was after on their home data system. The sound of soft, sophisticated jazz filled the air as Jordan poured the wine. They clinked glasses and sipped appreciatively as a tremor caused another piece of plaster to fall from the ceiling onto the kitchen floor.

Jordan placed her glass on the floor and stood up. She stepped up onto the coffee table and began to sway and move in time to the gentle jazz in their darkened lounge room.

"Is this your special dance?" asked Daniel.

"Yep," she said, continuing to sway with her eyes closed. "I always said I'd dance on a table on the last day of my life."

"It's a bit of a letdown, after all the build-up."

"I never said it was going to be brilliant."

"I thought you were supposed to be naked?" he asked.

"I'm naked underneath."

"True," he said, taking another sip of the fine red wine. "I suppose that counts. I'll let you off on a technicality."

"That's very gracious of you, Professor."

"Not at all. It's the least I could do, under the circumstances."

Jerem placed his glass on the floor beside hers and stood up. He stepped up onto the coffee table and put his arms around her, saying, "I'm not letting my wife dance alone on the last night of the world." He kissed her gently and they started swaying together as another tremor shook the house.

Daniel drained his glass and lifted Kelly to her feet. They held each other close and danced a slow dance, in time to the music. Outside there was a brilliant blaze of light as something streaked across the sky, burning up in the upper atmosphere: probably a small satellite that had fallen from orbit.

"They're putting on a light show for us," said Kelly, softly.

"I ordered it especially for you," Daniel said.

## 49

Daniel opened his eyes. He and Kelly were lying on the floor under their bed. At some point during the night, the two couples had retired to their bedrooms, to be alone with each other on what must surely be the last night of their lives. The constant shower of dust and plaster from the ceiling had eventually forced Daniel and Kelly to take refuge under their bed, where they had somehow both managed to fall asleep.

Daniel continued to lie there, not wanting to wake Kelly. Several minutes went by with no tremors or shakes. There was no wind yet, and the rhythmic sound of the surf could be heard, its steady crump and whoosh a soothing counterpoint to last night's tremors and earthquakes. Several more minutes went by, and still everything remained calm. No tremors. No earthquakes. The first waft of a warm breeze drifted in through the broken bedroom window, carrying the fresh, salty fragrance of the sea. A small, brightly colored bird landed on the windowsill and sang a morning reveille, as if to summon the sleepy humans from their beds. It gazed curiously at the inside of the room and, apparently deciding that it had done its duty, flew off on some other errand.

Daniel's brow furrowed. Something was not right. Or, at least, it *was* right, and that wasn't right. The light coming in the window from outside wasn't orange. It was … normal white light. There was no orange glow at all. He disentangled himself carefully from Kelly, who groaned softly and rolled over. Easing himself out from under the bed, he put his beach sandals on. He eased the bedroom door open and crunched across the plaster-covered loungeroom floor and out through the open sliding door.

Jerem was sitting on the edge of the verandah sipping a cup of lava tea. Daniel walked across the verandah and stepped off the edge onto the grass. He took a few more steps and then stopped, looking all around him in wonder. The sky was blue. The ocean was blue. Everything was the right color. At least it would be the right color if he was back on Earth. But this wasn't Earth. This was Atraya. How was this possible?

He looked toward the rising sun, already completely above the rim of the ocean. He couldn't look at it directly, but he didn't need to. That was not Tama. It was definitely not a Type-K star. It was a star just like Earth's: a Type-G yellow dwarf.

He looked back at Jerem who was still sitting on the edge of the verandah, staring at him intently. Neither man had yet spoken. Jerem was obviously giving him time to soak it all in.

"What's happened?" ask Daniel, incredulously.

"It's a miracle," offered Jerem, simply.

"The earthquakes?" asked Daniel, still trying to comprehend what his eyes were seeing.

Jerem shook his head. "Nothing. I've been up for an hour. There have been a couple of tiny tremors, but I think that's just the tectonic plates settling."

"I … I don't understand." Daniel pivoted around again, staring in wide-eyed wonder at a world strangely at peace.

"Neither do I. But I'm not complaining."

Daniel walked to the bedroom window and looked inside.

"Kelly! Kelly! Wake up!"

"Go away," she groaned. "Let me sleep!"

"No. You've got to see this! Get up!"

There was a thump and then, "Ow!"

"Oh yeah," said Daniel. "Remember, you're under the bed."

"Now you tell me," she said, rolling out from underneath and rubbing her head.

She put her sandals on and walked to the window, with her eyes barely open.

"What's so urgent that you ..." she ground to a halt. Her eyes opened wide, despite the glare from the rising sun. Her mouth opened in amazement, and she rubbed some sleep from her eyes as if that was the cause of the strange vista that she was seeing.

"What the hell?"

"No, I think it's a long way from hell, actually," said Daniel. "Quite the opposite, in fact."

Jerem had gone to wake Jordan, and a few minutes later they were all standing on the front verandah, still unable to believe their eyes. Looking inland, the damage from the tsunami was still evident. Fallen trees and debris littered the island, and there was a layer of mud over all the low-lying areas. In the distance, over the eastern rim of the ocean, smoke was rising, probably from the nearby archipelago where there had been a volcanic eruption yesterday.

But despite the damage, the world seemed somehow reborn. The local birdlife was going crazy in the early morning light, singing and screeching to one another as they celebrated the arrival of a new day with a strange new sun.

Jerem switched on the screen in the loungeroom. Most of the newsfeeds were offline, their power supply or transmitters probably destroyed in the Earthquakes. But Jerem managed to find one newsfeed still transmitting. There was world-wide incredulity. Angel City was in a stable orbit, as was Rios, Atraya's moon. But Jumea, and Helios, the other two planets, were gone. Not destroyed. Not decimated into a billion fragments. Just gone.

The neutron star was gone, too. It was not in visible range of their scanners, which was simply not possible.

Of course, the greatest mystery of all was the sun. They were now orbiting a completely different star. Bigger. Brighter. Yellower. And they were orbiting at a greater distance than they had orbited

Tama, which was just as well, because this was a much bigger, hotter star.

Speculation abounded, but there were no plausible scientific theories that could explain what had occurred. This was beyond any logical explanation. Scientists from the observatory in Angel City had also made a remarkable discovery. The whole starfield had changed. Not just a little bit. Completely. There was not a recognisable constellation, not a single known star, in the whole sky. Atraya was no longer in known space.

As well as confusion and speculation, in the aftermath of the near disaster, there was also profound grief. Hundreds of thousands of people had perished in earthquakes and tsunamis. Buildings and infrastructure had been destroyed. The clean-up would be long and messy, and it would probably take years to rebuild the technology and infrastructure that had been decimated.

But despite all that, there was immense joy and relief. They were alive! And their planet was inexplicably, perhaps miraculously, out of danger.

As the newsfeed continued to bring reports from all over the world, the four friends sat on their verandah, sipping lava tea and gazing around them.

"We're alive," whispered Kelly.

"And it's a bright new world," added Daniel.

"A miraculous new day," said Jerem.

"No offense, but this lava tea is crap," said Jordan. "We really need to get some coffee."

**50**

————

As Kelly and Jordan began sweeping up the mess inside the bungalow, and Jerem was investigating how to temporarily weather-proof the broken windows, Daniel took his neural interface cap and subspace communicator out to the edge of the grassy hill and sat down facing the sea. He connected to the quantum mainframe on Angel City and drilled down into the quantum subspace realm. Harry was the only one of the Newbies online.

"I've been waiting for you," said Harry.

"What's happened?" asked Daniel, without any preliminaries.

"Take a look for yourself."

Harry pointed him to the distinctive band of frequencies that represented Atraya. Its primary frequencies, including the complex bass frequencies that denoted it as a planet, were the same, but its address was different.

"The planet was moved!" Daniel said.

"Yes."

"Did you do this?"

"Of course not. The energy required to move a whole planet would be ... well it would literally be astronomical. The amount of dark energy needed would be ... unthinkable."

"So how did it move?"

"You tell me," said Harry.

Daniel thought about it and came up with the only possible conclusion.

"Someone a lot more powerful than us intervened."

"It's the only explanation," agreed Harry.

It was then that Daniel noticed the continuing presence of the strange set of frequencies that he and the others had seen yesterday. At the time, Harry's explanation had been that it was probably an artifact, an anomaly in the quantum foam of space-time, caused by the confluence of gravitational forces between the neutron star and their own sun. Now, however, Daniel was not so sure. In fact, he had a growing suspicion. He reached out toward the frequency spike and initiated direct contact.

"Who are you?"

"I've already tried that," said Harry.

Daniel ignored him and persisted.

"Who are you?"

Silence.

"Reveal yourself!"

No response.

"I'm not going away until you answer! Who are you?"

"Elori," came the simple answer.

Daniel was stunned. There was someone else in quantum subspace with them!

"Is that your name?"

"No. It is who we are."

"It's the name of your race?"

"Yes."

Daniel's mind was whirling. This was mankind's first contact with extra-terrestrials!

"You are not human?" he asked.

"That is correct. We are ... very different from your race."

"And you did this? You moved our planet?"

"Yes."

"How?"

"You are not yet ready to understand. Although you have started on the journey."

"You changed our subspace address."

"Physical location is an illusion. The Fold is everything."

"But the energy involved must have been monumental."

"A large star was sacrificed to save your world."

"Why? Why did you save us?"

"Because your destruction would have been a waste. You are the first race in millennia to have discovered the Fold."

"I assume 'the Fold' is what we refer to as the flux of subspace?"

"Yes."

"Why did you wait so long to save us? Hundreds of thousands of our people died."

"There was a disagreement."

"You were debating whether to save us?"

"Yes."

"Why wouldn't you save a planet full of people about to be destroyed? If you have the power to do so, why wouldn't you help? What is there to debate?"

"Those who abide in the Fold are not meant to interfere with physical space-time."

"But you did."

"Yes. We acted because you were the innocent victims of an attack."

"An attack? You mean that the neutron star wasn't a random event?"

"That is correct. It was an attempt to wipe out a race of people who might one day compete for dominance in the Fold."

"An attempt by whom?'

There was silence.

"Who did this to us?" asked Daniel, again.

"The Prymidians. They are the other race who have entered the Fold. They are ... lacking in honour."

"You can say that again!"

"They are lacking in honour."

"No. I didn't mean … Oh, it doesn't matter. Are we still in danger?"

"There is a slight possibility. The Prymidians are a highly competitive and aggressive race. But now that we have acted to protect you, they may not try to destroy you again."

"May not? That doesn't sound very definite."

"In order to watch you more closely, we have moved your world nearer to our own."

"Where are we exactly?"

"Your world is now in the galaxy you call, Andromeda."

"We're in another galaxy?"

"We believe you will be safe here."

"You believe? Once again, it doesn't sound very certain."

"There are forces at play that are beyond your understanding. It is complicated."

"What about the people we relocated to the new planet? Did you move them, too?"

"There was no need. They were not in immediate danger. Besides, it is a serious thing to destroy a star in order to move a planet. We hope never to do it again. It is the Creator's will that we care for the universe, and not destroy it."

"The Creator?"

"You have much to learn, but some among you see the truth: those who dare to examine the evidence with unfiltered eyes."

Harry, who had remained silent until now, interjected.

"Where are you? Where is your world?"

"That is not for you to know. I must leave you now."

"Wait!" said Daniel. "How will we contact you again if we need you?"

"Farewell."

The peculiar set of frequencies disappeared from quantum subspace, leaving Daniel and Harry stunned.

**51**

---

Later that day, the four friends ate a late lunch on the verandah of their hilltop bungalow. The usual brisk afternoon breeze had sprung up, whipping the surface of the deep blue ocean into a flurry of white-topped waves. They had made a start on repairing the damage to the bungalow, but it would probably be weeks or even months before it was fully restored. Jerem promised that he would help Daniel build a new cabin for him and Kelly, and discussions were already underway regarding its location. Kelly had her eye on the next hill up the coast, which was currently bare of housing.

A pair of gulls sat on the grass nearby, squawking, and Daniel threw them some crumbs which only made them squawk more loudly.

"Have you guys thought of any names for your baby?" he asked.

"I'm still getting my head around the fact that I'm going to be a mother," replied Jordan. "Having a baby wasn't something I ever thought I'd do."

"You're going to make a wonderful mother," Jerem encouraged.

"I just hope I don't end up looking like a beached whale," she replied.

"You probably will. But, hey, you're in the right place if you do," said Daniel, pointing to the beach below.

"Gee thanks, dude. You really know how to encourage a girl."

"You're welcome."

"What about you guys?" Jerem asked. "Any thoughts on names, yet?"

Kelly considered for a moment. "If it's a boy, I'd like to call him, Theo, after my grandfather."

"Nice," said Jerem. "And what if it's a girl?"

"I really don't know," Kelly replied. She looked at Daniel. "Do you have any ideas?"

Daniel thought about it for a moment.

"Yes, actually. I do. How about Elori?"

Kelly considered it. "Mm. I like it. How did you come up with that name?"

"Someone I spoke to, recently."

"A friend?"

"I think so."

She looked at him curiously but didn't enquire further.

After lunch, the four friends walked down the hill to where Daniel and Kelly's bungalow had stood. There was nothing left, not even any the slightest traces of debris to indicate that a dwelling had once been there. The sea had swept it all away as if it were as flimsy and insubstantial as a pile of twigs.

"It's all gone," Kelly said, wistfully. "It's as if there had never been a house here at all."

Jordan picked up a piece of driftwood and poked at a pile of seaweed that had been left by the receding ocean. "It's a metaphor for life," she said. "You live and work and labour to build something worthwhile, but in the end, it all gets swept away and there's nothing left."

"Not nothing," said Jerem. "Any life that was well-lived will continue to enrich the lives of those who follow. Even amid the ruin of death, there is always something of lasting value left behind."

"Hey! Check this out! Look what I've found!" exclaimed

Daniel, who had moved away and was squatting, looking at something in the silt where the house had stood.

"What is it?" asked Kelly, as they all rushed over to see what he had found.

Daniel looked up at them with a cheeky grin. "Nothing. Just kidding."

"Idiot!" said Jordan, laughing and giving him a friendly slap on the back of the head.

They wandered around the site for a few more minutes, finding nothing of significance. Finally, they stood together, gazing around them. Despite the damaged vegetation and the silt that seemed to cover everything, there was a feeling of renewal that could not be denied. A bright yellow sun hung suspended in a deep blue sky, and there was a warm tropical breeze teasing the leaves on the trees. All around them, birds were screeching in joyful chorus, as if they, too, shared the sense of wonder.

"Come on," said Jerem, turning to face the hill. "We've got a new life to build."

"Sounds good to me," said Kelly, taking hold of Daniel's hand.

"Yeah. To me, too," agreed Daniel.

"This new life better have decent coffee at some point, or I'm going to ask for my money back," said Jordan.

Jerem smiled and reached out his hand toward her. "I promise I'll get us some decent coffee," he said, drawing her to him and kissing her, tenderly.

"You'd better. People have divorced over less."

Together, they started walking back up the hill, with a warm breeze at their backs and the sound of the birds heralding a new beginning.

THE END

# SCIENCE STUFF

All good science fiction is based on existing science and science that can be reasonably extrapolated into the future. Here are some interesting facts that form the basis for this novel:

**NEUTRON STARS**

There are an estimated one billion neutron stars in the Milky Way Galaxy. Yes, these dudes really do exist! As was explained in this novel, they are the collapsed remnant of a star after it has gone supernova. They are between 10 and 20 kilometres in diameter and, apart from black holes and a few other hypothetical objects (white holes and quark stars), they are the densest objects in the universe. A teaspoon of the star's matter really would weigh almost as much as Mount Everest. I didn't make that up!

A neutron star's magnetic field is between 100 million and 1 quadrillion times stronger that Earth's and its gravity is 200 billion times stronger than Earth's. Neutron stars cool relatively quickly after formation. Initially they can have a surface temperature of up to 600,000 degrees Celsius (1 billion degrees Fahrenheit), but because there is no longer a nuclear reaction occurring at its core, this residual heat dissipates over time. Neutron stars that have cooled are, therefore, very difficult to detect and observe in the visual spectrum. They are detected most readily via their electro-magnetic and X-ray emissions.

After collapsing, the conservation of angular momentum results in the newly formed neutron star rotating at hundreds of times per second, emitting pulses of strong electromagnetic radiation in the process. These fast-spinning neutron stars are referred to as pulsars. The fastest spinning neutron star observed to date is known as PSR J1748–2446ad. It is about 18,000 lightyears from Earth, in the constellation Sagittarius, and it spins at 716 revolutions per second.

You definitely wouldn't want a neutron star wandering into your local neighbourhood. If it came close enough, its immense gravity would easily gobble up a whole planet. It would ruin your whole day! Of course, the chance of a neutron star encountering another star or planet is infinitesimal. That is because of the vast amount of empty space that exists out there. Thus, the encounter of the neutron star with Atraya, in my novel, was extremely unlikely as an act of pure chance, and was revealed, at the end, to have been the result of a deliberate act of aggression by a mysterious and extremely powerful adversary.

**QUANTUM SUBSPACE**

Quantum physics proposes that the underlying structure of the space-time continuum consists of quantum foam – a fizzing quantum realm of extremely small and extremely short-lived fluctuations in the fabric of spacetime. Quantum foam, so it is theorised, is a frothy, chaotic mess of constant eruptions of particles of matter and antimatter that are trillions of times smaller than atomic nuclei, and which last for trillionths of a second. Quantum physics also proposes that miniscule wormholes are constantly forming within the quantum foam of spacetime, forming extremely tiny and short-lived bridges through subspace between two points in the physical universe.

My own fictional addition to this theoretical base was to propose that objects in the physical universe have a corresponding, unique, identifying set of frequencies within the quantum foam of subspace. This came directly from the murky mists of my imagination! But who knows? Maybe one day such a thing might be discovered. If I happen to win the Nobel prize for science, posthumously, please leave the medallion on my gravestone.

Keep dreaming!

*"Somewhere, something incredible is waiting to be known."* – Carl Sagan

*"The science fiction of today is the science of tomorrow."* – Me! *(and a heap of others, too, but I'm claiming it).*

# LEAVE A REVIEW

If you enjoyed this book, I would be extremely grateful if you would leave a review on Amazon, Goodreads and other review websites. Reviews are hugely important for me as a self-published author. In Amazon's case, reviews impact Amazon's algorithms, helping the book to climb higher in the charts, thereby making it more visible to potential readers. Every single review really does help!

Leaving a review is very easy. To leave a review, just go to Amazon, search for my book and click on the reviews link next to the stars. A review of 4 or 5 stars is considered to be a positive review and a review of 3 or less stars is considered to be a negative review. (Unfortunately, Amazon only allows reviews from people who have spent at least $50 on Amazon over the preceding 12 months).

**Thank you!**

# SOMEONE ELSE'S LIFE

KEVIN SIMINGTON'S CRIME THRILLER!

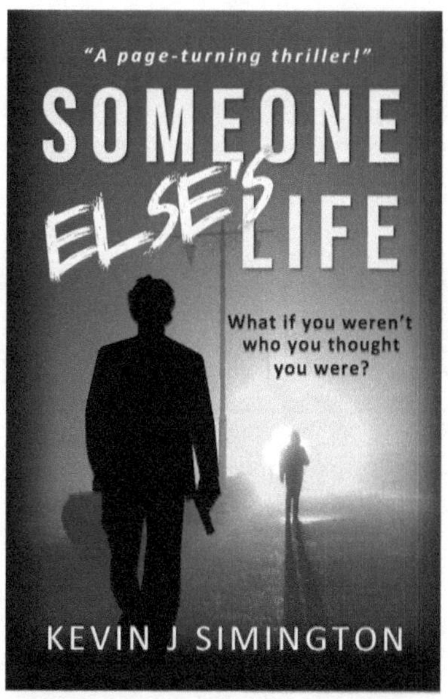


*"A page-turning thriller by a master storyteller!"*

*Much more than a simple detective story, this is a complex portrayal of a good man who is pushed to extraordinary limits.*

AVAILABLE FROM ALL MAJOR BOOK RETAILERS

# ABOUT THE AUTHOR

Kevin J Simington is an acclaimed fiction and non-fiction author whose books are renowned for their intelligence, clarity and wit. He is a very popular conference speaker on the topics of philosophy, apologetics and science. He also writes for several international magazines.

Website:
https://kevinsimington.com

Amazon Author Page:
amazon.com/author/kevinjsimington

# FREE EBOOK!

Join my mailing list and receive a FREE EBOOK. I will email you a complimentary copy of **"Welcome To The Universe: A Pocket Guide For Visitors"**. With stunning photographs and mind-boggling facts, the book provides a fascinating glimpse into the wonders of the universe and the many challenges of space travel. Just visit kevinsimington.com and tell me where to send your free copy!

## SEND ME A FREE COPY OF "WELCOME TO THE UNIVERSE"